Ba

Michael Cullen had been walking for close on an hour when he heard the sound, a thin, high vibration on the air. He stopped, tilting his head from side to side, listening. He had slipped into a numbed, semi-conscious state, his mind drifting, his body moving automatically, and he realised that he had been aware of the sound for a while before he actually listened to it.

He heard it again and stopped, turning to try and identify the direction of the sound. It was high pitched, barely audible, almost on the periphery of hearing. He felt his heart quicken, and he began to breath quickly. An owl? Some other nightbird? Some farmyard animal?

He turned around and hurried on, listening, watching. He was aware of the sound now, aware that it was approaching, growing louder, more insistent. And the pounding of blood in his temples and chest grew in tempo to match it.

And then he saw the light.

Small, round and white, it was moving towards him. Fast, incredibly fast, bringing the noise with it. He felt the vibrations through his feet, the thrumming deep in his head.

And then it screamed.

Also by Michael Scott
with Gloria Gaghan

Navigator

MICHAEL SCOTT

········ *Banshee* ········

Mandarin

A Mandarin Paperback

BANSHEE

First published in Great Britain 1990
by Mandarin Paperbacks
Michelin House, 81 Fulham Road, London SW3 6RB

Mandarin is an imprint of the Octopus Publishing Group

A CIP catalogue record for this book
is available from the British Library
ISBN 0 7493 0111 2

Printed in Great Britain
by Cox & Wyman Ltd, Reading

for Anna,
my own bean-sidhe

Knife-sharp, ice-cold, the cry lanced through the chill night, lingering briefly on the brittle air, leaving silence in its wake.

A shape – white, indistinct – moved through the desolate trees, almost invisible against the snowscape.

The wail broke the silence again, the sound as cold and as pitiless as the night. It was a cry of fear, of desolation, a cry of absolute loneliness.

A cry of hunger.

The shape moved through the trees, and screamed again . . .

1

Michael Cullen started awake as the engines of the 747 throttled down for their descent into Dublin airport. For a single moment the engine sounds and the cry in his dream remained one and the same, and then they separated, until all he could hear were the mechanical wails of the engines. He touched the papers in his lap, shuffling them together into some sort of order, while gazing through the window at the approaching ground, the green of the Irish countryside replaced now by the stone sprawl of Dublin city.

The dream was gradually developing, he noted abstractedly. The details becoming clearer and, unlike many other dreams, the details remained with him in his waking state. He could visualise the creature clearly, her features, her dress, only the exact sound of her bitter wail eluded him. But that would come in time. He took the top off his pen and boldly wrote a single word across the top of the page, pleased that he had finally identified the creature.

BANSHEE.

He grinned suddenly; he remembered when he had been researching the Norse legends for his MA, he had dreamt of the Fenris wolf for weeks, stinking hot breath and glowing red eyes racing through his nightmares, until he had managed to write the creature out of his life. Now that he had come to Ireland to research the lore and legends of the Irish race, was it any wonder that he would dream of the banshee, the wailing woman who warned of death?

Michael Cullen had come to Ireland on the first stage of a two-year research trip through the Celtic lands – Ireland, Scotland, Wales, Isle of Man, Brittany, Cornwall and parts of England – to study the folklore of the Celts for what he was determined would be the definitive collection of the folklore of the Celtic peoples.

The tall, slender man slipped his notes into his briefcase, his only luggage, and settled back into the seat to await the landing. He glanced at his watch, wondering briefly if his wife would be at the airport to meet him, and knew of course that she would. Karla had gone ahead some two weeks previously with the children, to settle into the house they had rented on the outskirts of Dublin for the duration of their stay. He had only managed to speak to her once in the two weeks, since he had been travelling, from New York to London, then Paris, back to London and now finally to Dublin. Now the serious work would begin . . . but first, a holiday.

It would be nice to spend a decent amount of time with Karla and the children. It would give him time to get to know his children properly, give him time enough to sort out his relationship with Karla and, perhaps, recapture a little of what they had lost in the fifteen years of marriage.

He took a deep breath as the plane touched down, holding it unconsciously, the final wailing of the engines reminding him briefly of his dream.

Michael Cullen strolled through the door that led out into the airport's reception area and found his wife and children sitting in the first row of seats that faced the automatic doors. The doors had barely hissed shut behind him when the children had ducked under the barrier and were hanging onto him.

'Daddy . . .'

'Dad!'

'You're strangling me,' he gasped as his daughter's grip around his neck tightened. 'Here, let me see how much you've grown in two weeks,' he grinned, 'well, not much, I suppose,' he added.

Michael Cullen jnr, MJ, bore the closest resemblance to his father, and already, at thirteen, was almost as tall and promised to be broader. He had his father's pale hair and grey eyes, but possessed his mother's straight, rather hard, mouth.

Christine, Chrissy, a year younger than her brother, was a mirror-image of her mother, the same dark hair, dark eyes and hard features. She still hadn't shed her puppy fat, and Michael seriously doubted if she ever would.

Michael walked around the barrier and kissed his wife. Her greeting was perfunctory, her manner offhand: she hadn't wanted to come to Ireland, she was sure his research could have been conducted in the university and college libraries in the States. She also bitterly resented the fact that she had been uprooted from the settled academic community, where her husband was a man of note, and shipped off to this godforsaken land. It also rankled that Michael had arranged to rent a house way out in the sticks rather than close to the city where at least she could have entertained herself with the theatre and shops.

'How are things?' Michael asked, as she led him through the half-empty airport.

'Fine,' she said shortly. 'How did your meetings go?'

He grinned, delightedly. 'I've managed to sell English hardback rights, paperback rights, and French language rights. There's also a chance that French television will do a documentary on it, and the BBC might be interested in a co-production with the Irish television network.'

'RTE,' Karla said automatically.

'What?'

'RTE. Radio Television Erin, or something like that,' she said quickly, the note of irritation creeping into her voice.

'I missed you,' Michael said quickly, catching her off guard.

Karla nodded briefly, but said nothing.

'This book could make us some real money,' he added.

She nodded, again; Karla had little interest in her husband's writings and in the additional money it brought. It kept him away from home, kept him locked into his study, and that meant that the burden of looking after the children fell on her. She resented the loss of freedom.

As they stepped out of the airport terminal, Michael paused to breathe in the damp air; it had rained recently, and the air smelled fresh and sharp, with none of the bitterness of exhaust fumes that tainted New York rain. He found himself grinning broadly, and he had to resist the temptation to congratulate himself on 'coming home'. It was something of a joke that every American tourist that came to Ireland said that they felt they had come home, but now he knew what they meant. He caught Karla's disapproving glare and the smile slid off his face, but even her ill humour couldn't dampen his high spirits.

Karla had rented a metallic-grey Volvo, which she drove hard and fast, and Michael had had to stifle a scream when he found she was driving on the 'wrong' side of the road, until he realised she wasn't. She sped out of the airport complex and turned left at a large grassy roundabout, heading northwards. She punched stations on the radio, finally settling on a pop station that could have been coming from anywhere in the world, except that the voices of the DJ's, with their Irish accents, sounded incongruous to his ears. He watched the countryside for a few moments, surprised to find that it really was as green as people said it was, and then he suddenly reached over and clicked the radio off.

'So tell me,' he said, looking straight ahead, but watching his wife out of the corner of his eye, 'how have you been?'

'I've been fine, I've been bored stupid, but I've been fine,' Karla said sharply, not taking her eyes off the road.

Michael twisted in his seat to look at the two children. 'And how have you two been? Do you like the house?'

'Dad, its neat,' MJ said quickly, 'there's fields and woods on one side, and there's even a ruined church with a graveyard. The sea is five minutes' walk away, and there's an island you can walk out to when the tide is out . . .'

'And the house is so big,' Chrissy added quickly, 'four bedrooms, and they're huge, and there's out-houses and barns . . .'

The children had grown up on campus and were used to a small, cramped apartment on the college grounds.

'Did my machine arrive?' Michael asked, looking from Chrissy to MJ.

'Got it set up and running, Dad.'

Michael Cullen had hired a computer and printer, identical to the one he used at college, and had brought his own word-processing and data base software with him from the States. He would write most of the book using the word-processing facilities on the machine in Ireland, store it on disc, and finish the final editing back in college.

'And what do you think of the house, love?' Michael asked, looking back at his wife.

'I don't. It's isolated, its twenty-two miles from the city centre. The house is draughty, the rooms are huge, impossible to keep warm, and the neighbours are incredibly nosy. You would not believe how many I've had around to welcome me, telling me how pleased they are that the American Doctor, that's you by the way, is coming to write his book in Loughshinny. Don't ask me how they found out.'

'Local Post Office?' Michael suggested, 'I wrote to them sometime ago telling them that we had rented the house and that mail would be arriving there shortly for us. Anyway, I don't think they're being nosy, I think they're just doing their best to make you welcome.'

Karla touched the brakes, slowing the heavy car, as the dual carriageway ended, after what seemed like a surprisingly short stretch of road.

'What's the speed limit?' Michael asked, his eyes on the speedometer, which was touching sixty-five.

'Fifty-five on the carriageway.'

'Just like home,' Michael said happily.

Karla slowed the car again, and began indicating. 'There's the turn . . .' she muttered.

'Mom's missed the turn twice,' Chrissy offered.

'It's opposite the gas station, Mom,' MJ offered.

'All right, you two,' Michael said good-humouredly.

Karla turned off the main road, onto a minor road, following the sign for Lusk and Skerries.

'Did you manage to do any of the things I asked?' Michael asked her carefully.

'Some. But you must remember I was just a little busy myself.'

He managed to bite back a retort. She had said she had little or nothing to do. Karla hadn't wanted to leave her friends and her settled way of life to come to Ireland, and she had managed to create countless little difficulties. The only thing he had asked her to do when she was settled in was to make contact with a few of the people and organizations in Dublin which might be some use to him in his researches. However, he should have guessed that she would do it half-heartedly. 'Well, whom did you manage to contact?' he asked eventually.

'I don't remember, all these Irish names sound alike to me.'

'You've an Irish name yourself, remember,' he said, attempting to lighten the mood. 'Cullen. In Irish that's O'Cuillin.'

'There's no Irish for Klein,' she said quickly, following the road to the right into the village of Lusk, and then turning left towards Skerries and Loughshinny. Karla's maiden name had been Klein.

Michael sighed. There was no way he was going to win. He settled back into the seat and watched the countryside flow by. Tonight, or tomorrow night perhaps, he'd take her out for a nice meal. Maybe that would improve her humour somewhat. If it worked, it would at least give him two or three days of relative calm.

Karla turned off to the right, down a narrow winding road. MJ leaned in over the seat and pointed off to the right.

'There's the castle. There's a tower and everything, and there's supposed to be caves leading down to the bay.'

'What's it called?' Michael asked, craning back to look at the castle through the back window, as Karla drove too fast along the narrow road.

'Don't know yet. But I'll find out,' MJ promised.

'We'll explore it first chance we get,' Michael grinned.

Chrissy suddenly leaned forward and pointed off to the right. 'That's the house Daddy.'

Before Michael had a chance to look at the house, Karla had turned in between two stone pillars and drove quickly up a tree-lined driveway. At the top of the drive was a second set of gates, which opened out into a semi-circular gravelled driveway. Karla stood hard on the brakes, spraying gravel, exposing the soft earth beneath. There were numerous similar scars all across the driveway.

'Keep that up,' he remarked, 'and I'll have to get the driveway resurfaced.' He smiled to take the sting out of the words, but Karla decided to take it seriously. Deliberately so, he thought. Shaking his head slightly, he stepped out of the car and turned to look at the house.

Blacklands was a large, rambling farmhouse, built sometime towards the end of the last century, or earlier this century, he guessed. The front of the house opened out onto the driveway, which was bordered by a broad, bush and tree-enclosed garden, while a tall, roughly-built wall separated the drive from a second, larger garden. He recognised apple trees over the top of the wall, and realised this must be the 'mature orchard' the brochure from the leasing company spoke about.

The house had obviously once been a simple, square box, but there had been extensive building at the back, and the stables had been converted into extra rooms. The exterior walls had been washed with what Michael guessed had once been yellow paint, but which had now faded to the colour of pale cream; the roof was of dark red slate, with the newer, brighter slates standing out like wounds.

It had a comfortable, homey feel to it, and on first impressions, he decided he liked it. He didn't even need to look at Karla to know she didn't.

Michael Cullen followed Karla, across the scarred gravel, to the glass enclosed porch that had been crudely added to the elegant doorway. She took out her key-ring and pulled off a spare hall door key, and handed it to him without a word. She stuck her own key in the lock and turned it savagely, pushing open the door and hurrying off down the uncarpeted hall, her heels clicking sharply. Michael turned from her and leaned back against the wall, watching the children, who had darted off amongst the trees and untrimmed bushes, their shouts and cries echoing off the stone walls.

And then he immediately noticed something else, the silence.

No, not silence. He stepped back out, onto the step, and listened. The air was alive with bird song, both close and distant, the buzzing of insects, the drone of a fly trapped behind the glass behind him, but after the constant bustle and roar of city traffic and the constant clamour of city life, it felt very good indeed. He breathed in the fresh country air, damp with earthy smells, touched with the salt from the sea, and nodded quickly. He was going to enjoy it here, whether Karla liked it or not. He turned back to the door and found an ancient, weathered, wooden name-plate screwed to the wall. There were shapes burned into the wood and he rubbed hard at the mossy letters, traced them with his fingertips. It was a name, 'St Jude'. Just a house name; in Ireland it was not uncommon for houses to be called after a patron or favoured saint. Smiling, he recalled something from his Catholic upbringing: St Jude was the Patron Saint of Hopeless Cases. Shaking his head, he stepped inside; he should be right at home here.

Michael Cullen spent the rest of the morning and early afternoon exploring the house. His earlier supposition proved to be correct; the original house had been a solidly-built, four-bedroomed farmhouse built towards the end of the last century, he found the date 1880 chiselled onto the broad, granite mantelpiece. Successive owners had added and expanded the original structure and now, while four original bedrooms remained, the attic had been converted to a fifth, which MJ had claimed, and another enormous bedroom had been added in the new wing at the back of the house. It was tall, and long, with arched windows set high up on both walls to catch the afternoon and morning light. Michael fell in love with it immediately; it was perfect for his needs. He walked along the length of the tall, airy room, and was amused to find that his son had loaded all his books and equipment into that room. Was he so predictable?

The computer and printer had been set up on a long table beneath the windows that looked out over the orchard. They would get the light in the morning, but he preferred to work in the evenings and at night, and this side of the garden would be in shadow then. He shaded his eyes and stared off into the distance to where he could see the deep blue line of the sea and the indeterminate shape of an island. Nodding his approval, the more he saw of this house, the more he liked it, he turned back to the room. His boxes of books and notes were piled up in one corner, untouched, but he was delighted to find a series of tall, deep shelves against the gable wall. There was a fireplace set into the wall, and he thought briefly about lighting a fire there on the cold nights, but immediately dismissed the idea: soot and coal dust would play havoc with the sensitive heads of the machine.

He strolled down to the kitchen, pausing to look in on the bathroom. He had been expecting something antique, a high brass tub, wooden-topped toilet, huge handbasin, but was pleasantly surprised to find that a completely modern bathroom suite had been installed . . . and a little disappointed too, he had to admit. The kitchen, too, had been completely modernised, dark mock oak cabinets and mock antique table and chairs. There was a split-level cooker and dish-washer against one wall, and a combination fridge-freezer behind the door. In a small utility room that opened onto the kitchen he found a washing-machine and tumble-drier, both of which looked new and unused.

When he stepped back into the kitchen, Karla was standing by the window, percolating a rich-smelling coffee. 'I like it,' he said, 'I like it a lot. I don't know what you're complaining about,' he added, looking around.

Karla hissed as hot coffee spattered across the back of her hand. 'Will you take that bloody silly grin off your face,' she snapped, 'you've had it ever since you walked out of the airport this morning.'

'Sorry,' he mumbled. He hadn't been aware that he'd been grinning, but he had to admit that his humour was particularly good, and had every reason to be.

'I'm taking the children home in August,' Karla said suddenly.

Michael, who had been peering into the fridge, looked up in surprise. 'What? But I thought . . .'

'There's no college here that even approaches their educational status,' Karla pressed on, not looking at him. 'The closest is in Dublin, and it would mean sending them into the city every day, and that's an hour's journey each way, either by car or train, and I'm not sure I want that. No,' she shook her head firmly, when he opened his mouth to protest. 'I'm taking them home in August before the Fall semester begins. You can remain and continue with your work.'

Michael took a deep breath. He could feel the old anger taking hold again. 'Look, we'll talk about it later, let's just enjoy a few days' holiday together.'

'There's no talking to be done. We're going home in eight weeks.'

Realising the futility of arguing at this stage, Michael nodded resignedly. 'What's for dinner?' he asked.

With the onset of night, the house and surrounding countryside assumed a different character. The daytime noises faded, to be replaced by an almost fragile stillness that was underscored by a gentle, barely audible, hissing. Michael Cullen spent about twenty minutes standing on the lawn, feeling the dew soaking up through his loafers, trying to identify the sound, until he suddenly realised that the sea was about ten minutes' walk away. He was hearing the sounds of the distant surf on the shore.

He breathed deeply, drawing in the chill night air, almost tasting it before turning back towards the house. He could see Karla through the uncurtained windows, watching a television picture that threatened to roll right off the screen at any moment. They were using an old-fashioned television aerial and weather and heat were distoring the picture. Even as he watched, she surged to her feet and snapped off the picture. He glanced at the luminous dial of his watch: not quite ten-thirty. He grinned, he couldn't remember when his wife had last gone to bed at ten-thirty. Obviously the extra sleep wasn't agreeing with her. He thought about going to bed himself, and then decided to give Karla some time to cool down.

Michael spent the next hour sorting through his books and notes. He had already made extensive notes for the new book and, within broad parameters, he knew exactly what he wanted to include. However, for the book to have any measure of success or credibility, he needed access to the folklore material in the National Library of Ireland and the vast collection in the archives of the Folklore Department of University College Dublin. And that was one of the principal reasons he had travelled to Ireland in the first place. He sorted through the boxes of books he had had shipped from New York, searching for the few which he considered vital to his research: an Irish-English Dictionary and Grammar. Unfortunately, he didn't speak any Irish.

It was close to twelve by the time he finished. He had been running on nervous energy since he had landed in Dublin Airport earlier that day and now he suddenly felt exhausted, completely drained.

Karla was asleep, breathing deeply and gently, when he reached the bedroom. Michael stood looking down at her while he undressed slowly; in repose her face was very like the face of the girl he had married fourteen years ago. It was a softer, gentler face, without the hard lines and edges it had assumed as time and circumstance had chipped away at their relationship. He slid between the chill sheets, his hands behind his head, staring out through the uncurtained window at the purple night sky. There was a tracery of shadow across the window cast by the branches of the nearby trees, moving gently in the sea breeze. As the exhaustion soaked through him, and sleep gradually claimed him, the branches assumed shapes . . .

Michael Cullen's last impression before he finally fell into a deep and dreamless sleep was of a face.

The creature stirred.

It had felt the presence earlier, dimly, distantly. The presence it was particularly attuned to. The presence had neared.

Soon it would touch the presence.

Soon it would feed.

2

Michael slept late the following morning, and he awoke to the sound of distant churchbells tolling noon. He lay in the bed, partially remembered images from his dreams vaguely disturbing him, before they finally settled back into his subconscious. He sat up slowly, feeling wretched; every muscle in his body ached and protested at far too many hours spent travelling. He dug the heels of his palms into his eyes and groaned aloud. But why had no one bothered to wake him? Karla knew he hated to sleep in. He hopped out of bed and then stood for a few moments, listening, but the house was silent, and not only silent, it felt empty too. Crossing to the window, he looked down onto the driveway where Karla had left the car, and he was somehow unsurprised to find it empty. Perhaps she had taken the children out of his way, to give him a few hours' extra sleep, he grinned sourly; he somehow doubted that.

He found the note stuck to the kitchen door with a length of green masking tape, 'Gone to city with children, back later.' He wasn't sure whether to be pleased or not: the extra few hours alone in the house would give him time to sort things out, and prepare his notes and books properly. But he still wouldn't have minded spending a little time with the children, considering he hadn't seen them in the past two weeks. When they returned, he would allow them to show him the house and gardens.

While the kettle boiled, Michael Cullen crossed to the back door and pulled it open, looking out across a small paved courtyard towards the orchard, breathing in the warm, slightly salty, air. Later in the year, he imagined the air would be rich with the odour of apples. The sun had moved off the back of the house, but the stones were still warm where they had baked through the morning. He hadn't felt so relaxed in . . . well, not in a long time. There always seemed to be so much else to do, his lecturing, his writing, his research. And, at the end of the day, there seemed to be very little time left for himself, for Karla, for the children. Karla, of course, had her own interests, her own circle of friends, that was one of the reasons she hadn't wanted to come to Ireland in the first place. There had been a time when they had had some interests in common, but that had been a long time ago, fourteen years ago, when they first married. The kettle whistled and as he stepped back into the kitchen to make the tea, he found he couldn't even remember what those interests had been.

Perhaps this holiday, in a country where time was appreciated differently, would help them on the road to a recovery or at least a reappraisal of their marriage.

He climbed the creaking wooden stairs to his study, a steaming mug of tea cupped in both hands. At the top of the stairs he turned to the left and stepped into the bedroom to collect his glasses where he had left them on the bedside locker. Glancing through the window, he could see the distant blue line of the sea, obscured in part by the trees, their branches inextricably woven together into tight knotted patterns. A slight sea breeze ruffled the tops of the leaves, the branches moving against one another, the patterns changing, forming pictures . . .

. . . the face was long and thin, the eyes slightly slanted, upcurved, the cheekbones high, the hair swept back, the chin pointed . . .

Michael blinked, blinked again, as he attempted to make sense of what he was seeing. The picture dissolved, and he suddenly found he was looking at a crow perched on one of the branches, staring in at him, its hard, black little eyes like stones. He took a quick mouthful of the hot tea; he really needed this holiday!

His study was pleasantly warm, heated by the morning sun, dust motes circling in the still air, faintly redolent of old wax and freshly cut wood. It was the perfect place to work, he decided, mentally comparing it with his tiny, cluttered work space back in New York. He spent the next few hours shelving the books he had brought with him, shaking his head in amusement as he found his own half-dozen publications among them. What had possessed him to bring those along? He had purchased most of the research material from the specialist bookshops in New York, and the remainder he had bought by mail order from two of Dublin's larger bookshops. However, that still left him with a shopping list that, he felt sure, would run to several hundred dollars worth of reading material. Luckily it was a reclaimable expense.

With the bookshelves in some sort of order, he set to work on the boxes which held the files, copy books and folders he had already prepared.

Finally, he turned his attention to the more important matter of an assistant. Michael Cullen preferred to work alone, doing his own research, his own writing. But this time he recognised the need for a research assistant. And his needs were quite particular: they would need to be reasonably fluent in Old and Modern Irish, have a very good knowledge of Celtic – not just Irish – folklore, and at least be conversant with computer technology. He was also convinced that his chances of finding someone who fitted those criteria were slim indeed. However, before he had come to Ireland, he had managed to secure introductions to some of the most eminent folklorists in the country, and he was hoping that they would be able to recommend someone. Which reminded him – he opened his diary, smiling at the large, blank areas that now occupied the centre of the book, by rights it should have been littered with scraps and notes, he was right – he had a luncheon appointment with Dr Patrick Byrne tomorrow. He flipped up Paddy Byrne's address and phone number in his diary; he had better ring and confirm.

There was only one phone in the house and that was in the hallway. After the warm, golden light that suffused his study, the hall was dark and dim, hot, and smelled faintly musty. Dust motes spiralled in the shafts of coloured light that came through the ornamental stained glass fan over the door. The house was very still.

Michael carefully dialled the six-digit number, and then waited while the phone clicked and buzzed to itself.

The screech made him drop the phone with fright and stagger back against the wall, his hands clapped to his ears . . .

'Hello . . . hello . . .?'

Shaken, Michael Cullen bent and picked up the receiver, holding it away from his ear.

'Hello . . . hello . . .?'

Michael pressed the receiver against his ear. His head was still ringing from the static howl, and his heart beating far too fast to be comfortable. 'Hello,' he ventured.

'Can I help you, sir?' The voice was female, the accent more what he expected an Irish accent to be.

'Doctor Patrick Byrne, please.'

'Whom shall I say is calling?'

'Cullen, Doctor Michael Cullen.'

'Hold the line.'

Michael rarely used his full title, and the receptionist seemed singularly unimpressed, but he supposed Trinity College secretaries got their fair share of doctors and professors not to allow a simple title to impress them. He changed the phone to his other hand, massaging his still throbbing ear with the palm of his hand. What a terrifying sound, good job he hadn't got a weak heart, eh?

'Michael!'

'Paddy. Good to hear you.'

'So you arrived in one piece.'

Michael smiled at the accent and intonation. Although Patrick Byrne, or Paddy as he preferred to be called, was American by birth, he showed absolutely no trace of his native Bronx accent. He spoke like an Irishman should, or rather, he spoke the way an American thought an Irishman should.

'We're having lunch tomorrow?' Michael asked.

'Table's booked for one-thirty.'

'Can I ask you to do something for me before then?'

'Ask it,' Paddy Byrne said immediately, and Michael could imagine his broad grin spreading across his round face.

'I'm going to need a research assistant, someone with old and new Irish and the knowledge of folklore. The ability to use a word-processor would be an added bonus.'

'Male or female?' Paddy asked.

'Does it matter?'

'It might to Karla,' Paddy cackled.

'You just find me someone who can do the job,' Michael grinned.

'I'll see you tomorrow, I've got to rush, I'm half an hour late for an appointment already.'

'Don't be late tomorrow, I'm still keeping American time, not your famous Irish time.'

'I'll be there.'

The line clicked and went dead, but Michael stood holding it for a few moments, expecting the static to howl down the line again, but aside from a few ghostly threads of conversation, there was nothing.

'And what did you do today?' Karla glanced up as her husband came into the kitchen. There were bags everywhere; Michael didn't recognise any of the labels on them, but even the bags looked expensive.

'Shelved some of my books, phoned Paddy Byrne to settle lunch for tomorrow, and was nearly deafened in the process with crackle from the phone, and then sorted out some of my notes. I should be able to start work on it tonight.'

Karla nodded non-committally.

'And how was your day?'

'Dreadful, absolutely dreadful. Traffic was abominable, and I couldn't find anything I wanted.'

Michael looked in disbelief at the parcels scattered across the kitchen floor.

'And then getting home was a nightmare; we were stuck in rush-hour traffic for an age.'

'Did you take the children around the shops with you?' Michael asked, second-guessing the answer.

'No, I dropped them at a cinema, and picked them up later. They had a great time.'

Michael turned away and headed towards the kettle, not wanting to start an argument. 'I was just about to make some tea.'

'That would be lovely.'

'What about dinner?'

'I thought we were going to go out?' K rla said, turning around, her eyes wide and surprised.

'Well, yes . . . but not tonight surely. I thought at the weekend . . .'

Karla stared at him for a moment longer than was necessary and then turned away, and Michael imagined he could feel the atmosphere in the room fall to freezing point. Well, it hadn't taken them long to fall back into their old ways. The tap rattled as he turned it, gurgling before it finally sputtered into life.

The water was a deep brownish-red, like old blood . . .

Blood ran into the stream, staining the waters a dirty brownish-red. Smoke curled over the battlefield, wrapping itself around the tattered pennants, the wrecked chariots, blanketing the dead bodies in a white pall. Ashes fell like snowflakes. A figure moved through the carnage.

The tap coughed and ran clear again.

'We'll go out,' he said quickly. 'Do you want to go into Dublin?'

Karla turned back to him, the wide-eyed, hurt expression gone from her eyes. 'No, there's a place nearby, in Skerries, that has a great reputation . . .'

'What about sitters?' Michael asked softly, concentrating on pouring the water into the tea pot.

'What for? MJ is thirteen and Chrissy's nearly twelve, they can look after themselves.'

'Well . . .' Michael began doubtfully, 'I don't like the idea of leaving them alone in the house at night.'

'This is Ireland, remember?' Karla said quickly, the sarcasm barely concealed, 'its not New York.' She was repeating something he had said before they had come to Ireland.

'Yes . . . but . . .'

'But what?'

'Well,' he said, looking around the modern kitchen, his unease seeming all the more ludicrous, 'well, this is an old house and they might be a little afraid . . .' he finished lamely.

Karla snorted rudely. 'I think you're forgetting where they were raised, they don't need lessons in security.'

'Yes, yes, I suppose so.'

'What time shall I arrange dinner for?' Karla asked, but had already walked out of the kitchen before Michael turned around to reply, two cups of steaming tea in his hands.

'Any time you wish,' he said to the empty room.

They never managed to keep their dinner engagement.

The argument started as they made their way into Skerries. They had left late because Karla had taken so long deciding what to wear, and unfortunately they missed the turning on the shortcut she knew, which meant that instead of coming into Skerries across country, they did a large loop, and ended up on the coast road on the north side of the town. She had driven, as she always drove, at high speed, with Michael holding tightly to the seat as the sea blurred past, seemingly just beyond his door. Finally, when Karla hit a corner too hard, and the tyres screamed in protest, Michael blurted, 'For Christ's sake, woman, slow down.'

Without looking at him, Karla snapped, 'I'm not driving that fast. And I don't want to be late for dinner.'

'Who made us late?'

The heavy car surged forward as Karla floored the accelerator.

'I don't want to end up in the sea.'

'You can swim,' she said savagely.

'Slow down,' Michael commanded, his voice unusually loud in the confines of the car.

Reluctantly, Karla allowed the speed to drop to something close to fifty.

'Slow down dammit,' Michael said, his voice tightly controlled.

'We're going to be late.'

'We're late enough already, a few more minutes either way won't hurt us. Now slow down or you're going to kill us both.'

Karla eased her foot off the pedal.

Michael glanced sidelong at her. There were no street lights on this section of the road, and the sky had clouded over, bringing an unseasonally early darkness, and the promise of rain. Pale green light from the dashboard lent her face a cold, hard cast, leaving her mouth a thin, hard line, her eyes deeply shadowed.

'Are you sure you wouldn't like me to stop altogether . . . or perhaps even turn back?' Her voice was sharp and bitter.

'You can do what you like,' Michael said evenly, turning away to look out the window, across the sea to where a string of lights picked out Skerries harbour.

Karla suddenly hit the brakes hard, the jolt throwing him forwards sharply, his seatbelt locking, wrenching him back into the seat.

'Just what the . . .'

'You didn't want to come, and now you're going to make the evening miserable,' Karla said loudly. 'You'd rather be back at the house with your bloody machine.'

'Look . . .'

'Well, I'm very sorry I kept you away from your work.'

'Look, I don't need this,' Michael said tightly. 'You know if this book works we'll have enough money . . .'

'We have enough money now!'

'Well, we won't have for very much longer at the rate you're spending it!'

'And just what's that supposed to mean?'

'You know damn well what it supposed to mean.' He hit the seatbelt release and pulled the door open. The cold sea air, rich with salt and seaweed brought him to his senses. 'I'm just going to stretch my legs,' he said quietly, his tone conciliatory. 'Look, why don't we both get a breath of air and calm down, and then we'll go on and have dinner. OK?'

He didn't hear what his wife said, didn't need to hear her reply as she floored the accelerator and screeched away, leaving him standing there, his hand still outstretched towards the open car-door. He watched the tail-lights disappear around the bend in the road, listening to the sound of the engine disappear into the night.

'Shit,' he breathed. The wind coming in off the sea was

invigorating all right, but it was cold, and he was wearing a light summer suit, silk shirt with no tie, and uncomfortable black dress shoes. He had two choices: continue on into Skerries or turn around and head back home. When he thought about it further, he realised that he really only had one choice. Although he didn't know where his wife had booked for dinner, and there was no guarantee she had gone there anyway, he had no idea of the way back, especially not with the 'shortcut' Karla had taken. All he could do now would be to continue on into Skerries and try and pick up a taxi to take him home. That's if he could find a taxi. Turning up his collar, and holding it closed across his throat, he set off at a stiff pace for the town ahead.

The road was deserted, and this seemed to be a particularly lonely stretch. To the left, over a low stone wall, the sea pounded against the beach, stones rattling, sand hissing in the dusty foam, while to his right, a long row of thick bramble bushes ran along the side of the road. There was a stand of trees beyond them and in the far distance, resting atop a hill, a grand old house was vaguely visible against the night. It was showing no lights and he wondered if it was deserted.

He wondered if he was far from home . . .

It was a long way from home.

A moon and more spent travelling through the Middle Sea and out through the Pillars of Hercules. Storms had taken them away from the coast, pushing them northwards into the colder, wetter climes. And when they had begun to despair, the coast had appeared. At first, a distant black line, then green-touched and finally a golden beach, with rich dark land beyond. The breakers carried their frail craft in swiftly, lifting it high over the jagged rocks that guarded the sheltered cove, bringing it crashing down into a trough, the water thundering, foaming.

'SHIT!'

Michael Cullen shouted aloud as a wave washed in, over the

low wall, soaking him with chill briny water. He stood for a few moments clinging to the wall, feeling his heart pound in his chest, the tightness in his lungs, the rubbery feeling in his legs. Christ, but that had frightened the life out of him. All he had seen was something white rush up over the wall and fall onto him. Before he had even had a chance to cry out, it had struck him an almost physical blow.

And now he was soaked through, there was even water sloshing around in his shoes. 'Pneumonia,' he muttered, 'I'm going to die in Ireland of pneumonia.' He felt the anger beginning to bubble up within him then: Karla had gone too far this time; abandoning him on a lonely country road was not funny.

He started to jog, attempting to keep warm, but the water had gone right through the light summer suit and his uncomfortable shoes were not designed for running. After a few hundred yards he gave up, his chest was burning, and his feet already felt raw and blistered. Realising that he was still on the seaward side of the road, he crossed to the opposite side and trudged along, hands deep in his pockets, head tucked down to his chest, trying to work out exactly how far he was from Loughshinny and the house. A couple of miles . . . four, five?

He should have divorced her when he had had the chance. There had been that time, three years ago, when he had suspected she had been having an affair with one of his fellow lecturers. When he had confronted her, she hadn't denied it, but he hadn't pursued it, afraid almost of what he might discover. He'd been busy working on a book then, and he didn't want, didn't need, the hassle. Perhaps that had been a mistake.

The wind had picked up and spat foam and grit across his face. Glancing out to sea, he noticed the heavy clouds massing on the horizon; there was a storm brewing. He pulled his hand from his pocket and glanced at his watch, a few minutes off nine.

He came to a junction and stopped, wondering which way. There was no signpost, but straight on continued along down the coast road, whilst the turn to the right led under a bridge and up a hill, moving on into the country. He couldn't remember the way they had come, but he had a vague idea that they had come down the hill and under the bridge, or had they? Christ, what a mess!

He turned under the bridge.

Michael Cullen had been walking for close on an hour when he heard the sound, a thin, high vibration on the air. He stopped, tilting his head from side to side, listening. He had slipped into a numbed, semi-conscious state, his mind drifting, his body moving automatically, and he realised that he had been aware of the sound for a while before he actually listened to it.

He heard it again and stopped, turning to try and identify the direction of the sound. It was high pitched, barely audible, almost on the periphery of hearing. He felt his heart quicken, and he began to breath quickly. An owl? Some other nightbird? Some farmyard animal?

He turned around and hurried on, listening, watching. He was aware of the sound now, aware that it was approaching, growing louder, more insistent. And the pounding of blood in his temples and chest grew in tempo to match it.

And then he saw the light.

Small, round and white, it was moving towards him. Fast, incredibly fast, bringing the noise with it. He felt the vibrations through his feet, the thrumming deep in his head.

And then it screamed!

Afterwards he realised that he must have shouted aloud too; with terror certainly, with relief too, and embarrassment at his own stupidity.

The train thundered past not twenty yards away.

3

'She did what?' Dr Patrick Byrne had already thrown back his head and was laughing as Michael repeated the story.

'She drove away and left me by the side of the road!'

'And what did you do?'

'I walked home. And I was drenched by a wave. And had the shit scared out of me by a mail train.'

Paddy Byrne wiped away tears from his eyes and shook his head slowly. 'Welcome to Ireland.'

The two men were sitting in Byrne's rooms in Trinity College, a pot of coffee grown cold before them as they had reminisced, and renewed a friendship that was fifteen years old.

Dr Patrick Byrne looked something like an older Michael Cullen, tall, thin, sharp featured, but his eyes, wide and deep brown, lent his face a warmth that Michael's lacked. And, whereas Michael's fair hair was already thinning, Paddy Byrne still possessed a thick thatch of unkempt, snow-white hair. Paddy Byrne was Michael's senior by nearly twenty years, Michael had been his student many years ago, but their friendship had been immediate, and had endured down through the years. When Paddy had come to Ireland some years ago to pursue his interests at a slightly more leisurely pace than back home, the two men had managed to keep up a sporadic correspondence. Occasionally, Michael would receive a copy of one of his articles that had been reprinted in one of the Irish or European folklore journals, and in return Michael passed on whatever material he thought might be of interest to his old mentor.

Paddy glanced at the clock on his desk and turned it towards the younger man. It showed one o'clock. 'We'll stroll out to lunch, I think,' he said. 'Just give me a moment.'

Michael wandered around the room as Paddy called his secretary on the intercom, advising her that he was leaving for lunch and an important meeting immediately afterwards.

When he turned back to Michael he was smiling broadly. 'That means she won't be expecting me back until four at least.'

Michael, who had been standing by the window, nodded down into the street below. 'Where are we now exactly?'

Paddy Byrne joined him and nodded to the street beyond Trinity's high walls, 'That's Nassau Street.' He pointed to the left, 'the second turn to the right down there leads to Kildare Street and the National Library. The museum's just beyond that too.' He reached for his coat and then decided against it, but grabbed an umbrella instead. 'Come on.'

They walked down the carpeted corridors in silence and down the stairs that led out into the side entrance to the college. Coming from the darkness into the sudden sunshine was blinding and Paddy had to stop for a few moments in the shadow of a thick-boled tree while his eyes adjusted to the light. 'Getting old,' he explained.

'We're all getting old,' Michael grinned. 'Where are we going?'

Paddy Byrne pointed with his furled umbrella, 'Up here,' he said, pointing to the street that lay directly ahead. They darted across the road and then strolled in a more leisurely fashion up the long, sunlit street.

'I take it things aren't so good between you and Karla then?' Paddy said gently, not looking at Michael.

The younger man paused before replying. 'She doesn't really want to be here,' he said slowly.

'Was there any need for her to come in the first place?'

'I thought it would be good for us as a family. Breathe in some clean air for a change.'

'I do believe she's a city woman,' Paddy said with a smile. He stopped and pointed to an ornate white-bricked house on the left-hand side of the street. 'That's the Lord Mayor's residence.'

Michael glanced at it out of politeness. 'She misses her friends, her own little world.'

'Well then, send her back to it.' He saw Michael's expression and said shrewdly, 'but perhaps you don't want her to go back on her own, is that it?'

The younger man smiled. 'You always were too smart for your own good.'

At the top of Dawson Street they turned right, squinting now in the bright sunshine. Michael looked in surprise at the broad expanse of trees and bushes that lined one side of the road. 'What's that?'

'That's St Stephen's Green, a couple of acres of public park, including a lake, right in the heart of the city. On a day like this,' he smiled, 'it'll be black with people. Mind you,' he added, 'I've found a few quiet corners tucked away here and there.'

'Where've you booked for lunch?' Michael asked on impulse.

'I haven't. I was going to take you to this French restaurant I know, marvellous food, and they know me there; we'll get a table.'

'Do they do takeaway?' Michael smiled, looking towards the Green.

Paddy Byrne grinned. 'No, but there's a few places on Grafton Street which do. Do you fancy eating American?'

'I'll force myself.'

'This is lovely,' Michael said, looking around.

Paddy Byrne nodded. 'One of my favourite places.' He wiped his hands on a paper napkin. 'So, tell me about this new book.'

Michael stuffed the remains of his lunch into a bag and picked up the styrofoam cup of tepid tea. He looked out through the trees and across the lake to where some children were feeding the ducks with pieces of stale bread. 'Basically, its going to be an encyclopaedia of Irish folklore.'

'Irish or Celtic?'

Michael shrugged. 'I'll do both if I can. But principally its Irish folklore I'm researching this trip. I've sold American hardback rights, there's interest in England from one of the paperback houses, and there's also French television interest.'

'Looks like you've got yourself a good deal,' Paddy nodded.

'If I play my cards right, I'll get one popular book and possibly one good academic book out of it.'

'It will have to be good though. Do you know how many similar titles there are on the market?'

Michael nodded, 'I know, I've seen most of them.'

'So tell me, Doctor Cullen, what makes your encyclopaedia different from all the rest?' Paddy asked seriously.

'Well, Doctor Byrne, research. The research for my book will be the most detailed, the most complete and the most up to date. I intend to return to the original sources for the traditional myths and to access the records in the Irish Folklore Commission and, armed with them, return to the localities where much of the local lore was collected.'

'And how long do you have to do all this?'

'About six months.'

Paddy's sudden shout of laughter turned heads. 'Six months! Impossible! I'd say it would even be impossible to achieve it in six years.'

'Most of the research is done.'

'How much?'

'Enough.'

Paddy Byrne leaned forward to stare into Michael's eyes. 'Then why come here. Most of the material you need would be available on inter-library loan, and some of the larger American libraries are better supplied with Irish folklore material than many of the Irish libraries.'

Michael nodded slowly. 'But I needed to get a feel for the place. I can read as much lore and legends as I like, but that doesn't bring me any closer to the people.'

The older man leaned forward and tapped Michael on the shoulder. 'Have a look down there,' he said pointing to the crowds of people lolling on the grass or simply strolling through the park. 'Look at them, how much lore do you think they know, how much of their own folklore could they tell you? These are city people, city born and bred; why, even the country people who work in the city would know just as much, or as little, of the country lore as their city cousins. Don't make the mistake of thinking this is a backward, primitive country, Michael, because let me tell you, once the locals find out, they'll never forgive you for it.'

'When I was doing my book on Esquimaux folkore . . .'

'There's a difference,' Paddy snapped. 'Many of the Esquimaux live out their folklore, their lore is part of them, Irish folklore has little or no place in this country.'

'But what about the cases I've read of people refusing to cut down trees because it's an ancient fairy thorn or something like that.' Michael swivelled to look up at the older man. 'What about the story I read that said that one of the reasons De Lorean had so much trouble with his car plant was because two fairy thorn bushes were uprooted when the gates of the factory were going in?'

'That's good newsprint,' Paddy said with a grin, 'and sure,' he continued putting on a thick Irish brogue, 'it wasn't the poor man's fault that he had all those problems, it was the wee folk against him.'

Michael ignored the jibe. 'Did you have any luck with an assistant for me?'

'Let's walk,' Paddy stood up and brushed off his trousers. Pulling on his jacket, he indicated the path to the right with his furled umbrella. They walked along the crowded paths, past the ornamental fountains and the carefully tended flowerbeds which were in full bloom now, surprising splashes of colour against the green and stone. Walking away from the main gates where the crowds tended to congregate, they found themselves in a slightly quieter portion of the park. It was also a lot cooler. As they walked past one of the small fountains, this one complete with a statue of three or four people, Michael noticed a young, dark-haired woman, wearing a simple snow-white dress, sitting on the low wall surrounding the fountain, and combing her hair, brushing it in long, even strokes. Its texture and colour in the muted sunlight captivated him, and it took him a moment to realise that Paddy was talking to him.

'I'm sorry . . .'

'I was telling you about your assistant,' Paddy said with a grin, 'but you were too busy.'

'I was watching that young woman . . .' He turned and looked back in the direction of the fountain. There was no one there. 'Ah, she must have left. It was a young woman with the most extraordinary hair.' He saw Paddy's smile and continued, 'You were talking about my assistant,' he reminded him gently.

Paddy nodded. 'I had someone in mind, but now I'm not so sure.'

'Why?' Michael asked in surprise.

'It's a woman.'

'So?'

'How do you think Karla is going to react if you suddenly start spending all your free time with a female research assistant?'

'But it's work,' Michael protested.

'I'm sure it is,' Paddy grinned. 'Well, it's your problem, and on your head be it. OK? Well, here's what it is. Finding someone who had a knowledge of Old and Modern Irish, as well as a grounding in Irish lore proved particularly difficult. However, I finally turned you up someone who fits all your qualifications, has done a BA and is studying for an MA.'

'In what?'

'Anthropology.'

'Excellent.'

'She has also written some popular books on Irish folklore for children, retellings of the old stories.'

'Sounds good. I don't suppose this paragon has any experience with a computer . . .?'

'Wrote her thesis and her books on a word-processor,' Paddy grinned. 'And, what's more, is familiar with your work and would be delighted to have the opportunity of working with the great American Doctor, and so on, and so on. In fact, I'm sure if I had asked her to do it voluntarily, she would have done so. As it is, she'll be delighted to take your money.'

'She sounds almost too good to be true. What's wrong with her?' Michael asked suspiciously. 'Something must be wrong with her.'

'There's nothing wrong with her, it's really a case of the right person in the right place at the right time. I've met her and I think she's perfect for your needs. She's intelligent, with an academic background, knows her folklore better than anyone I know, fluent in Modern and Old Irish, familiar with the workings of the Folklore Commission and, I think she views the opportunity to work with you as a chance not to be missed. She's made for the job.'

Michael shrugged helplessly. 'You've convinced me. When do I get to meet this wonder?'

'Half-past five in my office.'

'I noticed you didn't say anything about looks.'

'Didn't I?' Paddy Byrne asked innocently.

'You didn't.'

'Well, she's beautiful too.'

'Now that I can't believe!'

'Dr Cullen would not believe that along with the rest of your qualifications, you were beautiful too.' Paddy Byrne rose to his feet and came around the desk as Michael Cullen stepped into the book-lined college room.

'Why, what was Dr Cullen expecting?' The woman stood up and extended her hand to Michael, her eyes, bright, bright green, he noticed, locked onto his.

'I'm not sure,' Michael stumbled, 'something . . . someone older.'

'I'm not sure if that's a compliment,' the woman grinned.

'When I learned all your qualifications . . .'

'If you'll both let me finish,' Paddy broke in. They both turned to him and began to apologise, but he hurried on, 'Maeve Quill, Michael Cullen.'

They shook hands briefly, and Michael noticed that her grip was strong and firm, with calluses on her fingertips and the fleshy pads of her palm. She was, he guessed, somewhere in her mid to late twenties, and possessed a simple, natural beauty that needed no cosmetics to enhance it. Her face was oval, with strong cheekbones, and wide-set, bright green eyes. Her hair, which was thick and black, laced with occasional threads of silver, had been pulled back into a severe bun, which tended to age her, and this was emphasised by her clothing, a dark green suit and flat shoes. Michael guessed that she had dressed for the occasion. He also noticed that she was only slightly smaller than he was.

'It is a great pleasure to meet you, doctor, I've read many of your papers and all of your books.'

Realising that he was staring, he smiled and pointed to the chair she had just risen from. 'Please, please . . .' He waited until she had sat and then pulled out a chair for himself. He sat at an angle to Paddy's desk, so he could see them both at the one time. 'Paddy's told me a little about you . . .' he began, unsure now what to say.

'I've brought along my references.'

He waved them aside. 'No, no, no need. I'll take Paddy's word that you're perfect for the job and from what he's told me it does indeed seem to be serendipity. You know why I'm here?' he asked.

'You're researching a new book,' Maeve said. Her accent puzzled Michael; Irish, distinctly so, but with a pleasant burr that softened its edges.

'I am here mainly to complete my researches on what will be the definitive encyclopaedia of Irish folklore.'

Maeve nodded. 'One has been overdue for a long time.'

'But I need a research assistant,' Michael smiled. 'Someone fluent in Old and Modern Irish, familiar with the lore and legends and able to use a word-processor.'

Maeve smiled. 'I can do all those.'

'I'm here for six months, I've rented a house not far from Skerries, but my stay might overrun for a month, maybe two, certainly no more. But I am looking for a commitment for at least six months, with the option of another one or two at the end of it. With regard to salary, I was offering two hundred a week, plus travelling expenses, plus credit in the book.'

'That's fine,' she said without hesitation.

Michael was surprised, he was prepared to offer her a little more money and even willing to negotiate a percentage of the royalties if she wanted. Paddy had been right, she would have done this job for the love of it. 'Have you any questions?'

'What will you want me to do?'

'Researching original sources of the legends, and the local lore, some translating, verifications of facts . . . the usual.'

She nodded again.

'Anything else?'

'When do you want me to start?'

Michael looked at Paddy in surprise, he hadn't been expecting it to be this easy. 'Tomorrow . . . tomorrow?' he suggested.

'What time?'

'Well . . .'

'I've an idea,' Paddy said suddenly, 'I've got to close up shop here, but why don't you two go for a drink, and I'll follow on in about fifteen, twenty minutes.'

Michael looked at Maeve and she nodded. 'Do you know somewhere?' he asked.

'Buswells is very civilised, and it should be quiet at this time.' She looked at Paddy and he nodded quickly.

'Buswells it is then,' Michael smiled. 'Is it far?'

Maeve nodded through the window towards Dawson Street. 'Second left, then down on the right-hand side. About five minutes.'

They walked up Dawson Street in silence, and it was only as they turned left into Molesworth Street that Maeve spoke. 'Thank you for giving me the opportunity to do this,' she began.

Michael shook his head quickly. 'Not at all, I'm the one who should be thanking you. Any work of this nature involves a huge amount of reference and cross-referencing, and I'm only delighted I was lucky enough to find someone so highly qualified and so suited to the job. I think it must be some sort of lucky omen for the book.'

'Well, thanks anyway. I don't need to tell you how helpful it will be to have my name connected to a good scholarly work like yours, and the money will come in very handy too.'

'Yes, well,' Michael said, feeling embarrassed now because he hadn't offered her a better wage, 'if things go well, I'm sure there will be a bonus at the end of the day.'

'It's just here,' Maeve nodded to the quietly elegant frontage of a small hotel. Michael followed her inside, where she turned to the left into a small bar. It was deserted.

'I like it,' Michael said, looking around at the dozen small tables spaced around the room, complete with real leather armchairs. Glass panels had been set into one wall to give the impression of space, but it still managed to look homely and cosy. 'What'll you have?'

Maeve hesitated as if she were about to argue, but then said, 'A dry white wine, please.' While Michael went to get the drinks, Maeve made her way to the corner of the room and pulled in three chairs around the table. She sat with her back to the wall, watching the tall American buy the drinks and then make his way through the tables. He was a lot younger than she had expected, quieter too, with none of the brashness and loudness which so often characterised American academics. She had been dreading the job initially, but she needed the money and beggars couldn't be choosers. Perhaps it wouldn't be so bad.

'Paddy tells me you've had a few books published,' Michael said, placing the glass of white wine carefully down in front of her. She was surprised to see him slide a coke in front of his own place. 'I don't drink . . . well not too often, and usually for medicinal purposes,' he said with a shy grin, seeing the surprised expression on her face, 'don't know why, guess I just never got around to it. Tell me about your books,' he said, changing the subject.

Maeve sipped her drink and grimaced. 'Cold,' she gasped as the chill set her teeth aching. 'Well, there are four in print now, three are children's, one is adult. The children's are all retellings of traditional Irish tales, while the adult book is a collection of popular Irish legends and lore.'

'And they're successful, I hope?' Michael asked, sipping his coke, watching the woman carefully, noting how the professional reserve was beginning to slip now that she was beginning to relax.

She nodded. 'Very. I'm already in the process of putting together a second adult collection, and I've just finished another children's book.' She looked up at Michael and said quickly. 'But it won't interfere with my work for you.'

'Perhaps we'll be able to be of some assistance to each other.'

Maeve nodded and seemed to relax.

'Would you have any objections to spending some time with

me in the house I've rented?' He sensed, rather than saw the change in her expression, and hurried on, 'My wife and children have accompanied me on this trip and we're staying in a large old house not far from Skerries . . . do you know it?'

She nodded slightly. 'I know Skerries well, I used to go there on holidays as a child.'

Michael glanced surreptitiously at his watch, wondering what was keeping Paddy. 'Have you many brothers and sisters?'

'I was an only child.'

Michael noted her use of the past tense, as well as the sudden tightening of her lips and decided not to pursue the matter. 'I wonder what's keeping Paddy?' he said aloud.

Maeve glanced at her watch then finished the last of her drink in a swallow. 'I really must be going, I've some work to do at home.'

'Anything exciting?'

She shook her head. 'A little genealogical research for one of the heraldic shops; its boring, but it helps pay the bills.'

'Do you do much of that?'

'Tracing family histories, lineages,' she nodded glumly, 'a lot.'

'But this is amazing,' Michael said excitedly, 'one of the things I wanted to do while I was here was to research my family background. I'll never have a better chance. Would you do it for me? I'll pay of course,' he added hastily.

She hesitated a moment and then nodded. 'Of course I'll do it. If you get me as much family detail as you can, names, dates of birth, marriage and death, dates of departure, the port they left from, where they landed in the States. Anything you think might be relevant.' She stood up and Michael rose with her. 'I'm sorry for rushing, but I really must go.'

He nodded quickly. 'Of course, I understand.'

'When do you want me to start?'

'Can you come out to my place tomorrow? and I'll go through my notes with you, give you a better idea of what we'll be doing.'

'What time?'

'What time suits you?'

'Early.'

'Shall we say nine?' he suggested.

'Nine it is. Now, how do I get to your place?'

'Ah . . . yes . . . well, to be perfectly honest, I'm not too sure myself.'

'I'll tell you what, I'll get the train to Skerries and if you could pick me up there. I'll be on the one which arrives as close to nine as possible, give or take a few minutes either way.'

'That would be perfect.' They shook hands, briefly, professionally, and then, without another word, Maeve made her way through the tables and left without looking back.

Paddy Byrne entered seconds later, red-faced under his snow-white hair. 'Got caught with a student,' he explained. 'Met Maeve on the way out.' He collapsed into a chair.

'She had some work to do at home.'

'Well, what do you think?'

Michael raised his hand and began picking off points on his fingers. 'She reads Old and Modern Irish, she's familiar with Latin, an expert on Irish folklore and is pleasant, cultured and genuinely interested in the job. I think she's perfect and, added to that, she does genealogical research on the side, and you know I've wanted to look into my family background. She's perfect. Almost too perfect. She'll do,' he grinned.

'Well now, you can buy me that drink for finding you such a pearl.'

4

Karla's perfume was heavy on the warm bedroom air when Michael cracked open the door and stepped inside. The luminous display from the clock-radio shed pale-pink light across one corner of the room, one-fifteen reflected in the dressing-table mirror.

Michael undressed as quickly and as quietly as he possibly could, bearing in mind that he was more than a little drunk. His one drink with Paddy Byrne had turned into two and then three, and then he had lost count, but he had had far too many anyway. He had caught the last train into Skerries and then walked the four miles out to Loughshinny and then the one mile beyond that out to Blacklands House. The long walk should have helped to clear his head, would have helped to clear his head, if he hadn't had the small bottle of whiskey with him. 'To keep the night air off your chest,' Paddy Byrne had said, pressing it on him back in the hotel.

But now that he had finally stopped moving, he could feel the effects of all the alcohol in his system, and that, combined with the strenuous walk, had now left him feeling weak and nauseated. There was a dull throbbing behind his eyes that he knew was going to develop into the mother and father of all headaches. He was going to throw up. He stood still by the side of the bed, breathing in deep lungfuls of perfumed air. Although the night was warm and sultry he began to shiver, goose-flesh rising up all along his arms. He threw back the covers and touched the sheets, and stopped.

They were chill, cold and slightly damp to the touch. Surely Karla hadn't put damp sheets on the bed? He knelt on the rough carpet and brought his face close to the sheets, they smelt moist and . . . He frowned, desperately attempting to concentrate, wondering what the smell was. It was familiar, but vaguely so, like old mown grass or moss . . . moss! That was it, it smelt of moss, moss on stones.

In God's name, what was Karla thinking about? Was she out of her mind sleeping on damp sheets? He was reaching for the sheets when a bout of nausea hit him, rising up from his stomach, flooding his throat with bile. Clamping a hand over his mouth, he staggered for the adjoining bathroom, and then leaned over the sink, his forehead pressed against the cold glass. He remained there for a few moments, and then, when nothing happened, he ran the cold tap and splashed water over his face. He then filled a glass with the cold water, drinking it quickly to clear the taste from his mouth. But, if anything, the water tasted even worse, and he spat it out, but not before it had left a curiously salty, copper-metallic residue in his mouth. Old pipes, he thought. The nausea, however, had passed, leaving him covered in a fine sheen of sweat, shivering now as the night air raised ripples across his skin. He stepped back into the bedroom, and stopped.

Moonlight shafted in through the big windows, and splashed across the king-sized bed, washing it in stark shades of black and white. Karla had obviously thrown back the covers, or perhaps he had pulled them off himself, but now she lay on the bed wearing her long satin night-dress. The moonlight bathed her in a pale, ivory light, giving her a vaguely ethereal appearance. There were deep shadows around her eyes, and her dark hair had turned the colour of coal. For a single instant, he saw someone else, a stranger. He blinked and the image was gone before he even had a chance to absorb it.

Christ, but he had had too much to drink!

He pressed his hands to the sheets again, but they felt dry and cool to the touch, pleasantly warm where Karla had slept on them. He brought his face close to the bed and breathed deeply, all he could smell now was Karla's stale perfume. He crawled into bed, promising himself that he would never drink that amount again.

Michael Cullen lay on his back, his eyes closed, massaging his throbbing temples, suspecting that it would be a long time before sleep claimed him. He was wrong.

The dream came in waves, in fragments, in abstract images,

which suddenly, abruptly, coalesced into a coherent whole . . . and left him terrified!

The day was warm, a day close to the heart of the summer, still and silent. He was moving through a forest, an old, old forest, the trees grand and gnarled, covered with moss and vines, following a track that had obviously once been nothing more than an animal run, but which man had taken for himself.

He was following something, a thread of sound, a hint of melody, a trembling on the air . . . a perfume. He had first heard that sound during the battle, even above the screams of the dead and the dying, above the howls of the Foreigners, the din of battle, he had heard it. He had first smelled the perfume then, smelled it clearly, even though the air was tainted with the odours of blood and death, of fire and excrement.

The battle itself had been a blur, but he remembered nothing of it, indeed, he did not even know the reasons for it. The War Arrow had gone out to the clan chiefs, and he had been called to honour his pledges to his chieftain. The lure of the smell and the sound held him now, nothing else was important.

In the early part of the afternoon, the fighting had moved on, down towards the beaches, away from the position he and his clansmen had held on the low hills. Those still filled with the blood-lust had followed them, howling triumphantly, knowing victory was theirs, but he had simply turned his back and walked away. Through the trees, off to his right, he could see the tents where the king, Brian, held council with his advisors. There were supposed to be guards around the tents, but he saw none of them as he moved into the forest, still following the sounds, and the merest suggestion of the odour.

Twice during his search he lost it, the sounds and stench of the battlefield overwhelming his senses, wiping out the delicate fragrance and the elusive sound. But on both occasions they had returned, and each time they were stronger.

He found the woman in the latter part of the afternoon, just as the sun was beginning to sink and the shadows were claiming the forest. She was sitting on the mossy bank of a pool, her feet in the water, her head tilted to one side, combing her long black hair with a fine-toothed comb. She was humming softly to herself.

Without a word he sat down beside her, the rich, damp odour of the mossy bank rising up to engulf him. She turned to him, her face thin and pale, her eyes deep and shadowed, her lips parted, her teeth white. A cold, white hand brushed his face, touching his hair, and then the comb, made of etched bone, came around and sank into his thick, dark hair, moving easily through the tangled mess.

Something screamed.

Michael Cullen awoke, chilled and sweating, his head pounding, sick to his stomach, the image of the comb etched behind his eyes.

Another scream, and this time he nearly shouted aloud himself, but he had identified the sound this time. Reaching over, he turned off the alarm clock and rolled out of the bed. Ten minutes later, just as the long case clock in the hallway chimed nine, he raced out of the door, wondering whether he would be in time to meet the train.

The time table said nine-ten, but the train was late, finally crawling into Skerries station closer to nine-thirty. It stopped for what seemed like an inordinately long time before it finally moved away. There were four people standing on the far side of the track, and for a single moment, Michael thought that Maeve hadn't arrived, until one of the women looked up and waved in his direction. She then turned and disappeared down the steps that led to a tunnel running under the track. Michael was waiting for her as she reappeared a few moments later on his side of the track.

'Christ, you look like death.' She smiled to take the sting from the words.

'Thanks. If it's any consolation to you, I feel like it too.' Michael ran his hand down his face; in the mirror that morning it had looked pale and haggard, the eyes deep sunk and shadowed.

'A hard night?' she asked, falling into step beside him.

'Something like that,' he agreed warily.

'Paddy can drink most men under the table,' she said quietly, not looking at him, as they walked out of the tiny station into the morning sunshine. She raised a hand to shield her eyes from the glare while delving in her shoulder bag, finally retrieving a pair of sun-glasses.

Michael pointed to the car and started strolling towards it. 'Well, it wasn't just that,' he said, vaguely compelled to defend himself and his old friend, 'I didn't sleep too well. Nightmares,' he muttered, and then grinned, 'helped of course by the drink.'

Maeve smiled. 'I haven't been in Skerries for a long time,' she said, deliberately changing the subject.

'I must admit, I haven't seen too much of it myself,' Michael said, settling into the car, reminding himself that the gearstick was on the left-hand side.

'We were brought here as children,' she continued, throwing her bag onto the back seat, and settling comfortably into the front. 'It was a great seaside resort then. With the city growing so fast now, though, its being gradually absorbed into the suburbs.'

Michael nodded vaguely. He was concentrating on negotiating the narrow gateway from the train station. He drove slowly down the road, turned right at the bottom, heading towards a roundabout whose centre had been cleverly planted with scores of vari-coloured plants in a rigid geometric pattern. Now, at the height of the summer, it looked quite spectacular. He drove around the roundabout twice before finally taking the turn out under the arched bridge, which carried the railway across the road. 'Let's hope I can find the house again,' he said, only half joking.

'I could drive,' Maeve suggested lightly.

Michael shook his head. 'No, no, I've got to get used to the idea that you drive on the wrong side of the road and the gears and levers are on the wrong side of the car. I suppose this is the best way to learn, by doing it.' He slowed as they came to a crossroads. After a moment's hesitation, he turned to the left. 'This is the right way, I think.'

'What are we going to do today?' Maeve asked, partially to distract Michael's attention, his nervousness was making her edgy.

'I thought we could go over my plans for the book, the various fields of research I'm currently pursuing. I'll also show you what work I've done to date and that should give you some idea where the book is going, and what I'm trying to do with it.' He suddenly nodded as a ruined castle appeared on the right-hand side. 'Yes, this is the right road.'

Maeve read the sign as the passed. 'Baldungan Castle, never heard of it.'

'MJ, my son, Michael jnr, told me yesterday that it was built in the thirteenth century, on the remains of an ancient fort. There's supposed to be a tunnel leading from the castle to the caves at Loughshinny,' he added, looking at the building.

Maeve straightened in her seat. 'Do you intend to break any new ground with this encyclopaedia of yours?' she asked.

'What sort of new ground?'

'New research, outrageous theories, that sort of thing.'

Michael grinned and shook his head. 'No, I've neither the time nor the inclination for that. The book will simply be a scholarly compilation of all the classic stories and themes from Irish lore and legend. There will be a few appendices which will consider the ancient beliefs in the present day, the various cults and fringe groups which worship the old gods, that sort of thing.'

Maeve glanced at him. 'It seems out of place in this type of book.'

'I want to do an essay on the continuation of the old ways, and how the traditional beliefs have been carried down to the present day, albeit in a somewhat changed form.' Michael suddenly pointed to the right. 'There's the house.'

The shape moved through the trees, a shadow, a flicker, and was gone.

Michael hit the brakes, locking the wheels into a skid that left rubber on the narrow road, slamming Maeve forward against the seat belt.

'What's wrong?' Alarm had flattened her accent, taking the cultured edge off it.

He didn't answer her. Something had moved through the bushes that lined the road, he was convinced of it. Beyond the bushes there was nothing but open fields, and they were deserted at this hour.

'What's wrong?' Maeve demanded again.

'I saw something,' Michael muttered, fumbling with the gears, before finally finding first and taking off at high speed, engine whining.

'What did you see?' Maeve ducked her head to stare through Michael's window.

He shook his head. 'I don't know, a shape . . . a figure.'

Maeve sat back in the seat with a smile. 'Probably just a farmer, or it might be a trick of the light through the branches,' she suggested.

He nodded, and then smiled sheepishly. 'Or the drink. I'm sorry, I'm still feeling the effects of last night. I didn't sleep too well,' he added, his eyes on the mirror, watching the road behind him. 'Still jet-lagged I shouldn't wonder.'

Maeve nodded, but said nothing.

They drove the last few hundred yards in silence, both vaguely embarrassed by the incident. Michael was troubled by the partially glimpsed figure, and a little annoyed that it should have startled him in such a fashion. He wasn't usually so jumpy. Put it down to the drink again.

When they turned into the gravelled driveway that led up to the house, Maeve said, 'It looks like a lovely location.'

'We're renting the place for the summer,' he said shortly.

'Does your wife not think it's a bit remote?' she continued, watching the house appear through the trees.

Michael grinned. 'A bit, but she knows I need the peace and space to work. That's her now.' He hit the brakes a little too hard and the wheels locked on the gravel, biting deep gouges into the path. 'I'll never get used to these cars,' he muttered.

Karla remained standing by the door of the old house while Michael and Maeve approached. The air was still damp with the night's dew and almost completely silent, and the noise of their feet on the stones was an unwarranted intrusion. Maeve found herself automatically walking on her toes.

Without her make-up and the uncompromising early morning sunlight harsh on her face, Karla Klein Cullen looked closer to fifty than her forty years. She was wearing a thick knitted jumper and a pair of designer jeans that were at least one size too small for her and, even though it was still close to nine-thirty, she wore her jewellry. She looked at Maeve, her lips tightening into a thin line of disapproval, noting the lack of any make-up, the shapeless cheesecloth dress, and the sandals.

Michael Cullen imagined he could almost feel the temperature fall as the two women appraised one another, and he was careful to conceal a smile. From the moment he saw Maeve in Paddy Byrne's office he had guessed Karla wasn't going to like her. He wondered briefly at his motives, and the sanity, of hiring a woman researcher. He realised with a start that he was enjoying his wife's discomfiture.

'Karla, this is Maeve Quill.' He began to smile and then stopped, realising Karla would misinterpret it. 'Maeve is the expert Paddy found; she will be working with me for the next few months. Maeve, this is my wife, Karla.'

'Hi . . .'

'Pleased to meet you . . .'

Michael looked at his wife. 'Karla, love, how about some coffee, eh? I've got a pounding headache, and I'm sure Maeve would like a cup after her journey?' He looked to her, and she nodded slightly. 'Two cups then, if you would. I'm going to introduce Maeve to the machine, and give her a run-down on the work.'

Without waiting for his wife's reaction, he turned away from her. 'Come on, I'll show you the study first, and then I'll let you see the rest of the house.'

'Your wife seems . . . very nice,' Maeve said carefully, following Michael around the side of the house.

'I'm afraid she's becoming a little bored here,' he said, without turning around, ducking beneath a vine-twisted branch, stopped by a door that was deeply sunk into the wall and almost completely hidden behind the creeper that covered most of the old house. 'I discovered this door yesterday,' he continued in the same tone of voice, 'it leads up to the bedroom I'm using as a study.'

'Very handy.'

'Very.'

Michael disappeared into the darkness and Maeve followed

him, lingering a moment in the cool, musty gloom, allowing her eyes to adjust. She could just about make out a flight of stairs directly ahead of her leading up into the darkness; dry dust tickled at the back of her throat. There was a sudden splash of yellow up ahead as Michael turned on a light, and Maeve slowly and carefully climbed the creaking wooden stairs.

When Maeve entered the room, blinking against the wash of bright sunlight that streamed in through the high windows, he was sitting in front of the computer, the screen glowing a pale soft amber, reflecting in his glasses. 'Paddy tells me you're familiar with one of these,' he said without turning around. 'This is the same model I use in college back home, and I brought my own software with me.'

Maeve leaned over the back of his chair and peered at the screen. 'What are you using it for, word-processing and data storage?'

He nodded. 'I'd be lost without it,' he said. 'Now, if you'll pull over a chair, I'll run through this with you.'

'That's all OK Dr Cullen, I'll stand if you don't mind.'

'Michael or Mike, but not Mr Cullen, and never Dr Cullen,' he said with a grin. 'Even on campus the students don't call me Dr Cullen.'

'Sorry Dr Cullen . . . Michael . . . Mike.'

He turned back to the screen, and almost unconsciously his voice slipped into his lecturing tone. 'Now, the main body of the book proper is stored here.' He tapped FOLK onto the keyboard and the screen blanked momentarily to reappear with a new menu, this one obviously showing the chapters of the book, numbered 01 to 09 in sequence.

'My notes are kept here . . .' He called up a new directory, and here the listing was alphabetical, Banshee, Cluricauns, Leprechauns, Luricauns, Phooka. Michael looked at Maeve's reflection in the screen. 'If you discover anything new about any aspect of Irish folklore, add it in here, and then we can run the comparisons and correlations at a later stage. I've created similar data bases for the various folklore cycles – the Ulster Cycle, the Mythological Cycle, the Fenian Cycle and so on – and I'm in the process of setting up another which will deal with Irish history.' He smiled wryly. 'I'm afraid I've only just discovered that early Irish history is inextricably entwined with the myths and legends.'

'I'm very impressed,' Maeve said, 'you're very methodical.'

'You sound surprised.'

'I've seen how some lecturers work,' she said with a smile. She straightened up and looked around. 'I think it will be a pleasure to work in this room.'

Michael swivelled around in the chair to face her. 'That's what I thought.'

Maeve walked over to the bookshelves and tilted her head slightly to look at the titles. 'So, what do you want me to do?'

'Initially, I want you to read through my notes, and see if there are any errors, and then see if there are any gaps. I'm sure there must be. Once you've identified the weak areas, you can set to work filling them in. In the meantime, I'll be pressing on with the main body of the book, and of course, I'll call upon you when I need further information.'

Maeve nodded. 'Are these all your references?' she asked.

Michael stood up and walked over to the bookshelves. 'That's what I brought with me. Is there anything important missing?'

Maeve shrugged. 'You're missing a few I would consider to be essential, some of the Irish Folklore Publications for instance, and some of those published by the Dublin Institute for Advanced Studies.'

'Buy whatever you think I need.'

'They're not cheap,' she warned him.

'It's a tax deductible expense,' he grinned. He turned as the door opened. 'Ah, coffee.'

Maeve turned, expecting to find Karla standing at the door, but it was a boy whose likeness to his father was pronounced.

'This is Michael jnr, MJ for short,' Michael said, taking the tray from his son. 'If you've any problems with the machine, just ask him, I swear he knows more about it than I do.'

Maeve solemnly shook hands with MJ. He looked at her with a certain wariness that might have been hostility, and she wondered briefly if Karla had said anything about her.

'I'm going down to the beach, Dad,' MJ said, looking at his father. 'If the tide's out, we're going to investigate the caves.'

'Well, you be careful, and watch the tide,' Michael warned.

'There's plenty of fossils in those cliffs,' Maeve said quietly.

The boy looked at her with more interest. 'Real fossils?'

Maeve nodded. 'It's mostly sea mulch, shells, seaweeds, detritus, that sort of thing. When I used to come here as a child, we always went fossil hunting on the beach.'

'I'll look,' the boy said, a little more warmly, as he hurried from the room.

'He looks a lot like you,' Maeve said, sipping her coffee, walking around the room, and looking through the large windows onto the garden below. 'Have you only the one child?'

Michael joined her by the window. 'No, there's also Christine . . . Chrissy. She's a year younger than MJ, and very much her mother's daughter.'

'Are they enjoying their holiday?'

'I'm not so sure about the children, I think they are. Plenty of fresh air, the beach and the sea almost on their doorstep, caves, a castle just down the road. What more could they ask for? Karla though . . . well, Karla's a little bored as I said, she misses the bright lights and the big city.'

'I suppose she thinks Dublin is very provincial.'

'I'm afraid she does,' he grinned.

Maeve smiled. 'You mean she doesn't think its "quaint"?'

He shook his head. 'She definitely doesn't think its quaint.'

Maeve finished her coffee quickly, suppressing a grimace; the coffee had been instant and lukewarm into the bargain. She placed the cup and saucer on a box full of journals. 'Well, I suppose we should get started. What do you want me to do?'

'I was going to show you around the house and the gardens,' Michael began.

'Perhaps a little later, if you wouldn't mind,' Maeve said with a smile, 'it is a little early and just a little damp.'

'Of course, you must forgive me.'

Maeve shook her head. 'Don't apologise. I'd love to have a look around the house a little later. But right now, I think it might just be a little too damp to go tramping around the grounds.' She smiled at the American, taking the sting from her words. He was not quite what she had expected. He was far shyer, rather more nervous that she had first thought. And, from her brief encounter with his wife, she guessed that there was more than a little friction between them. But he seemed easy going, and was genuinely interested in Irish folklore. When Paddy Byrne had first approached her about the project, she had thought Dr Michael Cullen might be just another American academic trying to write another instant book about Irish folklore. It came as something of a pleasant surprise to realise that he was actually trying to do some solid work in the field.

They spent the next two hours going through the material he had already prepared, sorting through the various notes and files he had drawn up over the past eighteen months while he had been researching the subject. Maeve sorted through the large data base of references, deleting some and adding others, impressing Michael with her knowledge and familiarity with the field.

'Paddy said you were good,' he said quietly, watching her create a new data base to hold the names and locations of the various Irish supernatural apparitions.

'You sound surprised,' she smiled, not turning around.

'I am, a bit,' he admitted.

'Why?'

'I'm surprised he was able to find someone so perfectly suited to my needs.'

Maeve turned from the glowing amber screen and glanced back at him. The light from the screen reflected across her small circular glasses, sparking in her bright green eyes. 'You must remember that in Ireland, folklore is more than just the study of the past, more than just a collection of ancient stories. Irish folklore has been kept alive, is still kept alive, by the story-tellers. Its a tradition that is dying in the cities of course, but in the country, people are still able to tell the stories about the district they heard from their parents and grandparents. Some of these stories would be folklore, others would be legend, others just plain fiction. It was a way of educating people.'

Michael walked around the room, his hands deep in his pockets. 'Would many people, ordinary, everyday people, people in the street, be aware of many of the Irish folktales? I've found that within primitive cultures,' he continued quickly, developing his point, slipping easily into his role as lecturer, 'the ordinary people are intensely aware of their folklore heritage. Would that be true of Irish, or indeed, any of the Celtic lands?'

Maeve slipped off her glasses and smiled at the suddenly intense man. She could easily imagine him lecturing before a hall of students, she had seen his type before. 'I think you must draw the line between what is legend and what is folklore,' she said. 'But leaving that aside for the moment, I think you'll find many ordinary Irish people would be aware of some of the traditional Irish tales – the Children of Lir, the Cuchulain stories, Finn and his Knights, the St Patrick stories. They would also be aware, even if only in a casual way, of the various creatures that inhabit Irish supernatural myth – the leprechaun, the banshee, the phooka, the sidhe. Obviously, in the more rural communities, the folklore tradition would be stronger.' He had stopped by the window and was staring down into the garden below. 'Do you intend to travel to the south or west?' she asked.

He looked away from the window quickly, a curiously detached expression on his face. 'Yes, yes . . . to the west, I thought, to the Aran Islands maybe?'

'It's not necessary to go that far, but of course the west is a rich source of folklore. Are you all right?' she asked suddenly, 'you look very pale.'

'Yes, yes, I'm fine, thank you.' He smiled wanly. 'A late night, with too much to drink and too much fresh air.'

Maeve nodded, not believing him. He had been fine until he had gone over to the window, and she wondered if he had seen anything in the garden below. 'How about showing me the rest of the house or the gardens now? My eyes are beginning to buzz from looking at this screen.'

'That's a super idea.' He looked over his shoulder, craning to look down onto the gravel drive below. 'I don't see the car, it looks as if Karla's gone out. And the place is so quiet, it looks as if she's taken the children with her.'

Michael led Maeve down through the house, chatting excitedly about the book, and his plans for it, and the book he intended to do after it, and how he wanted to retire to Ireland.

Maeve stopped listening after a while. The man was nervous for some reason, and yet he didn't strike her as the nervous type. Intent, studious, keen certainly, but not nervous.

There was a note on the kitchen table, slipped beneath the sugar-bowl. Michael pulled it out and read Karla's spiky writing, 'Gone to Ball-Brigan.'

'Balbriggan,' Maeve gently corrected him. 'Its a town a few miles north of Skerries.'

'Wonder what she's gone there for?' he murmured, almost to himself. He crossed to the kettle and lifted it, tilting it slightly, listening to the water sloshing around inside. 'Some coffee, I think,' he said, glancing across as her, 'and the real stuff this time,' he added with a smile. 'Or would you like tea?'

'Tea would be lovely.'

'Right, tea for two then.'

Maeve crossed to the back door and peered out. Automatically, she tried the handle and the door opened.

Michael looked up in surprise. 'I wonder why Karla didn't lock it? In the States, our rooms on campus are like Fort Knox.'

'There's probably not much need for locks here,' Maeve said, pulling open the door and stepping out into the warm morning air. The garden, which had been allowed to grow free and uncultivated over the years, came right up to the back door, and the aroma of wood and growth was almost overpowering. Maeve breathed deeply, 'You can almost taste the air.'

'One of the first things I noticed,' Michael said from the kitchen behind her, 'was how clear and clean the air was.'

Maeve stepped out onto the few cracked flagstones outside the kitchen door. 'You can smell the sea,' she said, 'how far away is it?' When she got no reply, she glanced back over her shoulder. Michael Cullen was standing before the sink leaning forward, peering intently through the window. Water poured unnoticed from the overfull kettle. Maeve hurried back into the kitchen, wondering what was wrong. She glanced through the window, wondering what he was looking at, and found herself staring into the stone-black eyes of a crow. The creature suddenly pecked at the glass, the sound hard and sharp, making them both jump, and then the black bird hopped off the window ledge and disappeared onto the branches of a tree.

'Jesus!'

'Are you all right?'

'Yes, yes.' He turned off the tap and half-emptied the kettle. Maeve noticed that his hands were trembling. 'I'm sorry,' he said eventually, 'its just that it startled me.' He attempted a smile. 'When I looked out the window there, I thought it was a face, a tiny black face. It just startled me.'

She took the kettle from his still-trembling hands and plugged it in. 'The birds probably got used to coming up to the house for crumbs,' she said reasonably, 'I suppose you had better get used to them.' She paused and added with a sly smile, 'And all their country cousins, of course.'

'What sort of country cousins?' Michael demanded quickly.

Maeve shrugged. 'Rats, mice, voles, bats, owls, foxes, beetles, flies, bees, wasps . . .'

'Enough, enough,' Michael said, smiling. 'I get the picture.'

'I think I'm going to like working on the book,' Maeve said eventually, as she poured the tea for them both. 'It will be nice to have a genuine excuse to come out to the country every day. Might even get some work done on my own book,' she added.

'If there's any way I can help,' Michael said quickly.

'I might take you up on that,' she said with a grin.

'I mean it.'

'So do I.' She finished her tea quickly. 'Now what about work?'

Michael looked surprised. 'No, not today. I think you've done enough for the morning. You can take the rest of the day off, and we can start properly tomorrow.'

Maeve shrugged. 'You're the boss. But I tell you what I will do, I'm going into one of the bookshops later, I'll pick up a few of the books I think you really should have in your collection.'

'Great idea.'

'And I'll see you tomorrow, about nine.' She stood up.

Michael looked up in surprise. 'You can't go now. Karla isn't back with the car.'

Maeve jerked her head in the direction of the sea. 'I know there's a bus stop on the main road, and there's a bus . . .' she rummaged in her bag to produce a paperback bus timetable, '. . . there's a bus in twenty minutes.'

'Well, if you're sure,' he said doubtfully.

'I'm sure.'

He was still suffering from the after-effects of the previous night and he didn't feel inclined to argue. His brief encounter with the crow had left him feeling nauseous; when he had looked out the window he really had thought a tiny black face was peering in.

He stood by the hall door and watched the young woman stride down the gravelled path. She paused at the corner and turned back to wave, and when she had gone, Michael felt suddenly and unaccountably lonely. Pulling the door closed behind him, he walked aimlessly down the path and then turned off into the woods, following a well-worn track. He could see water sparkling through the trees.

The copse ended almost at the water's edge and he had actually stepped out of the trees before he saw the woman. She was sitting by the side of the stream, brushing her hair. She turned to look at him, and screamed!

5

Michael Cullen stumbled backwards, a scream caught in his throat. His foot caught in an exposed root, tumbling him backwards into a bush, briars clutching at his flesh, nicking his clothing. In panic he thrashed around, completely entangling himself, and it took him several moments to wrench himself free, and when he finally staggered to his feet the woman was gone.

The wood was completely silent, no sound, not even a birdsong, disturbed the stillness.

Had he imagined it? Would it be possible for someone to make their way through the copse of trees without making a sound? He sucked at a long briar scratch along the back of his hand. He had been making enough noise himself for any number of people to have successfully made their escape.

He walked around the small muddy pool, looking for any traces of the mysterious woman in the pool's margin or on the grass. The ground was hard, the mud baked solid by the sun, and he wasn't enough of a woodsman to tell if anything had passed over the grass recently. He ran his hand across the rough grass, parting it carefully – and spotted the long sliver of white. Hunkering down, he parted the grasses, not touching the object. It was a comb, a long, pale yellow-white comb that seemed to be made of a translucent plastic. A thin, wavering red line had been etched into the back of the comb, and the teeth seemed unusually large and thick.

Still squatting on the ground, he looked around for other any signs of the woman around it. But aside from the comb, there was nothing.

'It was probably one of the neighbouring children,' Karla said indifferently. She walked from the kitchen into the hall, to carry in another bag of groceries. 'They've probably been using the grounds as some sort of playground for the past few months. Goodness knows how long the house was empty before we came here.'

Michael nodded, unconvinced. He was standing by the kitchen table, removing the vegetables from the bag. He had returned to the house moments earlier, still shaken from his encounter with the woman by the pool, to find that Karla had returned from her shopping, and that the kitchen was strewn with plastic and paper bags.

When Karla came back into the kitchen, her lips were twisted in a thin smile. 'You probably half-scared the poor child to death.'

'I don't think she was a child,' Michael said slowly. 'I only got a brief glimpse at her, but she looked to be a little older, mid-twenties, something like that.' All he could remember about her was her hair, long, dark and lustrous. She obviously took very good care of it. He touched the comb in his breast pocket.

'What happened to . . . to, what was her name again?' Karla asked.

Knowing full well that she knew the name, he said innocently, 'Who?'

'The girl . . . your secretary.'

'Not a secretary, more of a research assistant.'

'What was her name again?' Karla persisted.

'Maeve.'

Karla nodded. 'What happened to her?'

'She's gone into Dublin to pick up some of the books I need for my research,' he said smoothly.

'Can we claim for them?' she asked immediately.

He nodded, and then, realising that his wife had walked out of the room again, shouted after her, 'Yes, they're a legitimate expense.'

'Is she necessary?' Karla asked casually, walking back into the kitchen carrying yet another bag.

It was the question he had been waiting for. 'She's vital. I need someone with a background in folklore who can speak Old Irish. I can't. In fact,' he continued, 'she may even enable me to complete the project a little quicker.' He looked around for a reaction from his wife, but she had walked from the room again.

Shaking his head in disgust, he slipped from the room, pulling the back door closed behind him. He was almost across the courtyard when he heard his wife calling from the kitchen. He ignored her.

Michael Cullen walked slowly around the house, keeping close to the wall, feeling the heat radiating off the sun-warmed stones, still vaguely troubled by his unsettling experience and annoyed by his wife's penny-pinching attitude. She was griping over a few books necessary for his research, yet she must have spent goodness knows how much on the groceries, and all the cupboards and presses were full and the chest-freezer was stacked high with frozen food. Even if they were to buy nothing for the next few months, he was sure they wouldn't go hungry.

Completing his circuit of the house, he eased open the door that led up to his room, and quietly crept up the stairs. He could still hear Karla calling his name, irritation lending it the shrillness of her New York unbringing, a twang and intonation that she successfully disguised most of the time.

The study was quiet, pleasantly warmed by the morning sunshine, and just a little stuffy. Traces of Maeve's perfume lingered on the air and he breathed it in, attempting to identify it, and failing. It was light, pleasant, vaguely floral, and seemed suited to her temperament. Karla preferred heavy, almost bitter, and very expensive, perfumes that left him with a pounding headache . . . and they totally suited her temperament and personality.

The girl was going to work out well, he decided. She was enthusiastic and knowledgeable, and he hadn't been lying to Karla when he said that she might help him to complete the work faster than he had planned.

He crossed the room and sat down at his desk, automatically switching on his machine. The computer hummed softly to itself and then began clicking softly. It blipped once, startling him from his reverie, and he sat looking at the blank screen for a few moments, before his fingers began to work on the keyboard, the muted clicking and the dull hum of the machine the only sounds in the long room.

Michael Cullen called up the files Maeve had been working on earlier. She had sorted through some of the files and he began by flicking through them, reading her notes and comments, pleased with her thoroughness. One entry caught his attention; Maeve had labelled it SUPERNATURALS, and its curious title intrigued him. He opened up the file.

Maeve Quill had sorted through his references and gathered together all the various elements and creatures that might properly have a supernatural explanation to them; werewolves, vampires, phookas, witches, banshees . . .

He hadn't realised Ireland had 'possessed', if that was the right word, werewolves. Scrolling up the screen, he began to read, nodding every now and again, scribbling notes to himself. Here was the opportunity to tie Irish folklore in with general European and some of the other lore that was world-wide in its distribution. Every nation possessed some form of the werewolf legend, with the animal always changing with the culture. However, the most commonplace was the man into wolf story; the Irish variant of which seemed to be man, or woman in this case, into hare. Maeve has also cross-referenced this entry with the one relating to witches and witchcraft. Thoroughly impressed, now, with the woman's professionalism, Michael quickly scrolled through that entry, reading it quickly for the main points. Interestingly, Ireland had never been subject to the witchcraft trials that had scourged England, and whilst frowned upon, the witch, in the form of the local wise woman, existed in nearly every village. In a footnote, Maeve had added that witchcraft was thriving in present-day Ireland, and that some of the covens were worshipping an Irish or Celtic mother-goddess. He made another note; perhaps the subject of witchcraft in Ireland would bear a little further research. However, that wasn't bad for a morning's work, the girl had already earned her pay. He flipped his notebook closed and stared at the screen for a moment. Then, on impulse, he closed the files and instructed the machine to open a new file entitled FAMILY.

CAN'T FIND THAT ONE. CREATE A NEW FILE. (Y/N)

He typed Y and the screen cleared.

When Maeve had agreed to do a little genealogical research, she had said she would need as much information as he had available, but now that he sat down to do it, he was surprised, almost shocked, to discover just how little he knew about his family's history.

His father, Thomas Cullen, had been born in Dublin in 1910, although his grandfather, also called Thomas, had been born in the Bronx in 1878, but his father, Michael's great-grandfather, had been born in those same slums of Dublin in 1830, and had fled, along with the rest of his large family in 1845, during the height of the Great Famine. He had sworn never to return to Ireland, although he had, lured back by a siren call he never fully understood. They had sailed to the land of opportunity on one of the many 'coffin-ships', leaking, disease-ridden hulks that separated many people from their savings. From a family of nine, only two, Michael and Elizabeth, his younger sister, had survived: the other seven, including a babe-in-arms, had perished on the rough crossing.

Michael Cullen sat back in his chair, the names and dates glowing amber against the black screen. Put so simply, so plainly, it said nothing, but he wondered what stories lay behind those simple stark facts. What was it like for a simple peasant boy to see his parents, mother and father both, three brothers and two sisters, die from starvation and disease and be thrown overboard. What must it have been like for a fifteen-year-old boy, stranded in a strange country, with no money and no prospects, and a ten-year-old sister to look after? How had they survived?

He had heard that his great-grandfather had been a hard man, a cruel man, and his own son, Michael's grandfather had possessed many of his traits. Was it any wonder?

He had seen a picture of his grandfather once, a tall, hatchet-faced old man, standing erect and still, proud despite his great age and the rheumatism which had crippled him in later years. The cracked and faded photograph, his father's, still managed to convey the man's great strength of will. Michael smiled wanly, wishing he possessed just a little of his grandfather's determination.

He sat back and switched on his printer with the intention of printing a hard copy of the file when he realised that the clattering of the noisy machine would bring Karla up. Better to give her a little while to simmer down.

Michael yawned, stretching in the seat, massaging his aching neck muscles. He was looking forward to actually starting to write the book; it was something he had been planning for a long time, and now, with Maeve's help, he was sure it was going to go very well. It was going to be a good book, and all he needed to ensure academic recognition and financial independence was one book, one good book.

> The boy woke suddenly.
>
> He lay on the rotting straw that served as a mattress, and breathed in the foul air of the hold. He didn't know how many people were stuffed into the belly of the leaking ship, he couldn't count that high, but there were many, too many. Too many people with not enough money, not enough food, and too many dreams.
>
> The fifteen-year-old boy lay still, his eyes still closed, breathing easily through his mouth, wondering what had awakened him. Over the past ten days, since they had sailed out of Cork harbour, he had grown used to the wails and moans of the travellers, who were all Irish, and he had now reached the stage where their cries no longer bothered him. He had quickly fallen into the habit of breathing through his mouth: the stench of unwashed humanity, faeces, urine, vomit, the sharp, bitter odour of the boat itself, the brine of the sea, were almost completely overpowering.
>
> Ten days out and three dead.
>
> His stone-grey eyes snapped open and he turned quickly, squinting in the dim light to make out the shapes of his family, his now, since his father had died two days ago. His family were bundled together in one relatively dry corner of the craft, and the boy quickly counted through them, moving his hand

across their faces, only relaxing when he felt their breath against his palm.

Two of them, his younger brother, James, and his sister Moira, still a baby in her mother's arms, were no longer breathing.

He sat still for a few moments, feeling the pounding build up inside like in a white-hot heat that threatened to sear through him. The anger flooded into his throat in a foul bile, and he spat it angrily into the darkness. Finally, he simply crossed himself; there was nothing he could do for them now, and at least they were out of their misery. His father, Michael, had died only two days ago, and before that his younger brothers, Sean and Thomas had died, one from the wasting sickness, the other just seemed to give up. And now two more. Where would it end?

He turned away, no longer wondering what had woken him. He knew now. He had first heard it in Ireland. At first he had thought it had been the wind howling through the bare trees, the sound thin and high, like a distant whisper. He had heard it often over the past few months, but it had always been remote, detached, plaintive, sorrowful, like a dog howling over the grave of its master. Lost. Yes, if he had had to describe the sound in any one word it would have been that. It had sounded lost.

And then he had heard it three days ago . . . only then the sound had been different, altered. It had sounded close, so close that it had brought him wide awake, fully expecting to find one of the women in the cramped quarters awake and screaming. But the decks had been surprisingly quiet that night. And the wailing had continued. Now it sounded triumphant, like that of a beast which has finally cornered its prey. There was something terribly savage in the sound.

The wailing had gone on through the night, the sound itself kept changing, the timbre altering, one moment sounding like the cry of a wild creature, and immediately afterwards, a woman's anguished sobbing. The sound had drifted in and through his troubled sleep, occasionally bringing him almost to the surface of consciousness, and once, when a sudden surge of panic overtook him, when he desperately wanted to come awake, the sound had settled into a soothing lullaby.

When he awoke the following morning his father was dead. And, somehow, he wasn't surprised.

Later that same morning, when they had been burying his father, throwing his blanket-wrapped corpse over the side, he had thought he heard the cry again. But it might have been nothing more than the wind whistling through the stays.

Two nights later, the sound wandered through his troubled dreams. Desperately attempting to come fully awake, he sought to identify the sound. Human or animal?

The cry was sharper now, clearer, with a keener, -hungrier?-edge to it. There were words which he could almost, but not quite, grasp. And laughter; the voice seemed to be always trembling on the edge of hysterical laughter.

The following morning two of his brothers were dead.

And now he had heard it again, and he had known, even before he had gone to check his family, that he would find that death had walked amongst them.

Where would it end?

Young Michael Cullen heard the song that warned, or promised, death twice more during the trip. When it had claimed his mother, it had sounded almost sorrowful, the cry sobbing like a wounded child, but when it had taken his sister, a year younger than himself, it had been triumphant, almost like a battle cry.

Michael Cullen awoke, confused, disorientated, the stench of salt and sweat, of vomit and urine still fresh in his memory. It took several long moments for him to reorientate himself, to realise that it had been nothing more than a dream.

He had been thinking about his great-grandfather, wondering what it must have been like . . . and he had fallen asleep . . . and dreamt.

He sat up, and stopped, staring at the screen before him. When he had been writing the notes about his family, he had been working on a file called FAMILY. But the screen was now blinking on his Irish folklore files. And the file it had opened was the one entitled SUPERNATURALS.

Memories.

It thrived on memories. Memories were all that sustained it through the dark times, the times between the feeding. Memories.

And now its memories were of a certain time . . . a time of hunger. It had walked fields turned to muck with the disease which took the potato. It had been strong then. It had fed often.

Memories.

Then there had been water, but water was not its enemy . . . distance was, and those who left the birthland drifted beyond its power. Many left home, many of its clan . . . and it had learned the emptiness of hunger. It had hungered for so long now.

Soon it would feed.

6

'Jesus, you look terrible.' Maeve turned from the glowing screen and pulled off her wire-framed spectacles.

Michael ran his hands through his thinning fair hair and stifled a yawn. 'I didn't sleep too well last night.'

Maeve nodded sympathetically, but said nothing. The man's haggard appearance and deep-sunk eyes suggested something else, and she wondered if she was working for a drunk. It wasn't beyond the bounds of possibility, many of the academics she knew were notorious for their drinking bouts. She also remembered that his friend, Dr Paddy Byrne, was more than a little fond of neat whiskey.

'Jet lag,' he said, catching her look, 'too many time zones, not enough time,' he added, attempting a smile.

Maeve turned back to the screen. 'I took the liberty of starting without you,' she said, her voice carefully neutral.

'Have you been here long?' he asked, attempting to focus on the wall clock.

'About half an hour.' The clock read nine thirty-five. She touched a brown-paper parcel on the floor beside her. 'I picked up some of the books you needed . . .' she began.

'Have you had coffee?' Michael interrupted her.

She stopped, surprised. 'Not yet,' she admitted.

'Look, I'll go and get us some, we can talk when I come back, when I've fully woken up,' he added bluntly.

Maeve sat back into the chair, listening to his heavy steps clump down the bare stairs. She pulled on her glasses and turned back to the warm, amber screen, looking at it but not seeing the words.

She wondered again if he was a drunk, if he was she'd quit; from experience she knew she couldn't work with a drunk. He didn't seem the type, but . . . well you could never tell. Her own father had been an alcoholic for most of his life and no one outside of his immediate family knew it. But Dr Cullen had written several very good books and papers, and would a drunk be able to do that? or had they been 'written' by research assistants like herself. She'd seen that happen too. But even as the idea came to mind she dismissed it; the man had already done far too much research on the present project. Her fingers began moving over the keyboard, calling up the directory where he was keeping his notes, and then changing to the sub-directory where the references were kept. She opened up the file and began reading through them.

There was a four-and-a-half page bibliography, roughly three hundred titles, and following that about the same number of academic papers in a variety of languages. Maeve wondered how many he had actually read. It was very easy to prepare lists of books and papers to lend weight to a book.

She heard a noise below and then Michael Cullen's steps sounding on stairs. She closed the file and changed directory, so as not to arouse his curiosity. But the doubt had been sown. And of course, here was an academic doing when he called the definitive book on Irish folklore and he didn't even speak or read the Irish language, in which the vast bulk of folklore material still remained untranslated.

'Here we are.' Michael Cullen walked into the room, balancing a tray loaded with two large, steaming coffee mugs, milk and sugar in matching bowls and a plate of biscuits. He put the tray down beside Maeve, took his cup and walked over to the window to perch on the deep sill, one leg stretched straight out along it, the other swinging loosely. 'I feel like I died last night.'

Maeve smiled. 'You look like it.'

Michael sipped his coffee and grimaced; when she was angry or annoyed, Karla had a habit of making coffee that could easily have have passed for creosote. 'I did a lot of travelling before I came here,' he explained, 'and my body clocks haven't adjusted yet. I made a couple of short hops to the West Coast to sort out a TV deal and then to France where I managed to get French television interested and finally to London. The BBC were cautious but,' he shrugged, 'I think they might.'

'Will it be a series?'

He shook his head. 'No, I'll make one long documentary,

120 minutes, something like that, and it will then be edited for the American and the British market. The French version will be dubbed of course.'

'I wish you the best of luck.'

'Thank you. And of course, your name will appear on the credits.'

Maeve smiled, her previous doubts beginning to solidify into certainty. If there was a television programme made out of his book, she very much doubted if her name would be on it.

'Now, what treasures have you brought for me?' he asked, finishing his coffee quickly and hopping down from the window ledge.

Maeve put down her cup, glad to have an excuse not to drink the foul coffee, and lifted the plastic bag onto her lap. 'I didn't manage to get everything I wanted, but I would consider these to be almost essential.' She lifted out four books bound in green cloth and blocked with a Celtic motif in gold. 'These are the *Lebor Gabala Erann, The Books of the Taking of Ireland.*' She handed one over to Cullen. 'They're bilingual and they tell of the various ancient invasions of this island, from the arrival of the Princess Caesir Banba from the island of Meroe in the Nile, to the arrival of the Men of the Gael.'

Michael picked up one of the books and checked through the contents. 'The names I recognise. The Tuatha De Danann, the Fomorians, the Nemidians, the Milesians. How much of this is considered authentic?'

'I think you would consider this to be the mythological history,' Maeve said with a slight smile. His ignorance was not only surprising, it was almost embarrassing.

'But a good place to start?' he asked.

Maeve shrugged. She didn't think it was her decision to make. 'Yes, as good as any, I suppose.'

'OK,' he said, 'I'll do some work on that this afternoon, and I'm sure there'll be questions that'll need answering.' He opened the top drawer of the filing cabinet and handed Maeve a single sheet of paper. 'Now, here's a list of questions which I've already made up. They're mainly references, and verifications of some of my sources.'

Maeve looked down the list of questions. 'Some of these I can answer immediately. Some of the references I'll need to check of course.'

'How soon can you do that?'

'It'll take some time. The Trinity College Library will have some of the answers I need, but I'll probably have to go out to the library in University College, Dublin.'

'But you think you would have all the answers tomorrow?'

'I'm sure.'

'Well look, we'll work until lunch, and then you can head back into town to do your research, if that's OK with you?' he added quickly.

Maeve shrugged. 'You're the boss.'

'I'm sorry if I sound dictatorial, I don't mean to be; I'm used to large classrooms of unwilling students.'

'I know what you mean,' Maeve said easily, turning back to the screen.

They worked quietly on through the morning. Michael Cullen spent most of the time reorganising his notes into sequence, while Maeve arranged the files into an order that corresponded to his book synopsis. 'This way,' she explained when they had paused for coffee around eleven, 'when you're doing your chapters on the arrival and influences of Christianity in Ireland, for example, you'll have your notes on St Patrick, the various legends surrounding him, the legends about his predecessors, the druids and the various pagan beliefs on the same files.'

'I could get very used to having someone like you around to organise me,' Michael smiled.

'Oh, I don't know about that,' Maeve smiled, 'all the material is here, all you have to do is to organise it.'

'I like to think I am organised,' he confessed, 'and I suppose compared to Karla I am, but, well . . . it takes someone like you to show me up for what I am.'

Maeve looked at him sharply. Was he in the process of admitting something? 'But I've read your articles and books, they're very impressive,' she said, waiting for his reaction.

'Painful births all of them,' he said with a grin. 'If I'd had someone like you working for me I would have either produced them in half the time, or produced twice as many.'

'Thank you.'

'It wasn't meant as a compliment, I was simply stating a fact,' he sighed.

Michael called a halt about twelve, and then offered to drive Maeve back into Skerries so she could catch the twelve-fifteen back into the city. They were both silent on the short drive to the station, each absorbed in their own thoughts. Although she found the work interesting, it fell neatly into her own fields of study, Maeve couldn't help but wonder how much of this book she was going to end up writing, and then of course there were her own books which needed work on, and since she had taken on this job, she had done no work on them. She had been hired as a research assistant, and so she couldn't really object to doing the research, but she was going to have to draw the line somewhere.

Michael interpreted Maeve's silence as exhaustion, and was almost glad of the excuse not to have to speak to her. Occasionally, far too occasionally now, he felt the excitement of writing, and when it happened he liked to capitalise on it. It was happening now and all he wanted to do was to leave Maeve and get back to work.

By the time he got back to his humming computer, some of that excitement had worn off, and he paced restlessly around the room, attempting to organise his thoughts. He was going to write the chapter about the arrival of the Princess Caesir Banba to Erinn in a time so far back it was considered mythological. She had been fleeing a flood that had raised the water level of the Nile and had threatened her island home of Meroe. He had been more than surprised to find that there actually was a place called Merowe still existing on the Nile today.

It was, as Maeve had said, a good place to start. These were the legendary first invaders to come to Ireland, these were the people who had given Ireland its first name, and there was also the added bonus in that it would allow him to draw comparisons with other 'flood' legends.

But when he sat down at the screen, the words wouldn't come, and almost reluctantly, he turned the machine off and sat listening to the hum descending into silence. After lunch, he would start after lunch . . . yes, lunch and a stroll . . . and he would be able to write.

MJ and Chrissy were just coming in as he came down to the kitchen. They had been down on the beach and trailed sand and the rich salt and iodine smell of sea and seaweed. For the first time in as long as he could remember, Michael thought they looked well, both rosy-cheeked, bright-eyed, and relaxed. Also they weren't arguing together, which made a pleasant change.

'Where've you been?' he asked.

'Beach, Dad,' MJ said shortly. He was absorbed in washing sand and grit off a long flat rock. He turned and held it up to his father. 'What do you think eh?'

Michael pushed up his glasses and brought the stone to his face. 'Trilobite,' he announced. 'Nice condition too,' he added, handing the fossil back to this son.

'You've got to come down to the beach with us Dad, there's whole seams of fossils.'

'And some gorgeous shells,' Chrissy added, tilting her bucket so her father could look in.

Michael Cullen made a deliberate effort to sort through the shells and show some interest in his daughter's collection, all the while marvelling that this was the same girl who had only shown interest in youthful pop singers and excessive make-up. His son, MJ, had previously only evinced an interest in computers, and if they both got nothing more from this holiday then Michael would consider it to have been well worthwhile.

'Tell me,' he asked casually, 'have you made any friends hereabouts?'

MJ shrugged. 'A few. They're OK.'

'Do they ever come here?'

Chrissy shook her head quickly. 'They won't. When the house is not in use, it's locked up and the walls are too high.'

'Are there walls?' Michael asked, surprised.

'Topped with broken glass,' Chrissy added seriously.

'There must be a way through, perhaps the wall is broken somewhere,' Michael suggested.

'Well, I haven't found it,' MJ said quickly, 'and I've gone round the grounds.'

'Would either of you know if there's a young woman, not a girl, living around here. Tall, thin, long black hair, pale face?'

Both children looked at him and shook their heads.

'Why Dad?' MJ asked.

'No reason. Just that I thought I saw someone out in the orchard earlier on, must have been mistaken though.'

'The only way in is through the front gates,' MJ said, 'and we spent most of the morning out on the front lawn before we went down to the beach. We would have seen them.' His sister nodded in confirmation.

'I must have been mistaken then, forget it. Now, where's your mother, eh?'

'Last I saw of her, she was in the bedroom, sorting through some of the new clothes she bought in Dublin,' Chrissy said.

'OK. Set the table, and I'll go and get her.'

'How about the beach after lunch Dad?' MJ asked.

'Well . . .' he saw the disappointment in his son's face even as the words were forming and smiled quickly. 'Yeah, why not.'

'Great!'

Michael found Karla standing before the full-length mirror in the bedroom, wearing a sky-blue dress that he certainly didn't remember seeing before. A black and cream plastic bag from the store had been tossed onto the bed, and even that looked expensive. He paused in the doorway, watching his wife carefully. She was completely engrossed in her image in the mirror. With her hair swept back off her face, highlighting her high cheekbones, emphasising her dark eyes, she was indeed the classic beauty he had married thirteen, fourteen? years ago. He had been very much in love with her then, the quiet academic marrying the rich beauty, the sort of thing cheap novels and poor soaps were made of. He wasn't sure if he could put his hand on his heart and claim in all honesty that he still loved her.

Karla caught his reflection in the mirror, and smiled. 'What do you think eh?' She turned, putting her hands on her slim hips. The gown was cut low in front, with a deep cowl neck, and tapered at the waist, with a classic cut and simple design that he knew must have cost a small fortune.

He forced a smile, resisting the temptation to snap a reply. 'I think it looks gorgeous. You look fabulous!'

'I couldn't resist it. And it was such a bargain.' She turned back to the mirror and he noticed that she hadn't mentioned the price.

'Are you coming down for lunch?' he asked, stepping into the room, and crossing to the window to look out into the garden below, his eyes drawn to the wooded and heavily overgrown section that he knew concealed the pool.

'I'll be down in a moment. I just had to try this on. Will you do the zip for me?'

Michael stood behind her as he released the zip, and now that he was close, the image of youth was slightly tarnished. There were lines around her eyes and etched into the corners of her mouth, lines that too much make-up couldn't hide, only emphasise, and beneath her chin, age was beginning to tell. Sometimes he forgot that Karla Klein was nearly ten years his senior.

'Your assistant went off early today,' she remarked, shrugging the dress off her shoulders and allowing it to pool around her feet. Beneath she was wearing the oyster coloured underwear he had bought her as a present for Christmas. It had been an outrageous price, but it was one of the few gifts he had given her that she seemed to like. He watched her dress quickly, efficiently, and he realised that it had been a long time since he had actually seen her naked.

Vaguely disturbed by the line his thoughts were taking, he hurried from the room. 'I'll start lunch,' he called back, 'I want to take the kids to the beach afterwards.'

* * *

It was close to five by the time Michael Cullen returned to Blacklands, exhausted but pleasantly so. Having decided that he was taking the afternoon off, he had been determined to enjoy himself, and had spent an enjoyable few hours with the children, which was something he did far too rarely, he realised. When he returned home, he found Karla sun-bathing in the rear garden, wearing a bathing costume that his mother wouldn't have been ashamed to wear, but perhaps the 50s look was in, he reflected, looking at the sharp-edged sun-glasses. There was a long glass of crushed ice by her side, a quarter inch of water in the bottom of the glass. He flopped down beside her and drank it quickly, wincing as the ice seared its way down his throat.

Karla stirred slightly. 'Did you have a good time?' she murmured, without looking at him.

'Great.'

'Where are the children?'

Michael smiled. 'I don't know where they get their energy from, they ran me ragged all afternoon and now they're off about the garden somewhere.'

'What time is it?'

'I don't know.' He squinted into the cloudless sky, the sun beginning to dip towards the horizon. 'Sometime after five, I should think.'

Karla stretched. 'I'll have a shower, I think, wash this cream off me, and then I'll start tea.'

Michael nodded. 'OK. I'll be working late tonight, so I might as well set it up now.'

His study was silent, pleasantly cool after the heat of the day. Dust spiralled in the still air, caught in the slanting sunlight, and Michael briefly wondered about the effect of the dust upon his machine.

The computer came to life with an ascending hum, and the hard disc whirred and squeaked. It blipped once and his fingers began moving over the keys, slowly at first, calling up his work directory and choosing a file.

He stopped when the first drop of blood spattered across the keyboard. Almost of their own accord, his fingers started moving across the keys, spattering them in red.

He looked blankly at the crimson stains, and then lifted his hands and looked at them: his left index and forefinger were sliced across the top, blood welling from the split flesh. He looked at the cuts, wondering where he had got them, and then his rational mind took over, telling him that he must have cut his fingers on the beach, perhaps on the sands, or the stones when they had been fossil hunting, and when he had started to tap the keys the split flesh had opened.

Blood.

There was blood on the air. And blood brought memories and memories were life.

7

Michael Cullen stopped working a little after midnight. His lower back was encased in a band of fire and his eyes felt gritty and sore. There was a sour taste in his mouth and lurking behind his eyes a pressure that he knew would develop into a serious headache.

He had been writing in darkness, the only illumination coming from the screen, but now he reached over and turned on the desklamp, wincing at the light. The darkness helped his concentration, cutting down the distractions, but it also meant that he tired more easily.

He stretched, his muscles popping and cracking, his eyes still on the screen, but not seeing the words, only the figures in the top right hand corner, ten, nearly eleven pages, single spaced, standard A4 size. He called up the word-counter programme and listened to the machine blip softly to itself and then the figure 5116 appeared on the screen. Five thousand words, not bad for a night's work. Of course, when he edited it down, he would be lucky if he got half that.

He'd get some tea, and maybe do another hour.

The house was silent, as silent as any old house could be, but he found the creaking and groaning oddly comforting. It was like listening to an old man settling down for the night. He stopped on the landing and looked in on the children, they were both asleep. A curious hissing sound brought him back to MJ's room, and it took him a few moments to realise that the clock-radio was now emitting a dull grey static. In the next room Chrissy was wrapped around her favourite teddy, a hideous creature of green and gold, which was now so old and had lost so much stuffing that it resembled a matchstick man.

He stopped and looked in on the master bedroom; Karla was asleep, curled up into a tight little ball, wrapped securely in the covers, and the room smelled warm and close, the air heavy with the scent of her perfume and the more pleasant odour of soap. He closed the door behind him and padded silently down to the kitchen.

Michael turned on the light in the hall, but left the kitchen light off, working in the light that came in through the open door. He filled the kettle and plugged it in, and then leaned foreward against the window, the glass cool against his forehead. He was bone-tired, but he was on a roll, and he knew from previous experience that if he continued working on into the night, he might get at least another five thousand words done. Now, it mightn't be very good, but at least it would be usable and could be shaped later.

But what he needed now was some coffee, laced with sugar.

The shape moved through the trees, blacker than the night, paler than the reflected moonlight.

Michael remained motionless, blinking hard, feeling his heart beginning to beat painfully. He moved his head back from the window and peered through the glass. Had he just seen a shape, tall, thin and black, move through the trees, or was it just the product of his exhaustion?

He continued staring out into the garden. He saw nothing, and now his eyes were beginning to play tricks on him, tiny splotches of colour and darts of light drifting across his retinae. He squeezed his eyes shut, digging the heels of his hands into them, and then, blinking hard, he looked out again, . . . and saw the figure.

There was a kitchen knife block on the draining board and he grabbed the first knife that came to hand, a black-handled short-bladed parer. The key was still in the back door and he turned it gently, pulling the door open as quietly as possible. He stepped out into the warm, close night.

He had seen the shape moving through the trees to the left, and that would bring it down to the lake, he realised. Gripping the small knife tightly, he skirted around the trees, his slippered feet noiseless on the grass. He was grateful for the moonlight, which at least allowed him enough light to see by, although beneath the trees, he guessed it would probably hinder more than help.

Michael stopped, head tilted to one side, listening, but aside from the thundering in his chest, there was no sound. He crouched low to the ground and peered through the trees. Initially, he could see nothing and then, as his eyes adjusted, he began to make out forms and shapes of the trees and bushes. He crept closer, and suddenly the small pool was a sheet of dappled silver in the light, and then the shape flickered before it.

He moved beneath the cover of the trees and attempted to make his way towards the small pool without making too much noise, but that was impossible. Leaves rustled, branches snapped or crunched underfoot, and every sound seemed magnified in the silence. With whatever chance of surprise now lost, he took a deep breath and burst through the bushes to confront the figure.

For a single moment he thought he had lost it, and then, smoothly, silently, it seemed to rise up out from the ground before him.

He might have shouted, he wasn't sure, but he brought the small knife up before his face and waved it before the shape.

'Who . . . who are you? What are you doing here?'

Something white moved in the shadows, rising up along the black and then a hood was pushed back, revealing the pale face of a young woman! Although he had only seen her briefly, he immediately recognised her.

'You . . . you're the woman I saw yesterday . . . with the comb!'

She nodded, but said nothing.

Michael lowered the knife and then, almost self-consciously, pushed it into his pocket. He stared at the young woman. Her face was long and thin, unnaturally white, although that was probably a trick of the moonlight, with high, pronounced cheekbones, and wide, slightly uptilted, almost oriental eyes. Her eyes were so dark that they could only have been black. Her hair was so black it took a lustre from the light and shone like strands of silver wire, completely framing her face. He guessed her age to be no more than eighteen or nineteen.

'What are you doing here?' he asked, his voice soft, almost gentle.

The woman brought her pale hand up to touch her hair and then mimed the act of combing it, and then she pointed to the ground. Finally she stretched out a bare arm, and it was as thin and as pale as the rest of her, and held out her hand, palm upwards. He noticed that her fingernails were long and seemed to be painted black, although that too, was probably a trick of the light.

'Who are you?' Michael asked. Why didn't she speak?

The hand moved again, moving upwards slightly, the fingers beginning to curl.

'Can you speak?' Was she dumb, he wondered.

Her hand went to touch her hair, and was then thrust forward again.

'You're looking for your comb. . . ?' he began, stepping forward, and the long-nailed fingers snapped closed around his throat!

In the few moments it took for the realisation of what was happening to sink in, the rigid fingers had tightened around his windpipe, the thumb pressing just below the point of his jaw. Holding him at arm's length, the woman began to lift him off the ground!

Michael scrabbled at her grip, but her fingers might well have been cast of iron. He could feel the gathering explosion of pain in his chest and skull, the creaking of his neck joints. His eyes were protruding so far it was painful.

The knife.

He remembered the knife in his pocket. Unnoticed, he sliced open his fingers pulling it from his pocket, and with his last few seconds of consciousness, he slashed at the women's bare arm. He saw the blade slice the pale flesh, felt it drag across skin, but there was no blood.

And then the woman hissed at him, the same sound a snake might make before it strikes, and although his head was afire, he thought he recognised words, vague, guttural words. And then she cast him aside, flinging him into the undergrowth.

When he came to she was gone.

Michael Cullen lay on the damp ground, desperately trying to work out what had happened. For a moment, he was inclined to dismiss it as a dream, but this was no dream: he could barely swallow and his entire throat felt crushed and raw. And then he began to shiver, and it wasn't from the cold.

'Well, there's nothing wrong with your throat,' Dr Patrick Byrne said reasonably. 'And if this young woman had a grip such as you described, and was strong enough to lift you straight off the ground, then she should have left marks clear enough for us to read her fingerprints.'

'I know there's nothing there,' Michael whispered, his voice hoarse and ragged, 'nothing visible that is, but I can feel her fingers here . . . here and here.' His fintertips touched his throat.

Paddy Byrne leaned back in his chair, his long fingers steepled before his mouth. 'How does your throat feel now?'

'As if someone tried to strangle me. I can barely eat, Karla thinks I'm coming down with something, even swallowing is difficult.'

'Even if it was psychosomatic, it would have left some traces on the skin, but there's nothing. Not a mark.'

'You don't believe me,' Michael said quickly, looking past Paddy Byrne, beyond the college walls and out into the busy street. Its mundane normality made his own experience all the more terrifying.

Paddy Byrne leaned forward and rested his elbows on the table. 'I didn't say that.'

'Well, what did you say?'

'I was simply stating the singular fact that there is no mark on your throat, but I never said I didn't believe you.' He laced his fingers together and looked at Michael, his eyes twinkling. 'But let us consider the facts if you will.' He began ticking them off on his long fingers. 'By your own admission, you had been working hard and intensively, and had managed to write more than five thousand words in one sitting. You had been writing in virtual darkness, the only light being that coming from the screen, a quick way to destroy your eyes,' he added in an aside, 'and you've also admitted you were completely exhausted.'

'Yes but . . .'

'But what?'

'I've written on into the night before.'

'Perhaps you have. But you've covered a lot of miles and time zones in the last few weeks. Your body doesn't know whether its coming or going.'

Michael nodded. 'You're right.'

'I know,' Paddy said shortly. 'Now, what could be more likely that when you went downstairs you nodded off while waiting for the kettle to boil, fell asleep standing up, it can happen!'

'I've thought about that,' Michael sighed, 'and I want to believe it,' he added, a touch of desperation in his voice, 'except that every time I swallow I'm reminded of this woman.'

Paddy Byrne ran his fingers through his snow-white hair. 'Tell me,' he said with a sly grin, 'what were your writing about before you saw this woman?'

'I was working on the first draft of the first story for the book, the arrival of the Princess Caesir Banba to Erin.'

'You'll forgive me if I get the facts wrong, but didn't she come to Ireland with thirty women and three men?'

'Something like that.'

'Hardly surprising then that you should have dreamt of a woman, especially an exotic, enigmatic woman. You dreamt of it with such clarity that when you awoke you retained the mental, if not the physical, reminders of your encounter. I'm sure a good analyst would provide you with several insights into the meaning of that dream in a psychosexual sense.'

'I didn't dream it,' Michael insisted.

Paddy Byrne fixed Michael Cullen with his sharp, hard eyes and asked very quietly. 'Well then, is there another explanation?'

'There has to be . . .' Michael began loudly, but his voice trailed away as he realised where Paddy's line of questioning was leading. 'But I don't know what that explanation is,' he finished lamely.

Paddy stood up and came around the desk. He stood behind Michael's chair and rested both hands on his shoulders. 'Come on, I'll buy you lunch.'

They walked slowly through the college grounds. Although it was summer and the college was closed for the holidays, it was still thronged with people. Michael pointed to a queue forming outside a simple wooden door. 'What's in there?'

'The Book of Kells.' Paddy grinned. 'I'll show it to you some other day.'

'I'm not sure I want to see it.'

The older man looked shocked. 'You can't go home without having seen the Book of Kells, its mandatory viewing.'

'Well, if you insist.'

'I do. But not today. Tell me,' Paddy continued, 'how's Maeve working out?'

Michael shrugged. 'I haven't seen a lot of her I must admit. She's been doing some research for me in the libraries here in town. However, what she has done has been excellent. She's thorough and efficient.'

Paddy nodded. 'She is that.'

'Is there a man?' Michael asked, curious.

'Don't even think about it,' Paddy grinned.

'I wasn't.'

'But you asked, and that shows some degree of interest.'

'Just curiosity, plain and simple, nothing more than that.'

Paddy turned to the left, heading towards the main gate. 'Well, there's no one that I'm aware of,' he said slowly, nodding to two students who smiled at him, 'although I have seen her in company with a young man occasionally, but I think they're only friends.'

Michael nodded. 'She has an independent air about her, she's very self-sufficient.'

'How does she get on with Karla?'

Michael smiled wanly. 'Ask me how Karla gets on with her.'

'Ah.'

They walked from the smooth cobbles onto the smooth wood flooring beneath the arched entrance to Trinity College. Pushing their way through the tourists, they stepped out into College Green, and then, taking advantage of a lull in the traffic, darted across the road. Paddy pointed to the right, to an impressively colonnaded building. 'That was formerly the Parliament Buildings,' he said, 'built in the early eighteenth century with numerous additions down through the years. It is now used as a bank.'

'Nice,' Michael commented.

'One of the most impressive buildings in Dublin and all you have to say is "nice". You're a Philistine, Michael Cullen, a Philistine.'

'I'm tired, sore and hungry,' Michael said with a weak grin. 'Give me the guided tour some other day.'

'OK.,' Paddy said gently. 'Do you like pizza?'

'I'm an American,' Michael said outraged.

'I know a great pizza restaurant.'

'Paddy sends his regards,' Michael said.

Karla nodded and grunted, her eyes never moving from the television.

'He said he might call on us some time over the next few days.'

Karla nodded again.

Michael shook his head and returned to the sheaf of paper he was correcting. He had arrived home just before six, relaxed and at peace with himself. He was grateful to Paddy, having only realised on the drive out to Loughshinny what the old man had done. Paddy had seen the state he had been in and had remedied it, and the good food, pleasant conversation and plenty of wine had combined to make the events of the previous night seem very distant indeed. His fingers automatically went to his throat. He could still feel the impression of the woman's fingers, but even that was fading.

Following a brief, virtually silent tea with Karla, Michael had retired to his study and powered up his machine. But when he had sat down and prepared to do some work, the words wouldn't come, and in the end, becoming irritated with the computer's low hum, he had printed up a copy of his previous night's work. He could sit with Karla and correct it; perhaps it might make amends.

Karla, however, was more interested in the television and after several fruitless attempts at conversation, Michael had turned on the stereo and plugged in the earphones. With Bach's 'Well-Tempered Clavier' on the turntable, he had settled down to work. And although he was seated beside Karla, with no more than two feet between them, an immeasurable gulf separated them.

In the soft warm silence of the night, a pale-faced figure moved through the garden, drifting around the still pool, eyes downcast to the ground, searching.

At first he thought it was the record, and thought no more about it. But the sound persisted and began to bother him, so much so that he put down his red pen and concentrated on the noise. Bach's 'Well-Tempered Clavier' was something with which he was intimately acquainted; like most writers he wrote with music on in the background, picking the piece to suit his need and humour, often adjusting it to match the piece he was writing. Perhaps it was a scratch on the record, a piece of dirt. He pulled off the headphones and stood up to cross the room when he realised he could still hear the noise.

It was a dull scratching sound, not unlike the sound of a nail being drawn down a blackboard, or the rusty hinge of a distant gate slowly creaking back and forth.

When he turned the record player off, the sound persisted. 'Do you hear anything?'

Karla didn't even bother to look up. 'Nothing.'

Controlling his temper, Michael strode from the sitting room out into the darkened hallway. He stopped, his head tilted to one side, listening, but the sound was fainter now, a mere irritation at the base of his skull. He opened the hall door and stepped out. The night was warm and heavy, and completely still, and now the sound was clearly audible, sounding almost close enough to touch.

It was the sound of someone, a young woman, crying.

8

It was a cat, nothing more than a cat mewling somewhere in the garden. A lost stray cat . . . a cat . . .

But he knew it was no cat: there was too much anguish, too much pain in that cry for it to be from any animal, only man had the capacity to express his pain in such a fashion.

Turning his head from side to side, he attempted to pin down the direction of the sound. It sounded so close, and yet it held the slightly echoing reasonance of a sound travelling over a great distance.

There, to his right.

He moved quietly across the gravel, his slippers making little sound on the stones, and stepped onto the grass. He had fixed the sound now, through the trees he could just about make out the metallic glitter of water. Somehow he was unsurprised.

She was waiting for him by the water's edge, her black cloak like a slice of the night. As he stepped into the clearing surrounding the water, her head came up, her face a pale mask in the dimness, her eyes black holes. There was a flicker of white and her bare arm came up, palm upturned, fingers closed in a fist. As he watched, the hand slowly opened, like some nocturnal flower.

'You want the comb?' Michael Cullen said slowly, his voice sounding numb and distant in his own ears.

The hand moved slightly, the fingers curling, the nails now visible, long and black in the moonlight.

'Who are you . . . what are you . . .?' His throat felt terribly contricted, throbbing where she had gripped it the previous night.

The woman's arms lifted, crucifying her against the night and her dark cloak split down the middle. She was naked beneath, her white skin gleaming like polished stone. She shrugged her shoulders and the cloak fell to the ground without a sound. Her body was that of a young woman in her late teens, with small high breasts, her nipples dark against the paleness of her flesh, her ribs gaunt and visible beneath. Her stomach was flat and she seemed to possess little or no body hair. She reached for him, both hands rising up to brush his arms, coming to rest lightly on his shoulders and her thin dark lips curled in a smile.

Michael Cullen sat up in bed, only to immediately collapse again with a groan. His head felt as if it was going to explode and his throat was raw sandpaper. There seemed to be a film over his eyes and he had to blink hard for several moments before they cleared. He looked around the room in confusion. Where was the woman, the pale-skinned woman? His trembling fingers came up to touch his throat, and then a pale face swam into view and he jerked back with a frightened whimper.

Karla and Maeve both looked down at him.

'The doctor said it was probably just overwork, coupled with exhaustion and jet lag. A few days in bed should see him well again.'

'He was looking tired over the last few days,' Maeve agreed.

'If you'll both leave off talking about me as if I'm not here,' Michael whispered, surprised at how weak he sounded. He sat up again, carefully this time. 'I've got a pounding headache.'

'I found you in the garden,' Karla said sharply. 'You had collapsed.' She made it sound like a crime.

Michael looked at her, his expression guarded. 'When was this?' he asked softly.

'A couple of hours ago,' Karla said firmly, although Michael noticed that her eyes were wary, almost frightened, and when she continued, he detected the break in her voice. 'I thought you were in your study, working,' she said quietly, 'and I went to bed. When I awoke about six and discovered you hadn't been to bed, I decided to investigate. I started to get worried when I discovered you weren't in your room. The room was cold, and your machine wasn't even warm, so I knew then you hadn't been working them. I checked the house, top to bottom, looking for you, and finally ended up out in the garden. I think I called out for you, I'm not sure. And I found you asleep down by the small lake in the trees. At least I thought you were asleep,' she hurried on, 'but you couldn't be roused. So I dragged you back here, and called the doctor. He helped me get you up here and then Maeve arrived. She's been a great help,' she added, reaching out and squeezing the younger woman's arm in a rare gesture of affection.

'Have you any idea what happened?' Maeve asked gently, watching Michael closely. She was worried by his haggard appearance; he looked as if he had aged since the last time she had seen him, and his skin was the colour of old dough.

Michael shook his head, his expression suddenly wary. 'I heard a noise outside, I thought I saw something down by the pool . . . I don't know what happened then. I must have fainted or something.'

'Maybe the moonlight sparkling off the water had some sort of hypnotic effect,' Maeve suggested. 'Anyway, it doesn't matter now. You're safe and well, and that's all that matters.' She looked at Karla, 'Why don't you try and get some rest, its been a fairly traumatic morning for you, and its not even half-nine. Go back to bed for an hour or two, I'll take care of the children's breakfast.'

'Thank you, that would be lovely. You're very kind.' Karla leaned forward to brush her lips across Michael's forehead. 'Try and get some rest,' she murmured, 'I'll be in the guest room if you need anything.'

Michael lay back on the pillows and waited until his wife had left the room before turning back to Maeve. 'Thank you,' he said suddenly.

'For what?'

'For everything. For helping.'

Maeve shook her head. 'Its nothing.' She turned away and went to stand by the window. Without looking at him, she said, 'Do you want to tell me what happened?' She turned quickly to catch his expression.

He looked at her in astonishment. 'I don't know what you mean,' he whispered.

'Come on,' she said in exasperation. 'I want to know why a native New Yorker would suddenly walk out into a pitch-black night to investigate a sound without a weapon of some sort. In fact, I would like to know why you went out to the garden in the first place. Why didn't you ring the police?'

Michael attempted a wan smile. 'I guess I wasn't thinking.'

'So what did you see down by the pool?'

'I didn't see anything,' he said defensively. 'As you said, it must have been the reflection of the moonlight on the water.'

Maeve stretched out her hand in a movement so reminiscent of the pale-skinned woman's that he flinched. In her hand she held the ornately-worked bone comb.

'What's that?' he asked innocently.

'You tell me; I found it by the computer this morning.'

Michael frowned. 'I don't remember leaving it . . .' and then he grinned, realising that she had caught him. He reached for the comb, but Maeve's fingers closed over the pale ivory.

'Do you know what this is?' she asked softly, her hard, green eyes locked on his face.

'Its a comb.'

She grinned humourlessly. 'Its a bone comb, carved, I would imagine, from the hind leg of some large animal, an ox or a deer. It is also, I would imagine, very old.'

'How old?' he whispered.

'I have no idea. I've seen similar, but smaller, types in the National Museum, dating back several hundreds of years.' She tossed it onto the blankets. 'Where did you get it?'

Michael regarded her steadily for a few moments, then he dropped his gaze, touching the comb with his fingertips. 'I found it,' he said very quietly.

Maeve nodded, but said nothing.

'Its true.'

'I'm not doubting you,' she said softly.

'Look, I'm tired,' Michael said quickly, 'I've a pounding headache . . . and I'm a bit confused. I seem to have lost at least a night of my life. I would like to rest.'

Maeve nodded, and then she leaned forward over to bed, her face so close to his that strands of her thick, black hair brushed against his forehead. 'Rest now. But later we'll talk about the woman. There is a woman in this isn't there? A pale-skinned woman?' And before he had time to nod, she had turned and walked away, closing the door gently behind her.

Michael lay back in the bed, his eyes closed, troubled, and just a little frightened. How had Maeve known about the woman? If there was an explanation, he didn't even want to consider it.

He dreamt briefly, terrifyingly, of the white-skinned woman. Her naked flesh was cold, so cold, and hard, like stone or polished alabaster, and he could look at her dispassionately, like a nude statue by one of the masters, perfectly formed, but soulless. And yet this creature wasn't soulless, quite the opposite. It had a soul.

And its soul was in torment.

Michael Cullen found Maeve in the study. She was standing before the long window, her arms folded, staring down into the garden. The computer was running, and there were numerous books and journals scattered all over the floor. He tapped gently on the door and stepped in, closing it behind him.

Maeve turned quickly. 'I thought you were supposed to be in bed.'

He shrugged. 'I've slept, and you know as well as I that I'm not suffering from exhaustion.'

'So, what is it then?' she demanded. She perched on the deep window-ledge and stared hard at him.

Her gaze was unsettling, and left him feeling ill-at-ease. And then suddenly he grew angry with himself and with Maeve, after all, she was his employee, she was working for him!

'Now listen here to me . . .!'

'Banshee!' Maeve whispered.

'I beg your pardon?'

'The woman you encountered is a banshee!'

Michael attempted a laugh, but the sound came out sounding strangled.

She hopped off the window-ledge and crossed the floor quickly, deftly manoeuvring Michael into the chair before the computer. Leaning across him, she began to tap the keys. The machine hummed softly to itself and then the amber screen cleared to show one of the files Maeve had created a few days previously. She looked at Michael, and then back to the screen.

'SUPERNATURALS,' he said slowly, reading the title of the file. 'I looked at this file. It contains details of . . .' he paused and then continued softly, 'Irish supernatural entities.' He tapped the keys, opening the file, the screen clearing on his command. He touched another key, and the machine threw out a question.

'FIND WHAT?'

He typed the seven letters very slowly. 'BANSHEE.'

'WAIT.'

The machine whirred and then the screen scrolled and stopped almost immediately, the cursor blinking beneath the word. 'BANSHEE.'

In growing disbelief, Michael Cullen read slowly through the classic description of the 'bean-sidhe,' the fairy-woman.

Maeve, who was leaning across his shoulder, read the description aloud. 'The banshee can appear in any of the three stages of womanhood; maiden, matron or hag. She usually, but not always, appears at night, and is more often heard rather than seen. In appearance, she is described as being unnaturally white and the length and texture of her hair is commented upon. She is often seen washing or combing her hair, and there is a separate body of legend surround the banshee's comb.' Maeve looked at Michael. 'Well?'

He nodded, his gaze fixed on the screen.

'Tell me about the woman you saw?'

'Her skin was white, stone white and cold, so cold,' he whispered.

'And her hair?' Maeve asked gently.

'Black, long, thick and black.'

'And she was young?'

He nodded.

'Was she looking for the comb?' Maeve asked.

'She never said, she merely put out her hand, as if she was asking for something.'

'Did she speak?'

'No.'

'But you heard her song, her cry?'

'A few times now.' He turned to look at Maeve. 'What does it mean?'

She looked away. 'To hear the cry of the banshee is generally taken to be a portent of death, either your own or someone very close to you.'

'Am I going to die then?' he wondered.

'We're all going to die,' Maeve smiled, 'sooner or later.' She squeezed Michael's shoulders. 'I don't know,' she whispered, serious now. 'I just don't know. Who knows: maybe this is nothing more than a product of your overtired imagination. You read this file a couple of days ago – you've admitted that, and that, coupled with your exhaustion, has generated a . . . a what? An hallucination.'

'And what about the comb?' he asked numbly. 'What about the comb?'

Maeve turned away and walked to the window. 'I don't know.'

'Where is it?' Michael asked, his voice suddenly sounding frightened.

Maeve took the small, long-toothed comb from her pocket. 'I was going to take it into the National Museum later today to compare it again the other old combs they have on display there.'

'Yes . . . yes . . . that's a good idea,' Michael said absently. He was watching the screen, and for a moment he thought it was his eyes, but even as Maeve spoke, her voice sounding strangled, he realised that what he was seeing was no trick of the screen or his eyes.

'Michael,' she whispered, her eyes fixed on the garden below, 'she's here.'

'I know,' he murmured, not turning around. The screen was gradually clearing, the letters blinking, then flaring brightly before disappearing in patches. There was a brief moment of screen interference, indeterminate figures and characters drifting across the screen in a random pattern, and then the file was gone, the last lingering words the title, BANSHEE, and then it too was gone.

'She's gone,' Maeve said in a horrified whisper.

Michael stood up and crossed to the window, holding the trembling woman. He felt surprisingly calm, almost detached, and he wondered if the doctor had given him anything, an injection to relax him perhaps.

'This is crazy,' Maeve muttered, her voice indistinct against his chest, her breath warm and damp through his pyjamas. 'Did I just dream that?'

'If you did, your dream just blanked our file,' Michael said quietly, his hands moving up and down her back, between her shoulder blades, his gaze fixed on the garden below. Had he just seen a shape move through the trees?

Maeve disentangled herself from Michael's arms and sank into the seat before the computer. She tapped the keyboard several times, but nothing happened, nothing appeared on the screen, nor could she exit from the programme. Finally she hit the three-key combination that effectively restarted the machine without having to turn it off and then on again. The machine began humming softly to itself, the hard disk whirring and blipping, until it finally returned to the main directory.

'Well?' Michael asked.

Maeve called up the file and then hissed with satisfaction. Her short, blunt nail tapped the screen. 'Well, we still have the Supernaturals file.'

'Is there anything in it?'

Maeve opened the file, and entered the search command.

FIND WHAT?

BANSHEE, she typed.

The machine blipped, the light flashing a few times and then the message appeared, COULD NOT FIND: BANSHEE.

'You have a backup copy?' she asked, looking up at Michael, who was leaning over her shoulder.

He nodded. 'Do you think we should run it just at the moment?' He didn't want to add, 'just in case,' but Maeve knew what he meant. 'Maybe it's the machine,' he suggested.

In the next ten minutes Maeve called up and ran every file

on the disc without a hitch. Without looking at him, she said, 'Its just the Supernaturals file, and the only section of that which is missing is the section dealing with the Banshee.'

'Can you recreate it?'

'I can.'

'Don't.'

Maeve turned in the chair to look at him, her eyebrows raised in a silent question.

'At least don't do it on the machine. Draw up your notes on paper, and keep a copy,' he added unnecessarily.

'You're taking this remarkably calmly,' she said.

'Well, what do you want me to do? I've collected folklore in just about every country in the world. I've watched Yacqui Indians fall into a trance and tell of what they have seen or heard some hundreds of miles distant; I've seen men die believing they were pursued by the Wendingo; I've watched an Inuit, an Esquimau, call the seals to a hole in the ice where he calmly clubbed them to death. I've seen the power of Voodoo, the Shaman, the Witchdoctor . . . so why should I find this supernatural creature all that startling?'

'This is a portent of death,' Maeve reminded him.

Michael nodded. 'And all we have to discover is whose.'

'Your coming here obviously triggered it,' she continued quickly, 'the women of the Sidhe are linked to a particular clan or family, obviously you are one of them. I dare say if we traced back through your family background, we would find your ancestors had been troubled by the creature.'

'Is there any way to exorcise the being?'

'Not to my knowledge.'

'Can you find out?'

Maeve shrugged. 'I'll try.' She was about to turn away when she paused. 'Can I make a suggestion?'

Michael already knew what she was going to ask even as she formed the question, and he had started to shake his head before she said, 'Please return the comb.'

9

'You've created it?' Paddy Byrne kicked at a half submerged piece of driftwood on the beach and shook his head. 'Tell me how.'

Michael shrugged. 'I'm not sure how. But it was something Maeve said to me.' He stopped, struck by a sudden thought. 'It was Maeve who sent you out here?'

Paddy grinned. 'She simply told me you had been unwell. Naturally as one of your oldest friends I felt compelled to come and see you.'

'She spoke to you about the Banshee?'

Paddy looked out across Loughshinny Bay to where a Martello tower perched on top of the cliffs. 'She mentioned it,' he said eventually. 'Can you get out to the tower?' he asked conversationally.

'I'm sure you can,' Michael said dismissively. 'What did she say?'

'She was concerned, Michael.'

Michael dug his hands deep into his pockets and turned to face the sea, his expression closed, his eyes hard. 'This is crazy. Here we are, two intelligent people, discussing the existence of a mythological creature.'

'Are you denying the evidence of your own senses? Are you saying it was nothing more than your imagination?'

'I didn't say that,' Michael said quickly defensively.

'You said you had created it,' Paddy Byrne reminded him, 'what did you mean?' He was standing a few steps behind the younger man. He could tell by his stance, the hunched shoulders and rigid back, that he was troubled.

Michael dropped his head, watching the tiny foaming rivulets of waters that lapped around his shoes. 'I came here to investigate various aspects of Irish folklore.' He spoke slowly and distinctly, choosing his words with care. 'Is it unreasonable then to suspect that this creature is nothing more than a manifestation of my own exhaustion, coupled with my expectations?'

'A creature from your subconscious?'

Michael spun around to face the older man. 'Exactly. A corporeal manifestation.'

Paddy Byrne held up both hands. 'Whoa. Now this is getting too deep for me. Lets keep this simple. You're saying that this creature, this thing, has appeared solely because you dreamt about it.'

'Yes . . . well no, not exactly.'

Paddy put his arm around Michael's shoulders and moved him away from the water's edge. They walked up the gently sloping beach in silence, heading for the small tarmacked car-park. Although it was close to noon, the beach was still relatively deserted, the more popular beaches of Skerries and Portmarnock, north and south, taking the bulk of the summer visitors.

'This is nice,' Paddy said eventually, looking around.

'I've grown to like it,' Michael said quietly, 'I've been thinking lately about retiring here.'

Paddy sighed. 'I doubt if I'll live to see you retire,' he said mockingly.

Michael shivered suddenly, although the day was close and warm. 'You'll probably live to see me down,' he said quickly. They walked into the car-park and then turned to the left, to stroll the few hundreds yards back to the house.

'You do realise that there is quite a body of folklore devoted to the banshee?' Paddy asked suddenly.

'Maeve said something to me about it. Why are you telling me?'

Paddy smiled thinly. 'Its just that I wouldn't be in such a hurry to dismiss the creature as a product of your imagination.'

'What are you saying, that its real?'

'It only has to be real to you,' Paddy said seriously, moving aside to allow a trio of deeply tanned bikini-clad cyclists to free-wheel past. He turned to follow them. 'I think I'll retire here,' he murmured. Sobering, he turned back to Michael. 'Do you believe in this creature?' he asked simply.

Michael turned to look at him, and his eyes betrayed him.

'OK.' Paddy said seriously, 'now all we have to do is to work out why this creature has appeared now . . .' He stopped as Michael began shaking his head.

'No, what we have to work out is whether this creature is real or a figment of my own fevered and exhausted imagination.'

'Maeve saw her,' Paddy reminded him.

'Shared hallucination,' Michael said quickly. 'Maeve and I had been talking about it, obviously she saw it.'

'The comb,' Paddy said, very gently.

'This is an old house,' Michael said immediately, 'formerly owned by a Dutch artist and his wife who collected antiques. Its probably something I picked up lying around the house.'

'The computer files?'

'Come on. How often have you lost information from your machine. Files disappear, get wiped out, or garbled for seemingly no reason. Could be a localised power surge.'

'And why that particular file?'

'All right; perhaps it was a sudden surge in static electricity between Maeve and myself when we were sharing our hallucination. How's that?' he added with a grin.

'You're trying very hard to convince yourself.'

They had reached the gates of the house, and as they pushed open the heavy wrought-iron gates, Michael looked at Paddy through the flaking black bars. 'What else is there for me to do? If its not something I've dredged up from my own imagination, what's left? An ancient Irish legend come to life.'

They walked up the drive in silence, each absorbed in their own thoughts. As they rounded the curve in the drive, they found Karla and Maeve sitting on the deep window-ledge, chatting quietly together, an empty wine bottle on the ground by their feet. The children's voices could be heard through the trees, and Delius drifted out through the open sitting room windows. Michael recognised, appropriately enough, 'In a Summer Garden.'

'Look at this,' Michael murmured, 'look around you and

then tell me that I'm being haunted by some supernatural creature.'

'Not all bogeymen come out at night,' Paddy said seriously.

Michael laughed. He walked past his wife, ruffling her hair as he entered the house to find another bottle of wine, and two more glasses.

There was danger.

It sensed danger.

Not danger like before, not from fire and sword, nor burning cross nor black-handled knife. This was different, a colder, calculating danger. This was the danger of knowledge, and knowledge was power.

It would have to be removed.

Dinner was a long, leisurely affair, prepared by Karla and Maeve, who had discovered a curious affinity following, what Maeve called 'Michael's turn'. Paddy's contribution to the dinner was to prepare the vegetables, while Michael and the children laid out the long table in the dining room.

The meal was a simple one; steak, covered with black and red peppers, cooked in a red wine sauce, with local vegetables, and too many decanters of the Paul Mason wine which Karla preferred, saying the European stuff was not to be trusted after Chernobyl. For dessert there was fresh fruit salad topped with cream and hazel-nuts. Although it was close to nine by the time they had finished dinner, it was still pleasantly warm, and the four adults decided to take their wine into the garden. Both MJ and Chrissy professed to be exhausted and retired to the sitting room to watch an imported American soap on the television.

It was remarkably pleasant in the garden. The insects had vanished and the leaden heat of the day had passed. The sky was almost colourless, except for a thin band of indigo along the eastern horizon where night was beginning to creep in.

The four adults sat in silence for a while, each lost in their thoughts, until finally Paddy stood up and stretched. 'Too much food, too much drink; I think I'll take a stroll around the gardens before setting out for home.'

Michael finished the last of his wine. 'I'll come with you.'

'We'll have some coffee when you come back,' Karla called after them. The two women watched the men walk slowly down the gravelled driveway, their footsteps the only sound in the twilight.

'They're going to end up at the lake,' Karla said sharply. The soft twilight had washed the lines from her features allowing Maeve to see what she must have looked like when Michael Cullen had married her, fourteen or fifteen years ago. 'Do you believe in this creature?' she asked Maeve suddenly.

'Do you?' the young woman asked immediately.

Karla smiled thinly. 'I've lived with Michael long enough to realise that folklore archetypes can often be powerful enough to assume a certain reality, what Jung called "exteriorization phenomena".' She laughed at Maeve's shocked expression. 'I have Ph.D's in psychology and metaphysics; don't look so surprised, in the late 60s it was quite the done thing.'

'Are you saying you accept the appearance of the creature?'

Karla shook her head. 'No, all I'm saying is that Michael thinks he saw it, and that's enough.'

'He's of the same opinion,' Maeve said quietly.

'I know.'

'I thought he wasn't going to say anything to you about it.'

'There's very little he doesn't share with me. I know we don't get on very well together on occasion; sometimes our opinions are so divergent as to be poles apart, and I know that there are times when I want certain things which he would never even conceive of.' She poured more wine, and Maeve suddenly realised that the woman was more than a little drunk. She offered the bottle to Maeve but she shook her head. 'I've got to get back tonight.'

'I didn't want to come here, you know. I was convinced, quite convinced, that Michael could have done the research for this book back home.'

Maeve found herself nodding. 'Well, most of it anyway. And the rest could have been done by correspondence.'

'But no, he had to come here himself,' Karla pressed on, her speech becoming more and more slurred. 'And what happens when he arrives? He sees a banshee,' she pronounced it *bansee*, 'and what's a banshee, only the ultimate female Irish figure.' She stopped, frowning, 'Or should that be the ultimate Irish female. Whatever. Do you know what I think?' she demanded fiercely. Maeve shook her head. 'Its a fantasy; a typical auto-erotic fantasy, the unapproachable woman, distant, mysterious. Did he describe her to you?' she demanded, changing tack. Without waiting for an answer, she pressed on. 'Young, slim, pale-skinned, unblemished, high cheekbones, beautiful. I used to look like that,' she added bitterly. 'And then I had two children, and that took care of most of that.'

'I think I'll go make some coffee,' Maeve said quickly, becoming uncomfortable with the older woman's drunken ramblings.

Karla didn't even seem to notice. 'A fantasy, nothing more than a fantasy,' she murmured.

'And this is where you saw her?' Paddy Byrne squatted down on the ground beside the small, dark pool of water.

'Right where you are now.' Michael stood well back from the water, surprised at his own reaction.

'The ground has been baked too hard for any marks,' the older man murmured. He stood up and walked to the waters edge. 'I wonder how high it gets in the winter,' he said, looking into the black water. The edge of the pool was clotted with dead and withered weeds and grasses, which had obviously died when the water receded. He turned back to Michael, 'And Karla found you here?'

Michael indicated the crushed bush and the flattened area of grass behind him. 'Just here.'

'Was there any moon?'

Michael pinched the bridge of his nose and squeezed his eyes shut, remembering. Already the events of the last few days had assumed a dream-like quality, and he found it difficult to relate them to himself. 'Yes,' he said eventually, 'yes. The first time I saw her there was a moon, but the next time the sky was clouded over. This was more than a trick of the light,' he added quickly.

'I didn't say that.' The older man brushed strands of hair from his eyes. 'Is there any incidence of epilepsy in your family,' he asked quietly.

Michael turned to look at him. Finally, he shook his head. 'You're thinking that perhaps the effect of the moonlight through the branches of the trees might have brought on an attack.'

Paddy smiled. 'The thought did cross my mind.'

'There are no incidences of epilepsy in my family.'

'Aah,' Paddy breathed. 'It was just a thought.'

'We still come back to the fact that the creature was here. I saw it, I felt it.' He shook his head in frustration. 'How can I prove it to you? Come on, lets go back to the house,' he turned away, leaving Paddy Byrne to follow on behind.

The surface of the water stirred as if a breeze had blown across it, but there was no breeze that night.

They found Karla dozing on the window-sill, the empty bottle of wine on the ground by her feet.

'I'll get her up to bed; how about seeing to some coffee.' Michael stooped and scooped Karla up into his arms with apparent ease. Paddy Byrne watched him carry her into the house and then heard him shouting for the children to make their way to bed. He picked up the wine bottle and Karla's glass and then stood still, breathing in the gentle night air, simply enjoying the balmy summer night. Finally he turned and went into the house, heading for the kitchen.

When Michael came back downstairs, about twenty minutes later, he found Paddy and Maeve chatting quietly together in the sitting room, a pot of coffee on the small table between them.

'All asleep, or just about anyway,' he added, hearing MJ's door close and the floorboards creak.

There was a Bach Harpsichord Concerto on the stereo, concerto number two or three, he thought, and he sank into the fireside chair, closing his eyes, allowing the gentle, almost ethereal music to wash over him. When the clock on the mantelpiece chimed nine he opened his eyes and looked up with a start.

Paddy spoke immediately. 'I'm sure you're aware of the value of therapeutic hypnosis?'

The sudden question caught Michael off guard and he looked from Paddy to Maeve and then back to Paddy in confusion.

'It is a process that has been used very successfully with people who have experienced unusual or unnatural delusions. Gentle probing under hypnosis can often detemine the case of the problem.'

'What are you suggesting?' Michael asked directly, although he already had a good idea what the suggestion was going to be.

'Allow me to hypnotise you, and regress you to your encounter with the banshee.'

'To what end?'

'We might discover something that would be of use, something that would help us determine if this was a real, if that's the word, or an imagined creature, something from your own imagination.'

Michael leaned forward, both elbows on his knees and stared at Paddy. 'And what do we do if we discover it's real?'

'I don't know. But at least it may allow us to draw up some sort of plan of action. Have it exorcised or something.'

'I don't think you can exorcise a banshee,' Maeve said. 'I've never heard of it being done.'

'When was the last time you heard of someone being haunted by a banshee?' Michael snapped.

'Far more frequently than you might think,' Maeve replied. 'In certain parts of the country it is accepted as being . . . well, almost normal.' She grinned. 'Why do you think we had no problems accepting your encounters with the creature?'

'I did wonder about that,' Michael admitted. He looked at Paddy Byrne and sighed. 'If you think it will help?'

'It won't hurt,' Paddy smiled.

The shape left the water's edge and moved towards the house. The need to survive was strong; the need to feed was even stronger.

'What, no watch, no "look deep into my eyes",' Michael asked, relaxing into the armchair. The tremor in his voice betrayed his nervousness.

'That's not necessary, that's a stage hypnotist's trick. But people are much more susceptible to hypnosis than you might think. Even now, subconsciously, you are prepared to be hypnotised, and that's half the battle.' He moved around behind Michael so that he was out of his line of sight. 'Now, I want you to look at the wall opposite and relax. Concentrate on your breathing, become aware of your breathing . . . now concentrate on the flower that is directly at eye level,' the wallpaper sported a muted floral pattern, 'and now, without moving your head, I want your eyes to drift upwards, until you are looking at the point between the ceiling and the wall. Continue to concentrate on your breathing and relax, and I think you'll find that as you breathe out you will become more and more tired. Your eyelids will become terribly heavy and you'll want to close them . . . don't fight this, allow it to happen. Now concentrate on your breathing, breathing in . . . and out . . . and relax . . .' and then his voice, which had become soft and almost gentle, took on a slightly more commanding tone. 'And now sleep. I want you to sleep, Michael.'

Michael's eyes obediently closed.

Paddy turned and winked at Maeve. 'Simple.'

She looked at him in astonishment. 'But that's amazing! I've never seen anyone do that before.'

'It's actually very simple,' Paddy confided. 'Michael was prepared to be hypnotised and, as I said, that's half the battle. He knew what to expect so his mind was working in that direction also. When I had him raise his eyes, without moving his head, I was in effect simply placing his eye muscles under a strain. The natural result would have been to close his eyes. All he needed was the suggestion.'

Maeve moved around to kneel on the floor before Michael. 'He looks as if he's asleep,' she said, her voice falling to a whisper.

'He is.' Paddy joined her, perching himself on the arm of

Michael's chair. 'And when we're finished he will awaken alert and refreshed, as if he had just completed a night's rest.'

'Can he hear us?' Maeve asked.

'He can.' Paddy pulled over his chair and sat down in front of Michael. Pitching his voice quietly, he began, 'Michael, listen to me. I am going to ask you some questions, and I would like you to answer them as fully as possible. Now, do you understand me?'

Michael Cullen's head moved slightly.

'Speak to me Michael. Can you hear me?'

'I hear you.'

'Do you understand me?'

'Yes.'

'Now Michael, I want you to think back. Two nights ago you met a woman, a strange woman, a woman you call the banshee.'

The creature felt a pulling, a tugging, a stirring of memories. In some vague way it felt it was being summoned.

'She was very pale, like polished stone. Her hair was black, jet black, and long, long. I don't know how long. Her eyes were dark, the same colour as her hair.

'How old was she?'

Michael frowned. He still had his eyes closed, and Maeve found the whole experience vaguely disturbing, as if he was detailing an intensely personal dream. Although his eyes remained closed, his face registered every expression, and he frowned and smiled as he spoke.

'She had the body of a young woman.'

'How could you tell?'

Michael frowned. 'She was naked and her breasts had barely formed.'

'Maiden,' Maeve muttered.

Paddy looked at her.

'The banshee can appear in any of the three states of womanhood; maiden, matron or hag.'

'How does his description fit?' he asked.

'Ask him to describe the face,' she suggested.

'Her face was almost heart shaped,' Michael replied to Paddy's question, 'and her chin was pointed. Her cheekbones were pronounced, and her eyes slightly slanted, vaguely oriental.'

Maeve nodded. 'It fits one of the traditional images.'

Paddy leaned forward to watch Cullen's face. 'Michael, did she speak?'

He shook his head.

'Did she want something?'

Michael nodded. 'The comb. She wanted the comb.'

'How do you know?'

'She held out her hand, palm up . . .' his own hand moved outwards in a mimicry of the movement.

'And then what happened?'

'Then . . . then she held me.'

Paddy looked at Maeve, and she shook her head slightly.

'How did she hold you?'

'She slipped off her cloak and pressed herself to me.'

'How did she feel?'

'Cold . . . so cold . . .' Suddenly Michael's lips began to turn blue and he began shiver. 'Cold,' he said again, his teeth chattering.

'She's gone Michael,' Paddy said urgently, 'the woman is gone, she's gone. You're safe now. Michael, I'm going to count downwards from three, and when I reach one you will awaken, alert and refreshed. You will also remember all the events you have just recounted to us. Now, three . . . two . . . one!'

Michael's eyes blinked open. He looked from Paddy to Maeve, his eyes wide and staring, and then he let out his breath in a long sigh. 'Jesus!'

Paddy Byrne sat back into the chair. 'So . . . that was interesting.'

'Does it get us anywhere?' Maeve asked, crossing to the sideboard and returning with an almost full bottle of Irish whiskey. 'I think we could all do with this,' she said, pouring three stiff measures into the dusty tumblers. She was annoyed to find that her hands were trembling.

They drank silently, and then Paddy said, 'Well, at least it has determined one thing.'
They both looked at him silently.
'The creature exists!'

10

By the time it had turned twelve, they had talked the idea through from every angle and still hadn't arrived at a satisfactory conclusion, and by that time too much drink had been taken for Paddy to drive safely and both the last bus and train had long since gone. Michael made up a bed for Maeve in the spare bedroom next to Chrissy's, while Paddy was forced to sleep on the couch. He threw Paddy a spare pair of pyjamas, warned him to leave something in the drinks cabinet and then walked Maeve upstairs to her room.

'I'll bet you're sorry you got involved in all this,' he said quietly.

Surprisingly, she laughed. 'No, not at all. I think I'm going to write a book about it, a big fat horror story. I'll call it *Banshee*. It'll be about an American academic who comes to Ireland to work on a folklore book and finds himself haunted by a banshee.'

'I'll sue,' he grinned.

'I'll change the names.'

He stopped outside the door to the spare bedroom. 'Chrissy's just here,' he said pointing to the next door, 'and MJ's beyond that. Karla and I have the last on the corridor.' He turned back to her. 'And thanks,' he said finally.

'For what?' she asked surprised.

'Well, for taking all this in your stride. I'm not sure anyone else would have taken the events of the past few days so equitably.'

'We'll get it sorted out, somehow,' she added doubtfully. She kissed him quickly on the cheek. 'Get some rest.'

But Michael shook his head. 'Not for a while. It must have been that hypnotic suggestion Paddy gave me about feeling refreshed, but I don't think I'd be able to sleep a wink. I usually do a bit of work at night anyway. I'll get a few hours in, catch up on my daily quota, eh?'

Maeve watched him disappear down the corridor before turning in and closing the door. She had to resist the temptation to lock it. She wandered around the large room, her arms wrapped around herself, unwilling to get into bed, even though she suddenly felt exhausted. She felt uneasy and there was a feeling at the nape of her neck, a tension which she had learned to associate with thunderstorms. Standing by one of the tall casement windows she looked up into the night sky, but it was completely cloudless in all directions and a silvery luminescence just below the horizon indicated that the moon would soon rise. Maeve leaned on the window-sill staring out into the night. Like most city-dwellers she was fascinated by the countryside at night, by the absence of lights and sounds, by the eerie silence. Yes, that was it she realised, that was why she was feeling so uneasy: she was missing the lights and sounds of the city. Maeve had a flat in Rathmines on Dublin's southside, right in the heart of flatland, with a twenty-four-hour shop just down the street, a late night take-away directly across from her, and a constant stream of traffic past her window. Even at dead of night, her bedroom was washed in the amber glow of the sodium street lights.

Curiously satisfied now that she had uncovered the reason for her unease, she began undoing the buttons of her blouse, still staring out into the night.

Michael Cullen plugged in and powered up the computer, and then allowed it to do whatever computers did before it finally blipped that it was ready for action. Although Michael used a computer, indeed, a variety of machines, both on and off campus, he was still remarkably ignorant of the inner workings. As long as it did what it was supposed to do, he was happy.

He called up the files he was looking for, arranged his notes, and then sat and stared blankly at the amber screen wondering where to start. Finally, he opened up the file he had been working on the night he had first seen the creature. He read through it slowly, discovering that, as usual, he barely recognised and remembered a fraction of what he had written.

He was still occasionally amazed at what percolated up from

his subconscious during the writing process. He found it curiously exhilarating, and sometimes vaguely frightening. He would do all the research, read everything readable on the subject, then let it swill around inside his head for a few days, before finally writing. He found that his subconscious made connections and assumptions that his conscious self never even recognised.

The chapter was entitled 'Arrival,' and sub-titled, 'The Arrival of the Princess Caesir Banba to Erin.' Unwilling to wake up the whole house by printing up a copy on the rattling printer, he began to read it on the screen, gradually scrolling the piece upwards.

Paddy Byrne settled the pillow beneath his head and pulled the blankets over him. He was tired; it had been a long, though interesting day, and the effects of the fine food and too much whiskey had left him pleasantly exhausted. It had been a long time since he had had such a pleasant evening, and the older he got the more important such simple pleasures became. Paddy had divorced his wife . . . twenty . . . twenty-two years ago, after a college scandal that had even made one of the national newspapers. He smiled remembering; it had all seemed so terrible then, now it was merely amusing. He wondered where Marion was nowadays. They had been married three years, three interesting years, and whatever her many faults, and she had many, her one saving grace was that she could cook. That was his abiding memory of her. There had been women since then, and one or two of those had lasted more than a month but somehow none of them could cook the way she could. Of course it was probably nothing more than his memory playing tricks on him again. Realising the whiskey had made him maudlin, he closed his eyes and settled down to sleep . . . only to open them immediately, as the door to the sitting room clicked open.

He sat up on the couch, rubbing his hand across his face, and found Maeve standing before him. He opened his mouth, but she raised her hand to her lips silencing him. She moved around the chair to stand before him, and then allowed the black blanket she had thrown over her shoulders to fall to the floor. She was naked beneath, her body slender and pale in the vague moonlight that came in through the windows.

Paddy started to shake his head, when she stepped up to him, bent forward and then kissed him, holding his head in both her hands. Her tongue parted his lips, and found his, and then she was moving on top of him, her legs wrapping themselves around his waist, her breasts against his chest. Still holding his head, she forced him back down onto the couch, and now one hand was tugging at his pyjama top, buttons popping in her haste to pull away the cloth. She pushed aside the single blanket, and then finally managed to tear off his pyjama top, the material ripping. Her hands, cold against the warmth of his skin, roamed across his hairless chest, and then moved down across his flat stomach. With a twist, she wrenched his pyjama bottoms open, the button clattering across the room. Paddy's hands, seemingly of their own accord, had come to rest on Maeve's back, supporting her as she moved her full weight onto him. For a moment he thought the drink might defeat him, but then he felt his body respond and he had never experienced anyone like Maeve. He had always got on well with her; he would have counted her a friend, but he'd never even considered her in any other way. He whimpered as she slid onto him, and then she crouched over, her head flat against his chest, her breasts against his stomach, her hands cradling his head.

Paddy stroked her back, his hands running up and down the satin-smooth skin. Christ, but she was cold. He remembered Marion was always cold too . . . she had cold feet . . . and there was that time he'd fallen in the frozen pond when he'd been in high-school . . . and the snow when he'd built his first snowman . . . it had been cold then . . . he remembered crying with the cold.

Memories
The creature thrived on memories.
Memories.
The creature, wearing Maeve Quill's face, sucked the memories from

Paddy Byrne, feeding on them, absorbing the experiences. The fingers flattened themselves against the naked man's skin, drawing the heat to itself. Already the lips had turned blue and a pallor had washed the colour from the body.

Soon.

When all the memories were gone, then the man would be gone . . . and the danger would be passed.

Michael Cullen went in search of Maeve. He needed to speak to her now; what he had discovered wouldn't wait. He stood outside the door to her room, hesitating, and then, with a tight smile – what would Karla say if she saw him entering a strange woman's room at one-thirty in the morning? – he pushed open the door and stepped inside.

And stopped in shock.

Maeve was laying naked on the bed, her legs outstretched. One hand was closed in a tight fist and lay across her large breasts, the other rested low on her stomach, the fingers splayed. She was moaning softly, her head jerking from side to side.

Blushing furiously, and feeling very much like a schoolboy caught peeping in the girls' dormitory, he was about to turn away when he noticed something liquid and black inch its way across her cheek. Abruptly terrified, he snapped on the light and discovered that her lips and chin were smeared with blood. Grabbing the bedclothes off the floor, he flung them across her, covering her nakedness, and then roughly shook her awake.

'Maeve! Maeve!'

She awoke suddenly, sitting up with a strangled scream that splayed blood from her split lip into his face. Unconscious of her nakedness, she whispered, 'Paddy.'

Truly frightened now, Michael raced from the room, almost falling down the stairs in his haste. He burst into the sitting room expecting to see . . . he wasn't sure what he expected to see.

There was nothing there. Paddy was gone.

Michael moved around the couch and almost shouted aloud. Paddy Byrne lay half on, half off the couch. He was naked and his skin was the colour of marble. His lips were so blue that in the half-light they looked almost black, and there seemed to be frost sparkling in his white hair.

Michael knelt and tentatively touched Paddy's throat, hissing with the chill that his skin exuded. Surprisingly, mercifully, he felt a pulse.

Maeve hurried into the room. She had thrown on a pyjama top and looked like a little girl in it, pale, lost and very frightened.

'Help me,' Michael gasped.

She came around the chair and helped lift Paddy onto the couch. Michael wrapped him in the blanket, tucking it in around the edges. 'Start rubbing his hands and cheeks,' he commanded, 'I'm going to get some more blankets.'

When Michael returned a few moments later, a bundle of blankets in his arms, she had succeeded in restoring a little colour to Paddy's cheeks, but his lips were still a shocking blue-black.

'Make some soup, and coffee too. And you can make both as hot and as strong as you like.' He started rubbing Paddy's skin vigorously, attempting to restore the circulation.

When Maeve returned to the sitting room ten minutes later, carrying a tray with hot soup and strong, black coffee, the room was sweltering. Michael had plugged in the electric fire and turned its setting to high. Paddy was looking a little better, his skin had lost its pallor, and his lips had assumed their usual shade.

'How is he?' she asked quietly, attempting to keep her voice steady.

'I don't know. His colour's returned; but I'd be happier if he'd wake up.' Even as he was speaking, Paddy's eyes fluttered, and he started forward, arms flailing. 'Easy, easy now, everything's all right.'

Paddy sank back against the couch, and began to tremble, but this time with shock rather than the chill. 'Jesus,' he said feelingly. He looked at Maeve as she handed him the bowl of steaming soup, and frowned, and then he looked at Michael. 'What happened?'

'Suppose you tell us,' Michael suggested.

'I'm not sure . . .' Paddy began, looking at Maeve again.

Michael glanced up at her and found a curiously embarrassed look in her eyes, and he didn't think it was anything to do with being in the same room as two men, and wearing nothing more than a long pyjama top. 'I'll start then,' he said with a slight smile. 'I went looking for Maeve about half an hour ago . . .'

'Why?' she interrupted.

'Because I was reading what I'd written the first night I saw the creature.'

She shook her head uncomprehendingly.

'A portion of it is written in Irish.'

'But you don't speak Irish,' Maeve protested.

Michael nodded, excitedly. 'I don't. But its there on the machine. So I went looking for you. I knocked on your door and went inside . . . and . . . and found you lying on your bed.'

She watched him closely, something like a smile playing around her lips.

'You . . . you were naked and seemed to be having some sort of erotic dream,' he hurried on. 'I was about to leave, when I noticed that there was blood on your face.' He reached out and touched her lips, where the faintest shadowings of a bruise were still visible.

'I must have bitten through my lip,' Maeve acknowledged.

'It frightened me, so I woke you. You came awake suddenly, and said Paddy's name in a strange way. Instinctively, I knew something was wrong . . .' He shrugged, and then attempted a smile. 'I'm surprised I didn't break my neck on the stairs.' He turned to look at Paddy. 'When I got here, you were lying half on the floor, looking like a piece of frozen meat, and feeling just about as cold. I thought you were dead,' he admitted somberly.

Paddy reached out and squeezed his hand. 'I very nearly was, I think. You've saved my life.'

'What was happening?' Michael looked from Paddy to Maeve.

'I don't know,' she admitted suddenly. 'I was dreaming . . .

at least I think I was dreaming . . . that I was making love to Paddy.' She looked at the older man, and blushed. 'Its not that I wouldn't . . . its just that I've never even thought . . .'

Paddy smiled. 'There's no need to explain. I know what you mean. However,' he added, 'I too dreamt, or at least I think I dreamt, that Maeve came into the room shortly after we broke up. She came around the chair here,' he traced her movement with his arm, ending up almost in the exact spot she was standing in. Almost unconsciously, she stepped away. 'You, or should I say your dream-self, were wearing a black blanket around your shoulders. You allowed this to fall away to reveal that you were naked.' He stopped suddenly. 'Except that it wasn't Maeve!' he said excitedly.

'What do you mean?' Maeve asked.

'This woman, this dream figure, had small breasts . . . whereas yours, if I may say so, are a little more developed.'

'Did she speak?' Michael asked quickly, attempting to spare Maeve any embarrassment.

'No. There was a point when I was going to speak, but she put her finger to her lips.'

'What happened then?' Maeve asked.

'We made love, I suppose. I remember touching her, and thinking how cold she was . . . and then I remember thinking back on the times in my life I can recall being cold, really cold.' He smiled. 'I even remembered the time I built my first snowman, and I was so cold I cried because my toes were numb in my boots. I'd forgotten that until now. And when the creature lay down on top of me, it was as if all the heat in my body was drifting out of the pores. I can see the images in my head, all memories, some good, some not so good, but memories. I thought your whole life flashed before you only when you were dying,' he grinned.

'When I found you, you were icy to the touch, your lips were blue, and there was what looked like frost sparkling in your hair.' Michael took a deep ragged breath. 'So what have we got here? Do you need me to remind you that it's the middle of Summer. It's so warm, I've got every window in the house open. I've got text in Old Irish on my machine. We've got one shared erotic dream, and one guy nearly frozen to death in my sitting room! Just what in God's name is going on here?'

'I was just going to ask that same question. Is this one of your regular orgies, or can anyone join in?' Karla wandered into the sitting room, took the coffee cup from Maeve's hand and swallowed it in one go. She grimaced, but the bitter taste managed to awaken her slightly. 'Do I get an explanation? It's nearly three in the morning, and you three are having a pyjama party down here.'

'I wish it was that simple,' Michael said feelingly. 'Look Karla, let's just say it looks as if the banshee struck again, only this time at Paddy.'

'Why?' she asked directly.

Michael looked at Paddy and then at Maeve. 'Any ideas?'

The both shook their heads.

'I thought banshees were supposed to scream and wail,' Karla said with just enough doubt in her voice.

'I heard nothing,' Michael admitted.

Paddy grinned. 'I heard plenty, but none of it was screaming.'

'Let's go and see what's on your machine,' Maeve suggested.

'Could it not wait until morning?' Karla asked quietly.

'I'm almost afraid to leave it to morning,' Maeve admitted, and both Michael and Paddy nodded in agreement.

11

Maeve Quill sat before the screen, staring at the amber letters on the black screen. Without her glasses, the words were slightly fuzzy, and she knew she was going to end up with a blinding headache. Her lips moved as they formed the words which shouldn't have been there, which had no right to be there. The text on the screen was in Old Irish, the ancestor of the Modern Irish language. It was a language barely a hundred people in Ireland understood; it was a scholar's language, an academic's language. It was an extraordinarily difficult language to learn, and Michael Cullen didn't understand a word of it!

She started as he draped a coat around her shoulders, and then stood behind her, staring at the incomprehensible language as she began to read:

> 'From the Land of the River we came.
>
> 'Our number was three and fifty: the Princess Caesir Banba; the warrior-maid Cipine and fifteen of her women-warriors; Ain, the Huntress, with the same number of her dark female clan; Trayim, the craftswoman, with a similar number of her most skilled craftswomen and the Sorceress.
>
> Of men there were but three: Bith, father of the Princess Caesir Banba, Fintane, her betrothed and a man, Ladra, a boatman, skilled in navigation.
>
> 'In boats of reed and hemp we came, fleeing the rising waters of the River, the Giver of Life, the Taker of Souls. Perhaps Hapi, the Lord of the River had fallen prey to Set, the Evil One in the eternal struggle between the Light and the Dark, and the Evil One had caused the waters of the River to rise against us, driving us from our home. He would have taken delight in such a ruse, for he delighted in evil and

mischief. We left Meroe, our island home, and began the long journey down the River of Life. There were signs of destruction on all sides; the waters had claimed many souls, and where once there had been villages and towns now there was only the River.

'The Gods were good and after much travail we reached the Water. Many had not seen such an expanse of water before and were afraid, but the Princess Caesir Banba comforted them, saying that this was the Middle Sea, but that it was circumvented by land.

'The Sorceress bespoke directions from the gods, and they answered her prayers and her sacrifices, and the sunset that night was truly a gift from them.

'There was fire in the heavens.

'As the sun set in fire and light across the skies, colours, the like of which had never before touched the clouds, ran across the heavens, as if some artisan had spilled his tinctures or dyes. We took it as a sign, and set our course into the west, following Herak-ekhty, the God of the Setting Sun.

'There was suffering on our voyage, hunger and thirst betimes, and only with the grace of our Lady Isis did Princess Caesir Banba maintain order aboard our sodden craft.

'We sailed through the gates of the Water and into a sea that was colder and rougher than any we had yet encountered. Unlike the first Water, this rose and fell, like the bosom of some water god. There was a chill about it that did not dissipate during the day and at night it grew bitter.

'We kept to the coast now, for the Sorceress said that our destination lay to the north. Her vision gave us great encouragement in the darkest hours of our travel, for we knew that a new land would be ours, a green and pleasant land, safe from the Waters which threatened to engulf the world, sweeping all back to Chaos. Even here, in the Waters at the Edge of the

World, the seas were rising, and had claimed much of the lowlands around the Water; even here, so close to the Edge of the World, there was little safety.

'Oft times our nightly encampments, which were always situated well above the high water mark, would find the seas lapping at its edges with the onset of morning. Even the weather changed: the skies were clouded then, and the very air tasted of grit and smoke and death. We saw not the Lord Horus during the day and at night even the stars were hidden from us.

'And when the Sorceress worked her magics, she spoke of great waves engulfing whole cities, of mountains spitting fire and ash into the sky, burying towns beneath their filth, of the earth opening like the maw of a huge beast, swallowing villages whole.

'Truly it was a time of terror.

'Forty days and forty nights, as men reckon time, we travelled from our homeland, homeland no more, for it was gone beneath the Waters of Life, swallowed, countless souls swallowed with it. But on the morning of the fortieth, having passed much land, the Sorceress pointed to an island that had appeared with the dawn and said simply, 'That is the Isle.'

'We reached it near noon of that day and we named it, in honour of our princess, "Banba."

'It was a green land, rich and fertile, blessed with many lakes and streams. There were great forests of thick dark wood the like of which we had not seen before, and even the sands differed to that of our own land.

'There were animals aplenty, birds and beasts, some gentle, others less so, but the Huntress attended to these.

'And there were the Beasts.

'Like men they stood, but hairy, and Ain the Huntress, who hailed from the warm lands to the south of the lost Isle of Meroe, said that were they were not dissimilar to the hairy tribes of her own homeland; creatures that were neither man nor beast, but something in between, as if the Gods had remained undecided whether to make of them men or animals.

'We would have lived in peace with them, but they were brutes and attacked us, and our numbers were few enough, and the loss of even one threatened our ultimate survival.

'And so we slaughtered them; male, female and newborn babe we butchered, for they were animals and deserving to be treated as such. In a single day and a night we wiped them out, and their corpses we gathered together and buried in a mound in the heart of the country, away from all civilised habitation.

'Little did we know but that we had paved the way for our own destruction.

'For a time our land prospered, and Isis blessed many of the women, making them fertile, and in time young were born to us, and our small tribe increased.

'And then the vermin arrived.

'Big were they, bigger than those we were accustomed to in our homeland, where they raided the barns and stores. Black they were, with long pointed heads, and hairless tails; these were evil, dangerous creatures, wont to attack without warning or provocation.

'We slaughtered many thousands, but for every one we killed another three seemed to take its place, and so we set forth to track them to their lair. And found it to be the great mound where we had buried the beastmen. The vermin had sprung from the corpses of the beasts and fed off their rotting flesh to assume their present proportions and ferocity.

'We ringed around the mound with fire and slew many of the squealing, screaming creatures, but even though we destroyed them, it was too late for us then.

'Plague struck at us; plague grown strong on the bodies of the dead beastmen and nurtured by the vermin. It took many, the old and the young first, and then the hale and healthy. Finally, it took the entire tribe of Caesir Banba, and later invaders, thinking themselves the first to walk this isle, would wonder at the bleached bones they found in a sealed cave. Little did they knew they were the mortal remains of the Princess Caesir Banba and one of my greatest regrets was that I had not the skill to embalm her in the traditional way, and I am unsure if our Gods hold sway over this land.

'And when the tribe of Banba had gone, I alone remained.

'I am the last of my race.'

Maeve finished suddenly, her voice hoarse. 'That's it,' she said, 'that's where it ends.' Almost without thinking, her fingers touched the keys, closing the file, returning to the main menu, and then she stopped. On the menu before her the files were listed in alphabetical and numerical order, and alongside them, the space they occupied in memory, expressed in terms of K. 'Michael,' she said, without turning around, 'how many K would a six-page, closely written file like that take up?'

Michael Cullen leaned forward to look at the screen, immediately realising what Maeve was getting at. 'Between eighteen and twenty K,' he said very softly.

The file, which Maeve had just read, took up just two K.

Paddy leaned over Maeve's left shoulder. 'Open the file again.'

The screen scrolled down to reveal the Irish text, with Michael's few English notes at the top of the page. Paddy tapped the screen, 'That's what's taking up your two K.'

Maeve jumped to the end of the Irish section of the file. A series of numbers appeared at the top of the screen, which told her the number of pages the file took up, as well as her exact position within the current page. 'There are six and a bit pages here. It should be taking up more space.'

'Delete my notes, so all you'll have in that file is what you've just read, and then close it down,' Michael said decisively. 'And when you've done that, copy it onto a disc.' He pulled one of the flat, black discs from its envelope and slid it into the machine's disc drive. Maeve typed the sequence that would transfer the data from the machine's hard disc onto the floppy disc.

The message flashed across the top of the screen almost immediately: FILE NOT FOUND. 0 FILE(S) COPIED

'So, the machine thinks its not there either,' Michael said softly.

'Perhaps its for our eyes only,' Maeve suggested quietly.

And then they heard the scream.

It began as a low cry, almost below the threshold of sound, and then it climbed in register, growing in volume and power. The scream sounded almost triumphant, like the snarl of a big cat when it has caught and killed its prey. It went on and on, undulating through the house, setting teeth on edge, tearing at nerves, fraying tempers.

And then Michael looked at the screen.

And although Maeve had closed the files, the text was back on the screen again . . . and then the document began to flicker, blinking furiously, words disappearing with every second.

Until finally, silence.

It was almost shocking in its suddenness. The screen was blank, the machine humming softly to itself, and there was a brief moment in which they all wondered if they had simply imagined it.

'The cry of the banshee,' Maeve whispered, crossing herself.

Both Michael and Paddy nodded, glad to have it confirmed.

'A cry of death,' Maeve said, looking from Paddy to Michael, 'to hear its cry is to be warned of impending death, and sometimes it acts as an indication that a death has taken place. But it is always described as a sorrowful cry, a cry of loss, of pain.'

'There was nothing lost in that sound.' Paddy said.

'I'm going to check on Karla and the kids,' Michael said, suddenly troubled.

MJ and Chrissy were asleep, apparently untroubled by the terrifying sound that had ripped through the house. He glanced in on Karla but she was resting peacefully. He was about to turn away, when he noticed that the window was open. He crossed the room to close the window, the night had grown chill, and stumbled on some bedclothes Karla must have kicked off in her sleep. She was wearing a night-dress that had been fashionable when his mother was a girl, and he smiled at the thought. If it did nothing else it would certainly keep her warm. Nevertheless, he picked up the clothes to cover her up, and his fingers touched the heavy cotton of the night-dress.

It was crusted with ice.

Sated, the creature retired. There had been failures and triumphs this night. There would be more triumphs . . . but for now there were memories to be examined . . . and memories were life.

The autopsy was a brief formal affair; Karla Klein Cullen was found to have an extraordinarily high blood-alcohol level, the result of drinking most of the bottle of wine, on top of an assortment of gins, and at least two Irish coffees. The verdict, accidental death caused by inhalation of vomitus, satisfied the police, and forensic examination of the sodden sheets and Karla's night-dress revealed the liquid to be nothing more than body sweat, rich in salt and alcohol. 'A tragic accident,' was how the Coroner described the death.

The funeral was a naturally small and private affair, with only Michael, the two children, Paddy and Maeve in attendance. Her remains were cremated in the crematorium in Gasnevin Cemetery and Michael made the necessary arrangements, with the American Embassy in Ballsbridge in Dublin, to have the ashes flown home.

A few days later, Karla's parents arrived in Dublin airport. They stayed at the airport hotel, and flew out on the next flight, taking the two children with them.

Michael Cullen remained, 'to tie up some loose ends,' and promised he would be home within the week. It was a promise he had no intention of keeping.

12

The full enormity of what had happened only really struck Michael Cullen when he eventually returned to the empty house in Loughshinny.

He was alone now. Karla was gone, and the children had returned home with Karla's parents. He had watched the children grieve with a curious sense of guilt because he couldn't cry out his own grief, couldn't share their sorrow. And when they had grieved, they had seemed to come to terms with their loss, and accept it so very easily. And that, in itself, shocked Michael, perhaps even more than Karla's death. Granted, she had never been a great mother, it was a task she had taken to almost reluctantly, and during her two pregnancies had constantly bemoaned her lost figure, but neither had she been what Michael would have called a bad mother. Her greatest crime was perhaps a simple lack of interest, a selfishness that he was also guilty of.

The last two weeks had been a strange, an almost abstract time. There were occasions when he felt that he was an outsider looking in on some strange play, in which someone who looked like Michael Cullen was taking part. Paddy and Maeve had arranged the funeral, and it had been a quiet dignified affair, for which he was truly grateful.

In the days prior to the funeral, while they were waiting for the autopsy to be performed, Maeve had been an almost constant visitor to Paddy's house, where they were staying, taking the children out each day, giving Michael time to himself: time for him to make plans for his future, for the children's future.

In those strange, twilight days between the death and funeral, he made many decisions, some short-term, others far longer reaching.

And he took one oath.

* * *

Michael wandered through Blacklands House, touring the rooms. Already, the house smelled musty, even though it had only been closed up for a little more than two weeks. In the few weeks he had lived in it, he had grown accustomed to it, become familiar with its many little traits, the stair which squeaked, the door which stuck, the floorboard which squealed, but now he felt a stranger there once again. The house felt dead he suddenly realised. The life, or lives in this case, had gone out of it.

He walked the length of the landing, twice, before finally venturing into his bedroom. It felt strangely alien, almost apart from the rest of the house. The bed was still stripped, the mattress propped up against one wall, and there was an odd, slightly medicinal odour in the air.

He pulled open the wardrobes; Karla's clothes were still hanging there. Maeve had said she would come out and help him pack them up for shipping, but as he walked down the long lines of dresses, he couldn't help wondering why she had brought so many. His fingers trailed along the edges of the various cloths, lingering on the silks and smooth, soft wools, and he wondered if Maeve would be interested in having some of them. After all they were no use to him, and Karla's sisters really wouldn't appreciate them; he experienced a sudden snap of anger, and they weren't going to get them anyway. He'd instruct Maeve to take whatever she wanted, and then dispose of the rest through a charity. They'd find a use for them.

In the bottom of the wardrobe there were shoes, dozens of them, and he was quite convinced she hadn't brought that many with her. No wonder she hadn't liked living so far from the city centre, she wasn't able to spend her money as often as she wanted.

In the bottom of her wardrobe, hidden beneath a box of shoes, he found her jewellry box. It was a simple, leather-covered padded box he had given to her on the eve of their first wedding anniversary. He ran his fingers across the soft hide; he remembered telling her then that it was to keep all the presents he was going to buy her down through the years. And he'd kept to that promise. He had brought her back something of value from every country he had visited. But it was only when he pressed the catch and opened it that he realised quite how much she'd acquired herself.

Michael carried the box over to the table beneath the window and began to work through the pieces. Some, no most of them, he'd never seen before, and he certainly never remembered seeing her wearing them. He knew a little about jewellry, and from the little he knew, he guessed there was a tidy sum here. There were rings, earrings, bracelets, bangles, pearls, chokers, three watches, one of which was a real Rolex, which he certainly hadn't bought her, and a lot of junk.

He lifted the top tray out of the box . . . and underneath he found the comb.

Michael Cullen sat looking at the small bone comb for several long moments. He couldn't imagine how it had ended up in his wife's jewellry box; the last time he had seen it, it had been sitting beside his computer in his study. In the early afternoon light, the comb looked yellow, the ivory worn by time, and the intricate design worked onto the flat side had a curiously disturbing air about it. He felt that, if he concentrated long enough, the etched design would suddenly become comprehensible. He reached in with his left hand and lifted out the comb.

A thin tendril of pain lanced up his fingers and across his palm. He gasped with shock, turning the comb in his hand, to find that one of the tines had pierced his index finger. He pulled the comb away, and blood, dark and red, welled from the wound, curling down into the palm of his hand, splashing onto the comb itself. The thread of crimson ran into the ornate curling motif, nestling there like part of the pattern, and then it vanished, seemingly absorbed into the bone comb.

Blood.

There was blood on the air.

And blood was the very essence of life.

Michael Cullen hurried into the bathroom, the comb clutched in one hand, the fingers of his left hand curled back on themselves, allowing the blood to twist down into his palm. He dropped the comb onto the window-sill and ran the cold water on his finger, gasping with the sudden chill and the sharp sting. When the blood had been washed off, the wound was virtually invisible, and all that remained was a tiny puncture on the fleshy pad of his finger. Picking up the comb, carefully this time, he slipped it into his breast pocket and made his way back to the bedroom. Looking at the jewellry, he decided that he'd finish going through Karla's things at a later stage, and unceremoniously swept the jewellry back into the box and stuffed it in the bottom of the wardrobe.

He wandered through the rest of the house, opening windows and leaving doors ajar, allow some air to circulate, finally ending up in his study. The long room felt warm and close, and as he moved across the room, he imagined he could almost feel the heavy air parting before him, like some breathy blanket. He opened the long window and leaned against the sill, looking down into the garden below. From where he was standing he couldn't see the small dark pool, but he imagined he could feel it as an almost palpable presence. What was the creature's connection with the pool? Was it a home? A base? Some relic from the past?

Coming to a decision, he crossed to his machine and plugged it in. He hesitated a moment before finally turning it on, and then sat watching the screen slowly come alive with letters and symbols. It blipped, the sudden sound startling him, to signify its readiness. His fingers moving quickly, he called up a new file and gradually began to list the things he needed to do.

He needed to discover more about the banshee; about its habits, its history, its origins. He also needed to discover more about his family's past: had anyone else been troubled by the creature, and if so, how had they coped. He also needed to know whether it possible to destroy one of the creatures.

Unwilling to trust the file to remain intact on the machine, he turned on his printer and printed out two copies, one for himself, one for his files. He then opened up the SUPERNATURALS file, systematically checking the contents against the material in the file.

With one exception, it was intact.

The section devoted to the banshee, which Maeve had culled from her numerous sources, was missing. Well, if Maeve was still interested in working with him, he'd get her to replace that, but on paper this time. He looked at the clock, wondering if he should phone; he needed to know if she was still interested in acting as his assistant. He fervently hoped so; he needed her skills, not only as a folklorist, but also as a genealogist. He was convinced that when he had established the link, either mythological or historical, between his family or himself and the creature, he would have found the means to destroy it.

He worked on through the evening, on into the night, stopping only briefly around ten that night to grab a cup of coffee. He spent most of the time working through his folklore references, extracting all they had to say about the banshee, and committing it to paper. It was laborious, exhausting work, but the very fact that he had tiresomely to write every sentence down, ensured that what he'd read and written remained imprinted on his memory. By twelve, he'd covered nearly forty foolscap pages in his small neat handwriting. He was exhausted, his head buzzing, his eyes gritty. He knew what he was doing, deliberately working himself to the limit so that he would fall into a dreamless sleep.

At least that was the plan.

He dreamt.

The dream was not a particularly vivid one: the images were vague, shadowy, and all that remained with him were two distinct emotions, loss and hunger. He wasn't sure which was worse: the loss, a terrible, immediate sense of hopelessness, of rage and devastation, mingled with a terrible rage. The hunger was a deep gnawing pain, and not a stomach pain. This was an urge that seemed to consume his entire body, and his every conscious moment was directed towards alleviating that hunger, and the hunger, too, seemed to be touched with a curious sense of anger.

The dream itself wasn't particularly frightening or ominous, merely curious and disturbing, and when he awoke, slumped across his desk, the computer still humming, he couldn't ascribe any meaning to it. It was probably nothing more than his own unconscious, attempting to make some sense of Karla's death.

He sat up slowly, stretching his arms wide, hearing his shoulder muscles pop and crack. He had a good, solid headache that he guessed he wouldn't shift all day, no matter how many tablets he took and his stomach was twisted with cramps; probably from lack of proper food and the awkward position he had slept in.

He was rising to his feet when he spotted the comb. It was lying on the table before him, inches from his fingertips, and yet the comb had been in the breast pocket of his coat . . . and his coat was hanging across the back of the chair!

He nudged it with his pen, as if it were some sort of venomous creature, and then, on a whim, he took an envelope from his desk and slipped the comb inside. Unwilling to bring it close to his mouth, he sealed the flap with a length of sellotape, and then shoved the envelope into his inside pocket.

Although the dawn was grey against his windows, he was unsure of the exact time. He glanced at his watch, but it had stopped, and he remembered then that he had neglected to wind it over the past few days: there had been little need, he had nowhere to go, and he was in no hurry to get there. He called up the time on his computer, four fifty-five, and then set his watch by it. Leaving the machine still running, he stood up and stretched, working his shoulders and neck to ease the kinked muscles and then headed downstairs to make himself some breakfast.

The house was deathly silent; the nocturnal creakings having long since settled as the house had cooled, while outside the dawn chorus hadn't started up yet. He shivered, chilled through to the bone. In the kitchen he switched on the radio simply for background noise, but the Irish radio station, RTE hadn't come on the air yet, and RTE 2, which broadcast throughout the night, played pop music, and Michael Cullen discovered he was in no mood for that.

He filled the kettle and plugged it in and was standing before the kitchen window looking out into the garden, when he distinctly heard footsteps walk across the floor of the room directly above. His bedroom, Karla's room.

He stood before the sink, rigid, unwilling, unable to move. He tried telling himself that it was nothing more than the floorboards settling, or his imagination, or . . . or what? What was he frightened of? He chided himself bitterly, aware of his shallow breathing and the too fast beating of his heart. The worst it could be was a banshee . . . and he'd already met one of those and survived. Unlike Karla.

Moving as quickly and as quietly as possible, he raced out into the hallway and back up the stairs. The study, the first room he looked into, was empty, and everything seemed untouched. Michael walked around the room, checking everything and then just to be certain, checked every other room on the landing, before finally coming to his own bedroom. He stood for a few moments with his hand on the handle, summoning up the courage to open the door.

'Shit,' he whispered, and swung the door open. The room was empty. He stepped into the room and looked around. Everything was in order. The room felt cold, but that might have been his imagination, and the room was in shadow, facing away from the rising sun.

Just his imagination then.

He had reached the bottom of the stairs when he heard a door slam above. He didn't turn back, obviously he'd neglected to close a door properly and the draught had pulled it closed. He didn't even want to think about the fact that all the downstairs windows were closed, and there should be no draughts. And he was quite sure he had closed all the doors upstairs.

Michael walked back into the kitchen and pressed the switch on the kettle again. Hot steam dampened his face, and the footsteps, firm and solid, sounding almost purposeful, walked across the floor upstairs. This time he didn't investigate and, when half an hour later the sun rose out of Loughshinny Bay, he took his cup of tea and went to sit on the steps to watch the sunrise in the chill morning.

He was still sitting there nearly four hours later when Maeve drew up in a much-battered Mini.

'Kind of early to be up and about,' she said conversationally.

'Getting a bit of work done.' He nodded towards the car. 'I didn't know you could drive.'

'I can't . . . well, not really, all I have is a provisional licence.'

'What does that mean?' he wondered.

'Means I'm not supposed to drive unless I'm accompanied by an experienced driver.' She paused on the bottom step, looking up at him. 'I wasn't sure whether to come today or not . . . but I thought I'd try anyway.'

'You could have phoned,' he said.

'Yes well,' she said, looking vaguely embarrassed, 'I suppose I could, but I wanted to see how you were.'

'I could have told you over the phone.'

'I wouldn't have believed you.'

He stood up, moving stiffly, and pressed both hands into the small of his back.

'How do you feel?' Maeve asked.

Michael shrugged. 'I've felt better.' He glanced at his watch, and was vaguely surprised to find it was just past nine. 'I'll make some breakfast,' he mumbled.

'How are the children,' she asked, following him into the house. Although the morning wasn't warm, the house itself felt positively chill, and she suddenly shivered. Michael, however, seemed unaffected, and she wondered if she were imagining it.

'I don't know. I've heard nothing from the States. I assume if anything was wrong, I'd be contacted.'

Maeve nodded. She pulled her long, woollen cardigan tighter around herself, folding her arms to keep it closed. The house was definitely cold, far colder than it should have been. And it felt empty, deserted; she had been in houses that had been vacant for months, and had not experienced the same feeling of emptiness she was feeling now.

'I'm sorry, I've no food,' Michael said with a wry grin.

'I'm sorry . . .?'

'I've nothing I can offer you for breakfast, except tea or coffee.'

'Tea would be fine.'

Maeve stood by the kitchen door, watching as Michael stood over the kettle, waiting for it to boil. 'Have you made any decisions yet?' she asked.

He shook his head without turning around. He was staring out into the overgrown garden.

'But you're staying here?' she persisted.

'For a while,' he said eventually.

'To finish your book?'

He shook his head again, and she could see the tension tighten his shoulders. 'I don't think it'll ever be finished. I've lost heart in it, I think.'

'But it was going to be your most successful, you told me so yourself. What about the money you've already received in advance?'

'I'll return it.'

'Well, if you're not going to continue with the book, what's keeping you here?'

'A little unfinished business.' He turned around and Maeve almost recoiled at the expression on his face. His teeth were pulled back in a grimace, and his pupils had shrunk to tiny pinpricks completely surrounded by white. 'The book killed my wife. If I hadn't started it, I wouldn't have called up this creature, and she wouldn't have claimed Karla like some blood sacrifice.' He suddenly snatched a knife from the draining board and held it up before his face, the point almost touching his cheek.

Maeve stifled a scream.

The fixed expression slowly faded from his face, and his eyes lost their glassy stare. He looked at the knife in his hand, almost in embarrassment. 'A black-handled knife will supposedly slay one of the fairyfolk,' he said dully, allowing her to see the black plastic handle on the knife. 'I'm going to find out though.'

'What do you mean?'

'I'm going to kill the banshee!'

13

'I don't like the term witch,' the Reverend Charles Woland said with a smile, reaching out and swallowing Michael's hand in his huge paw.

'Charles, you're impossible,' Maeve said, brushing by the huge man, pecking his cheek, 'last week you were a witch, and the week before that a warlock.' She stopped, smiling at Michael's bemused expression, 'He changes his title as often as he changes his religion.'

'A gross calumny,' the big man murmured, stepping back and allowing Michael to precede him down the long, dark hall into the interior of the huge house. Michael followed Maeve and was almost startled when she opened a door and entered a room with a breathtaking view out over Killiney Bay.

Michael still wasn't sure what he was doing here. He had gone along with Maeve willingly – there was little enough for him to do in the house in Loughshinny, and she had promised that they might get some leads on the creature that had killed his wife. Michael was cynical, but at this stage he realised he had nothing to lose and so he had agreed.

In Maeve's battered and uncomfortable Mini, it had taken them an hour and a half to get into the heart of Dublin City and then another half hour as they drove through the suburbs on the southside, through Ballsbridge, and Blackrock, and into Dun Laoghaire, and finally into the exclusive Killiney area, where the houses were discreet, well shaded from the road, and very expensive.

Maeve had turned into a short, gravelled driveway that led up to, what at first had seemed to be, a small single-storied house, and it was only when she had stopped the car and Michael had followed her up what looked like a small private road, that he realised that the house was actually built into the rock, with the ground floor set at an angle into the side of the cliff.

The door had been answered almost on the first ring. The man standing in the doorway was tall and bulky, with iron-grey hair cropped close to his skull, and looked like just about every Marine Sergeant Michael had seen. He was wearing a vaguely clerical garb, black jumper over a grey shirt, but without the white clerical collar. Maeve introduced him simply as 'the Reverend Charles Woland, a witch.'

Michael had almost turned and walked away then but, the large man had his hand, and before he knew it, he had been deftly manoeuvred into the house.

He followed Maeve into the sitting room which ran the length of the house. The tall, airy room was all soft woods and natural stones, and one entire wall was of sliding glass doors which led out onto a veranda that overlooked Killiney Bay.

'Drink?' the Reverend Woland asked, coming up behind Michael, startling him.

'Ahem, no . . . not for me thanks . . . a little too early in the day.'

'Coffee?' he asked, and this time Michael caught the trace of an American accent.

'Yes, that would be lovely thank you,' he nodded, realising that the big man was watching him with intent grey eyes.

Without turning around, the Reverend Woland called out, 'Maeve, be a pet and make us some coffee. Michael and I, I can call you Michael?' he inquired and then hurried on before the question was answered, 'we'll sit outside.' He crossed to the sliding doors and stepped out onto the metal veranda, settling his bulk into a solid cane chair. After a moment's hesitation, Michael joined him, sitting in the chair opposite.

In the sharp morning sunlight, Michael looked closely at the Reverend Charles Woland. The man was taller than he first imagined, at least six-two, six-three, and bulky, two hundred and twenty or two hundred and forty pounds, but with his height he carried his weight well. Everything about him was big, his hands were enormous, the knuckles and palms callused and ridged from manual labour and his feet, now tucked under the pine table, were size twelves or larger. He had a pleasant round face, and with the tight military-style haircut, Michael wasn't sure if he was balding or not, and he had a close-cropped goatee beard. His eyes were cold, sharp grey, the colour of granite.

'What do I call you?' Michael asked, to break the silence that had grown between them. He was also beginning to wonder how Maeve knew her way around the Reverend's kitchen, indeed how she knew someone like the Reverend in the first place.

The big man shrugged. 'You can call me anything you like; the newspapers do. But I think Charles or Charley will do.'

'Is your title merely a courtesy then?'

The big man looked affronted. 'It is not. I trained to be a Catholic priest for five years, I just never completed my final year. However, I supplemented my training with an American evangelical church and received my credentials of ministry from them.'

'He paid twenty-five dollars for a fancy certificate,' Maeve said with a smile, as she stepped through the sliding doors onto the veranda.

Charles Woland shook his head in despair. 'Aah, how can you disillusion this young man, what faith will he be able to place in me after hearing that?'

Maeve sat down between Michael and Charles and poured coffee from the tall metal pot. 'We'll let Michael make up his own mind about you,' she said.

Woland nodded and then tilted his chair around to look down over the bay. 'As you wish my dear.' He squinted up at the sun shining almost directly overhead from a cloudless sky. 'Do you think I'll get a tan?'

'No, you'll burn,' Maeve said quickly, and then, turning to Michael she added, 'you really must ignore him, he's nothing more than a child sometimes.'

The Reverend Charles Woland grunted but drank his coffee and remained silent.

Maeve ignored him, watching Michael. 'Charles is an old friend, he's one of those people I've known for so long now that I can't even remember where we met. In fact, I can't remember a time when I didn't know him.' She turned away, looking down over the bay. 'If you can ignore the title and his arrogance, he is actually quite an authority or the growth and development of the recent revival in witchcraft and the Wicca movement.'

'My dear, I was instrumental in orchestrating it,' the Reverend Charles Woland interrupted.

'He didn't,' Maeve contradicted him immediately, 'he's been involved for so long now that most people only think he did.'

Michael nodded politely, wondering where all this was leading. He felt curiously detached, as if he were standing outside himself, watching an actor who looked like himself take part in a flat two-dimensional play.

'But leaving all that aside, he is an authority on the principals of Celtic magic and ritual,' she continued.

'You've read my book? You must read my book,' he continued when Michael shook his head.

'He's also done extensive research on the feminine principal in Celtic folklore,' she said softly. 'It is the subject of his next book.'

Michael sat up, suddenly interested, and Charles Woland turned around, and the jovial, pleasant figure was gone now, leaving in its place an intent, hard-eyed man.

'Maeve tells me you've encountered a bean-sidhe,' he said gently, using the Irish pronunciation, *ban-shee*.

Michael nodded. 'It took my wife.'

'I know,' the big man said gently, 'and I am truly sorry.'

'I'm going to stop it. I'm going to kill it!'

The Reverend Charles Woland laughed mockingly. 'Might as well try and kill a part of yourself.'

Michael shook his head. 'I'm not sure I understand.'

'It is my belief, based upon my researches and observations, that the bean-sidhe, in any of her incarnations as maiden, matron or hag, is nothing more than the physical manifestation of the feminine principal that exists within all of us.'

Maeve snorted rudely.

Michael Cullen shook his head stubbornly. 'What I saw was real. What touched me was real. What killed my wife is real,' he said flatly.

'I'm not doubting that you believe it to be real,' Woland pressed on. 'It exists because you believe it exists. It exists because it is part of you; it exists in all of us. You were merely experiencing another part of yourself. Like the schizophrenic, who may be unaware of his other personae, so too you would be unaware of the female that lurks within you.'

Michael rounded on Maeve, suddenly angry. 'I didn't come here to be given some bullshit yin and yang lecture!'

'Tell Charles about the item which appeared on the machine,' Maeve said, unruffled by Michael's outburst.

'Why?' he demanded.

'Do it,' Maeve insisted, looking from Michael to the Reverend Charles Woland, who was now sitting back in his chair, watching Michael carefully, his blunt fingers steepled before his face.

Michael turned to the cleric. 'There was a . . . a message of some sort left on my word-processor. A message . . . a history . . .' he floundered, 'a story of how the first invaders came to Ireland.'

'The Caesir Banba?' the priest asked.

Michael stopped, surprised. 'That's them.'

'You said there was a message "left" on your machine. What do you mean by "left" exactly?' the big man asked.

'It was written in one of the Old Irish dialects, Charles,' Maeve interrupted, 'and Michael has no Irish.'

'And although it ran the several pages on the screen, it took up no disc space,' Michael added.

Maeve leaned forward to look at the Reverend Charles Woland. 'There's something else you should know Charles. Michael's friend, Paddy Byrne, tried hypnotic regression on him, and he was able to speak quite clearly about his encounter with the woman. He certainly visualised a real character, and he definitely believes that his encounter with the creature was real.'

The cleric nodded. 'We will come back to that. I'm slightly more interested in the material which appeared on your machine. You say it was present in the electronic memory, but not on disc or tape. Is that correct?'

'That's correct. It would be as if I had done a night's writing. But not actually "saved" it; while the machine was on it would exist, but once the machine was turned off, it would disappear.'

The Reverend Woland leaned forward across the table, staring intently at Michael. 'And had you encountered the creature before, during or subsequent to the machine being turned on? Now think man, it could be important.'

Michael nodded. The events of the last few days were chaotic enough without trying to recall the days before Karla's death; they had assumed an almost unreal air. 'That was a crazy night. That was the night we tried the hypnosis, and then we talked in the early hours of the morning,' he frowned, remembering. 'Maeve and Paddy went to bed; Maeve was upstairs and Paddy down on the couch in the sitting room. I went to do some work.'

'Is it your custom to work late at night?' the Reverend Woland interrupted.

'Yes, I do my best work then.'

The cleric nodded. 'Continue, please.'

'I started to read the first chapter of my new book, which is an encyclopaedia of Irish folklore. The first chapter deals with the arrival of the Princess Caesir Banba from the island of Meroe. I had written a few lines, little more than notes really, when I discovered pages and pages of Irish text. Naturally, I went to look for Maeve. There was no reply when I knocked on her door, and so I opened it and went in. She seemed to be having some sort of dream, she was tossing and turning, and I was about to leave, when I realised that there was blood coming from her mouth.' Michael suppressed a smile at the clergyman's startled expression. 'She had simply bitten through her lip in her dream. But the moment she awoke she said Paddy's name. I raced downstairs to find him ice cold and near to death, I imagine. However, when we revived him, he told of a dream in which Maeve had come and made love to him.' He looked to Maeve for confirmation. 'That's the correct sequence of events, I'm sure.' She nodded.

'So you invoked, through the hypnosis, the creature, which came to Maeve and Dr Byrne in their sleep, which nearly claimed Byrne, and which left something, an electronic message on your machine. It would have been running at that time, presumably, it was running when the creature entered the house; it would only take a second to imprint the information into the machine's memory.'

'I thought you said this creature was something from my subconscious?' Michael said accusingly.

'I would still hold to that belief. I am merely conjecturing now. Interesting.' He stood up suddenly, chair legs scraping on the metal veranda. 'Come then; let's see if we can find something.' He turned away and headed back into the house.

Maeve linked her arm through Michael's. 'We're going into the library now; don't be surprised at anything you see.'

'This is one weird guy.'

'Ah now, he's calmed down a lot since I first knew him.'

'Remind me to ask you how you met him,' Michael whispered as they stepped into the house, blinking hard as his eyes adjusted to the dimness.

The library ran the entire length of the first floor. If there had ever been windows, they were long gone now, either bricked up or lost behind the shelving which covered every available inch of wall space. Long, glass-fronted cabinets ran along the centre of the floor. Michael stopped to look in one, half-expecting to see esoteric or arcane implements, instead it held carefully catalogued fragments of what looked like Egyptian papyri. He looked up to find that Maeve and the clergyman had walked on towards the end of the long room. Michael strolled after them, looking around in open curiosity. In one corner was an Egyptian sarcophagus, in another, the upper half of a suit of armour, and on the floor beside it, a fourteenth-century broadsword. Pinned to the shelves at regular intervals were an exotic collection of knives and short swords, and none of them looked like reproductions.

At the far end of the room was what Michael recognised as a typical altar, with candlesticks, a sword, a chalice and several small bottles. He looked at the Reverend Charles Woland curiously. The man caught his look and grinned. 'Don't look so nervous man, I'm not going to do anything to you. Well, not much anyway,' he amended. He gripped Michael's shoulder and eased him around the altar to where a tapestry of a golden five-pointed star, on a crimson background, hung on the wall. With a sweep of his arm, the Reverend pulled back the tapestry revealing a door.

'My study,' he smiled at Michael's shocked expression.

The room inside was surprisingly bare. It was almost completely circular, and windowless. There was a single table set in the centre of the floor and a high-backed wooden chair beside it. The table was bare. For a moment, Michael wondered where the light was coming from, and then he realised that lighting strips had been recessed into the walls, close to the floor and ceiling.

'This is my sanctum,' Charles Woland said proudly, 'I designed it myself.' He touched a switch on the wall and the ceiling suddenly blurred, and turned transparent, bathing the room in brilliant morning sunshine. 'Polarised glass,' he explained. He touched the switch again, plunging the room in to comparative darkness. The big man led Michael to the chair. 'People assume that the study of the occult sciences involves incantations and various arcane rites. Well, it does I suppose, but there is also a great deal of study and introspection involved. For a ritual or rite to work, you must have complete confidence in it, and to do that, you must have complete confidence in yourself.' He moved Michael into the chair and then stepped away. Maeve had remained standing by the door.

'What . . . what are you going to do?' Michael asked, suddenly nervous.

The Reverend Charles Woland rubbed his large hands together. 'How badly do you want to get rid of this creature?' he asked quietly.

'I want to destroy it!' Michael said fiercely.

The cleric shook his head. 'That may not be possible; if it is part of yourself, as I suspect, then by killing it you may in effect destroy the feminine aspect of your being. What I may be able to do, however, is to . . . shall we say, banish it.'

'How?'

'With your permission, I will attempt to exorcise it!'

14

Michael had been expecting some sort of magical ritual, some ceremony, but there was nothing, and he later realised that had the Reverend Charles Woland even attempted such a ceremony, then he wouldn't have gone through with it.

The large man had simply requested that he sit quietly in the darkened room, concentrating on his breathing, staring directly ahead at the wall, thinking back over his encounters with the creature. Michael was aware that the priest was manoeuvring him into an almost hypnotic state. His own feelings about the banshee were mixed, and he still couldn't separate in his own mind whether he had actually dreamt his encounter with her – it had certainly assumed that quality now – or whether she had actually appeared. Paddy Byrne certainly thought she had appeared, so did Maeve . . . and of course there was Karla. Something had killed Karla, her death had been no tragic accident, he knew that. Thinking of her brought the image of the banshee, the sharp features, the dark, slightly slanted eyes, sharply to mind, and he clutched at that image, holding tightly on to it.

Unknown to Michael, the Reverend Charles Woland stood behind him, pressed flat against the wall, his arms folded across his broad chest, his head slumped forward, his breathing light and shallow. He had long since gone beyond the use of symbols or ritual to achieve the level of consciousness necessary to 'work'.

Initially nothing happened.

Michael's head dropped forward and he began to breathe deeply as he slipped into a light sleep.

On a conscious level the Reverend Charles Woland was aware of his own physical presence in the room, and knew that Michael Cullen was seated before him, but on a deeper, intuitive level, he was becoming aware of the subtle changes taking place in the room. The temperature had fallen slightly, no more than a degree or two, and while it wouldn't register with his physical, conscious body, subconsciously he had noted it. Although he was prepared for what was happening, and had encountered it on many occasions, it still managed to frighten him. That was one of the reasons he was such a good magician, only the fools ignored the fear and refused to accept it. The fear itself was as much a part of the working than any ritual.

In a confused, vaguely frightening dream, Michael slowly became aware of the woman walking towards him. She was young and naked.

'Maiden,' the Reverend Charles Woland acknowledged, raising his head and bowing slightly.

In the cool dimness of the room, the vague figure of the pale, naked woman glowed softly. It was as if a small pot, placed on the floor, had issued thick white smoke, and that smoke had coalesced into the body of the banshee. But while her head, shoulders, upper torso and arms down to her waist were perfectly formed, her legs were shadowy, lost in the smoke which wreathed her body.

The creature's arms came up and it's mouth and eyes, black holes in the whiteness of its face, opened wide. It seemed to lunge towards the seated figure of Michael Cullen and then it stopped, suddenly, as if it had struck a wall.

'You are bounded by the circle,' the Reverend Charles Woland said, the words echoing slightly in his head, his lips unmoving. In his mind he could clearly visualise the three circles set into the polished wood of the floor. The Circle of Power, which held the creature at bay, the Circle of Protection, within which Michael sat and the Circle of Working, in which he stood. As he named them they seemed to turn to flame on the floor, the symbols, usually invisible in the wood, beginning to glow, the arcane glyphs sparkling in the gloom.

The young woman touched her small, high breasts, cupping them, and then reached out for Michael, her intention and intent obvious. Her lips were parted and he could see her tongue against her small, perfectly white teeth. And then she stopped, as if she had been struck. Her face contorted, her mouth opening wide, revealing her overlong teeth, and her darting tongue was now dark, her chin flecked with spittle. She recoiled, turning away, twisting, crouching down, the swirling mist covering her body, and then she straightened up.

'Matron,' the Reverend Charles Woland said quietly. The creature's body had changed, matured, filled out. The face had broadened, although the cheekbones were still high and pronounced, the body had thickened, the breasts were larger, fuller, the nipples darker, and the stomach was slightly rounded. Her hair was still long and thick and, although he couldn't be absolutely sure, it seemed to be streaked with silver.

In the chair Michael moaned, his head turning from side to side.

Again the creature reached out, attempting to touch either man, and again, it was pushed back by the invisible barrier. This time the alteration was much more rapid, and more startling, and although the Reverend Charles Woland was expecting the transformation, it was still shocking. 'Crone,' he whispered.

An old woman looked at him through hate-filled eyes. The face had collapsed into itself, the cheekbones now nothing more than gaunt remainders of its former beauty, lending the face a skull-like appearance. The breasts had flattened and hung in ugly flaps against the withered chest. The stomach drooped, and the creature's entire body was seamed with wrinkles. Only the hair remained and it now clung to the head in scabrous patches, an ugly yellow-white. It too reached for Michael.

And the man in the chair recoiled, nearly toppling onto the floor.

Woland's arm shot out, grabbing Michael by the back of the neck, holding him within the Circle of Protection; once outside the circle, the crone, although still trapped within her own circle, would be able to exert influence over him, and very possibly call him into her circle.

But the spell was broken and the image of the creature seemed to fold in on itself and dissipate. The big man breathed a sigh of relief. Breaking the contact so suddenly had been a risk, but allowing Michael to fall onto the floor would have been a greater risk. Still holding onto Michael with one hand he cancelled the ritual, cleansing his mind of the tripartite images of the creature, erasing all the emotions the three stages of woman had called up in him: such creatures, the simple elementals, tended to feed on those emotions and would latch onto any remaining trace. When he was finally satisfied that he was clean, he stepped out of his own circle and eased Michael Cullen's comatose body to the floor. His breathing was now deep and regular, and Charles peeled back his eyelids to reveal the whites: he was simply sleeping. Stooping, he caught the man and lifted him with an almost casual ease and carried him out into the library.

'Jesus!'

'It's all right, it's all right,' the clergyman assured a startled Maeve, 'he's sleeping. He's had a trying time, but he should have something useful for us when he wakes up.'

Maeve brushed damp strands of hair from Michael's forehead. 'So it was interesting?'

The Reverend Charles Woland smiled tightly. 'It was very interesting. I know what I saw, but I'd be much more interested in what our friend here saw.'

'I feel like shit,' Michael sipped the hot, sweet tea, grimacing with the sticky taste. He could feel his teeth beginning to ache with the sugar.

'You look like shit too,' Maeve said, coming around the table to sit beside him, tapping his shoulder gently. She touched the rim of the saucer with her fingernail. 'Drink your tea.'

Michael obediently lifted the cup to his lips.

Charles Woland sat down opposite Michael, ice tingling in the tall glass of water he was sipping. He knew if he drank tea or coffee after 'working', the caffeine, combined with the residual effects of the adrenalin in his system, would give him the jitters.

The three were sitting around a low glass table in the long sitting room. The sun had gone from the balcony and a sea breeze drifted up from the bay and in through the open windows, leaving the room pleasantly cool. Michael had slept for nearly two hours, curled up on Woland's king-sized bed in a foetal position. Maeve had wandered in and out of the room, watching over him, worried despite Charles assurance that Michael was merely sleeping off the effects of his encounter. The priest meanwhile, had busied himself in his library, going through his folklore and occult references, and by the time Michael had awoken he had amassed nearly fifteen pages of notes.

Michael finished the last of his tea, looking with distaste at the thick residue of sugar in the bottom of his cup. He shook his head when Maeve lifted the squat-bellied pot, offering more.

'Do you believe me now?' he asked Woland suddenly.

The big man shrugged. 'What I encountered was interesting,' he said, choosing his words with care. 'But I have seen such creatures before, they are nothing more than primitive elementals. Although,' he added, 'this one is slightly more cunning than most.'

'But you admit it exists?' Michael persisted.

Surprisingly the priest shook his head. 'No, these creatures have no existence outside of your own consciousness. You believe they exist and your faith, your belief, may very well have given them substance.'

'That's nonsense!' Michael snapped. He rounded on Maeve. 'I thought you said this man might be able to help,' he demanded. 'I didn't come here for some sort of mumbo-jumbo, and cheap psychological crap.'

Maeve rested her left hand on Michael's arm. 'Bear with him, listen to him for a few moments, please. He does know what he's doing.' She looked at Woland. 'Please Charley, tell him without attempting to analyse it.'

The big man nodded and smiled an apology. 'You'll have to forgive me, I'm used to doing things in my own dramatic fashion. I am sorry if I offended.'

Michael shook his head tiredly. 'There was no offence.'

'Well, I'll tell it as straight as I can. If you're asking me, do I think you're being haunted by a banshee, well then the answer is yes. Or at least you believe you're being haunted by a banshee.'

'It's the same thing,' Maeve snapped.

The Reverend Charles Woland nodded and hurried on. 'But at this time, I cannot determine whether these manifestations are malevolent or not. The answer to that however,' he added quickly, seeing Michael's disappointed face, 'lies in your past. Undoubtedly the banshee contacted your family in previous generations, all you have to determine is how they fit into your genealogy. He touched the notes on the table, moving them slightly. 'You see, certain families, and Cullen is one of them, are blessed or cursed by a banshee, a fairy woman, to look after them. Sometimes she can warn of impending death, sometimes she actually causes it.' He looked at Maeve. 'Can you do some research in that direction?'

She nodded. 'I've already started to do the preliminary work.'

'I think she brings death,' Michael said suddenly, startling them both. He looked from Maeve to Charles. 'I can . . . see. Yes, I can see her in my mind's eye, and around her there is nothing but sorrow, people crying, pain, anguish.'

'Where do you see her?' the clergyman asked quietly.

Michael shook his head. 'It's just an image.'

Woland leaned forward across the table, resting his elbows on his knees. 'Perhaps it is more than an image. Inside, when I conjured up the banshee, I saw her in all her aspects. You were asleep, but I would be curious to know how she appeared in your dreams and images.'

Michael shook his head again. 'I don't know . . . I can't.'

'You can,' Woland said fiercely. 'Now concentrate, this is important. You say you can see people crying; describe them to me. What are they wearing?'

Michael squeezed his eyes shut, attempting to capture the elusive images. Again and again the image of the banshee, young, pale and naked, her arms open and inviting, drifted before his gaze. Her eyes were pits in her face, dark deep pits into which a man might sink and lose himself.

'Michael!'

Woland's command snapped him back to the present, and he opened his eyes to find that he was bathed in a cool sweat.

'Tell me about the people,' Woland urged. 'Are they shod, have they shoes?'

Michael concentrated and then nodded. 'Yes, no!' He looked at Maeve in frustration. 'They're wearing sandals, flat sandals, open toes, with thongs wrapped up and around their calves.' He started to shake his head as the image faded, and then, suddenly, it popped back into his head, complete and graphic in very detail. 'There's a man lying in tall grass, there's blood all around him, dark blood, red-black. I can see his sandals, there's a crack across the sole of one. His bare legs are dirty and he wears a tunic of dirty cloth with some sort of leather hauberk over it. There's a sword sheath on a thick leather belt, but there's neither sword nor knife present. The man is wounded, there's blood seeping from a long gash across his stomach, and it has dried red and black against his tunic. He's alive.'

'His face,' Charles prodded gently, his voice barely above a whisper, 'describe his face.'

There was a long pause and then Michael said in a voice so soft that both Charles and Maeve had to lean across to hear him. 'He has my face.'

'Is he alive?' Charles asked.

Michael frowned, and then nodded slightly. Although his eyes were wide open, he was staring straight ahead, and obviously saw no one, and was barely aware of his surroundings. 'He's alive,' he said finally.

'Are there others around you?'

'Only the dead. This is a battlefield . . . a battlefield after the battle. Only the dead remain. I can see the sea in the distance, and longships.' He breathed deeply, and then sighed. 'She comes.'

'Who's coming?' Woland asked quickly, his fingers resting against Maeve's arm, squeezing gently, warning her to say nothing.

'She's coming. The woman. She's old, old and tired. She's moving amongst the dead, touching them, looking for signs of life. Now she's leaning over me. I can see her face, old and tired, lined and worn, and her eyes, they're old, so old. Aaah, she's singing, singing . . .'

Michael began to sway slightly in the chair, moving from side to side.

'She's calling me, and the pain is gone, and . . .'

'Michael!'

Michael Cullen's head snapped back, and he looked around the room in dismay. 'Could I have some tea please?' he asked Maeve.

'It's cold, but I'll make some more.'

Michael looked at Woland when she had left the room. 'It was so vivid,' he said quietly.

'Obviously.'

'Is it from my past?'

'Perhaps. I just wish we knew when. Maeve can research the costume, and you were lying in sight of the sea and there were longships on the water, so it should be possible to pin down the period. We also know that the banshee in her crone aspect, brings release.' He caught Michael's puzzled expression and continued. 'She sang to you, releasing you from your pain and you,' he shrugged and grinned, 'you died. So we can speculate that the crone aspect of the banshee is benign.'

Michael shivered suddenly. 'Where do we go from here?' he asked.

'I've told you the answer lies in your past,' Woland said with a smile. 'You've got to explore that past, and determine when and where the banshee first appeared and how your ancestors treated her. You've heard her sing, you've seen her, only you can determine whether she means you harm or not.'

'And you must give back the comb,' Maeve said, returning from the kitchen with a fresh pot of tea.

Charles Woland nodded. 'Immediately.'

But Michael shook his head stubbornly. 'I feel I've some sort of hold over her while I have that. While I have that, she'll keep coming back.'

'I don't think that's anything to look forward to,' the clergyman said sharply. 'The next time she returns, she might just take you with her!'

15

'Have you made any decisions yet?' Maeve asked, turning to Michael. They were sitting on a seat overlooking the lake in St Stephen's Green in the heart of Dublin. It was late afternoon and the park was crowded, with every available inch of grass occupied by sun-bathers. Couples strolled arm in arm around the shaded paths, and from the children's playground, on the other side of the lake, delighted screams and shouts were vaguely audible.

'Pardon?' Michael turned to look at Maeve, the distant look fading from his eyes.

'I wondered whether you had made any decisions yet?' she said quietly.

'Just one,' he said coldly, 'and you know what that is.'

She looked at him, saying nothing.

'I'm going to kill the banshee!' he whispered coldly.

'Michael!' she said insistently.

'Where did you meet the Reverend Charles Woland?' he asked, deliberately changing the subject.

Maeve simmered for a few moments and then decided there was nothing to be gained by sulking with Michael Cullen. In his present state, he probably wasn't even aware of the fact that she was annoyed at him. Maeve was frightened, if her studies had revealed nothing else, then they had shown that the banshee represented a very real and very immediate danger.

'I met him shortly after I'd graduated,' she said quietly, sitting back against the slatted wooden bench, half-closing her eyes against the glare of the sun, wishing she'd brought her sun-glasses. 'Like you, he had come to Ireland to research a book,' she smiled tightly, 'only his was on Irish witchcraft. He was my first research "customer". He never wrote that book to the best of my knowledge, perhaps he's still writing it, but we grew to be good friends.'

'A strange character,' Michael remarked.

'In the beginning he terrified me. I read about him in the American papers, about how he had run this cult in the Mexican desert, and how he'd been high priest of some satanic church in California. You should talk to him about it, he's very amusing on the subject. That's where he made his money apparently,' she added.

Michael nodded. 'Religion's a ticket to print money, especially on the west coast. Every crackpot and crank sets himself up as the church of this or that, and no matter how stupid the idea, how ludicrous, you'll always find some poor suckers willing to shell out a few dollars to be a priest or a minister, complete with credentials of ministry and a framed certificate.'

Maeve shaded her eyes and tilted her head to look at Michael. 'But Charlie is different, he actually believes in it and there's no denying that he has some strange powers. Well, you saw that for yourself today.'

'I'm not sure what I saw,' Michael said stubbornly. He shrugged. 'Hypnosis perhaps. I've seen Voodoo shamans and Indian fakirs perform extraordinary feats.'

'And the banshee, did you see that, or was that a product of your imagination, or just some hypnotic suggestion?'

He remained silent for a long time and then he stood up abruptly. 'I saw that,' he said, walking away.

Maeve hurried after him. 'And where are you going now?'

'Home.'

'Home?'

'Back to Blacklands.'

'Well, this way then.' She slipped her arms through his and steered him around onto a side path. 'The car's in Dawson Street, we can cut out through here.'

They walked through the side gate that led onto the north side of St Stephen's Green and darted across the busy road, heading down Dawson Street. Michael stopped to look at the Mansion House, the home of the Lord Mayor of Dublin on the right-hand side of the street, and he read the inscription on the enormous candle in its glass container outside the building.

The candle had been lit to commemorate the Dublin Millennium in 1988. Maeve had parked a few doors further down the street outside the Royal Irish Academy, and while she was fumbling for her keys, Michael leaned across the roof of the car and looked at her. 'I'm going to need your help,' he said suddenly, startling her.

Maeve straightened up and rested her elbows on the car roof, her fingers intertwined, the metal hot beneath her bare flesh. 'In what way?' she asked cautiously.

'Let's forget for a moment what I said about killing the creature, let's leave that to one side for a moment. Would you be willing to continue to do research for me?'

'What sort of research?'

'Historical, genealogical.'

'What do you want me to do, Michael?'

He attempted a smile, but it only succeeded in curling his lips. 'Do some digging into my family background. See if any of my ancestors have been troubled by this creature. Perhaps you might be able to pin-point unusual or unnatural deaths.'

Maeve nodded slowly. 'We could do that certainly. A generation or two back is no problem, but you know that the further you go, the more difficult it becomes. It also depends on how much information you yourself possess.'

'I've got a lot on my father, my grandfather and my great-grandfather, and bits and pieces on my great-great-grandfather.'

'Well that's a good start anyway.'

A sudden blast of a car horn startled them both, and they turned to see someone in a bright-red Sierra pointing to their parking spot, eyebrows raised in a question.

The journey back to Loughshinny was conducted mainly in silence, simply because there didn't seem to be anything further to say. Michael dozed in the heat of the car, his all night session, coupled with the other events of the day, catching up on him.

Maeve concentrated on her driving; she had failed her test twice already, and the last thing she needed now was to be caught by one of the speed traps on the main airport road.

She knew she had to be out of her mind to continue associating with this man. There was danger here, terrifying, terrible danger, she was convinced of that. She'd already had one close encounter with the creature and that was one too many. She could still remember that dream with terrifying vividness; every time she thought of it, her cheeks burned with shame. She had had her share of boyfriends, and she'd slept with two of them, but she'd never felt as aroused or as fulfilled as she had by that dream. And now, whenever she saw Paddy Byrne, she felt vaguely embarrassed, and guessed by his own attitude towards her that he felt the same. But what was really strange, the really frightening part, was that she had never harboured any erotic feelings or fantasies for Paddy Byrne; he was a good friend, but that was it.

A lorry thundered by, snapping her back to full awareness as she fought to hold the steering steady as it bucked against the slipstream. She blasted her horn, regretting it as Michael awoke from his doze.

'What's up?'

'Oh nothing. Just some eegit driving too fast in a truck. Sorry I woke you.'

'It's OK. Eegit?' he asked with a smile.

'Slang for idiot,' she smiled. 'There are other words.'

'How come you only have a provisional driver's licence?' Michael wondered, suddenly feeling guilty for falling asleep on her.

'Oh, I've had two tries at the real thing.'

'No go?'

She shook her head, 'No go.'

'Why not; you seem perfectly capable to me.'

'Oh I can drive,' Maeve said quickly, her green eyes sparkling, 'but there's these things called the "Rules of the Road".'

'I think I've heard of them,' he said with a smile.

'Oh, I've heard of them, in fact, I know most of them by heart, but its just a matter of applying them to the real world.'

Michael nodded.

'And of course, there's the speed limit.' She laughed quickly, the sound surprising him, it was the first time he had heard her laugh in a long time. 'I failed my last driving test because I drove at fifty-five miles an hour,' she glanced at him and added, 'in a thirty mile an hour zone.'

Michael joined in her laughter. 'Karla was a demon for speed. I was always telling her it would kill her,' he said, and then immediately regretted it. Silence, as thick and as cold as a sea-fog descended between them.

Eventually, when they had travelled four or five miles, Maeve asked softly, 'Did you love her?'

Michael hesitated before replying. 'I'm supposed to say yes, aren't I?'

Maeve said nothing, concentrating on her driving, regretting the way the conversation had turned.

'Well, I suppose I did love her, once. Lately though, we seemed to have drifted apart. She had her interests, I had mine; she had no interest in my writing, except for the money it brought in. Even then she was independently wealthy and didn't really need my money. And I suppose I didn't share her interest in clothes and trivia. But I'd grown used to her and that's not as callous as it sounds. She made me what I am, I owe her that, I owe her a lot. Oh, she could be a bitch at times, but as the rhyme goes, when she was good, she was very, very good. I miss her now. I suppose I'm feeling sorry for myself,' he added, forcing a grin.

'You've every right to.'

He shrugged uncomfortably. 'I don't know about that.' He glanced sidelong at her. 'Have you ever lost someone close to you?'

'My parents,' she said, immediately.

'I'm sorry, I didn't mean to pry.'

'I can talk about it now. But I do know what you mean; you can't help feeling guilty somehow. And then you feel guilty because you can't be grieving all the time.'

Michael nodded. 'You're right, I feel guilty. I can't help feeling that if I hadn't insisted she and the children come to Ireland with me, and if I hadn't been doing this book, and if I hadn't found the comb and . . .'

Maeve heard the break in his voice and reached out to

squeeze his arm. 'You couldn't have prevented it,' she said earnestly. 'You've got to believe that. If you start to think otherwise, then you're in trouble.'

'I know. But . . .'

'The world is full of "ifs" and "ands" and "buts",' Maeve said quickly.

'Ignoring them won't make them go away,' he said. 'I suppose I'll always wonder "what if": what if Karla and the kids had stayed at home, what if I'd chosen a different country for my book, a different area of research, what if . . .'

Maeve let him talk. She realised that this was his way of coming to terms with what had happened. She marvelled at how well he seemed to have taken the tragic affair, and she had had her own suspicions about the state of his marriage with Karla Klein. They had seemed so ill-suited, and yet obviously, at one time, there must have been an attraction of sorts; they must have been in love once. She couldn't make up her mind whether Michael was stil in love with her or whether he was feling guilty because he wasn't.

Maeve slowed for the turning to Loughshinny. She turned to the right and headed down the narrow country road, past the scattered houses and cottages. In the distance she could see Baldongan Castle, it was her landmark, and she knew the house lay beyond that on the right-hand side. She hadn't come this way before, although she had managed to make her way to the house earlier, she had come in through Skerries and then taken the coast road. It was a few miles longer, but at least she knew her way. They passed the ruined castle on the right, and she was just beginning to think she had missed the house, when she saw the red barn buildings appear over the tops of the trees. Immediately beyond them lay Blacklands.

'How long will you stay here?' she asked.

He shrugged. 'I don't know, as long as it takes.'

Maeve slowed and indicated to the right although the road was empty, and then she carefully turned the Mini in through the high stone pillars, and up the gravelled driveway.

'Will you not have to return for college?'

'I can take leave of absence, I'm due some time off and I can also claim compassionate leave.' Even though he was speaking to Maeve, she noticed that he was staring into the bushes and trees that lined the avenue, and as they drove into the circular driveway in front of the house, she saw that his eyes went to the thicket of trees and bushes that concealed the pool. She pulled the car around in a tight circle, gravel crunching beneath her tyres, turning the car to face the way they had come. When the car stopped, Michael stepped out, but she remained in the car.

He squatted down beside the open door. 'Aren't you coming in?'

She shook her head. 'I don't think so. I'll call tomorrow, but I better be getting back. At this rate I'm going to be hitting the city just as the evening rush hour is building up.'

'Why head back?' Michael asked. He saw her surprised look and hurried on. 'I mean, if you were going to come out here again tomorrow, what's the point? Stay the night here.'

Maeve looked at him steadily, considering his suggestion. If it had been anyone else, she wouldn't have even thought twice about it. She glanced at her watch. Five o'clock, she'd be hitting the city at half past or a quarter to six, right in the middle of rush hour. It would take her the best part of an hour to get across the city to Rathmines, which meant that she'd be getting in around seven or so. And then she'd have to think about getting herself something to eat.

Maeve turned off the engine and unsnapped her seatbelt. 'I hope there's some food in the house,' she said lightly, 'I'm starving.'

It had fed.

For the first time in an age it had fed, and that feeding had sated a hunger, but that same feeding had awoken old memories, memories of a happier time, a bygone age, full of light and life. It had never gone hungry then. Those memories had kept it fulfilled in the lean times, for it thrived on memories, and those same memories had made it hungry.

It had fed, and it was still hungry.

It would feed again.

Michael and Maeve walked along Skerries harbour, not touching, but close enough and comfortable in one another's company. There had been no food in the house, nothing edible at any rate, and so Michael had suggested they drive into Skerries for something to eat. The town boasted a couple of fine restaurants, and they had finally settled on a small restaurant overlooking the harbour. They both chose the fish dish which had been prepared, they were assured, from fish brought in on the morning tide. The meal had been long and pleasant, and the talk had been light and inconsequential, neither of them speaking of the events of the past few weeks. Maeve spoke of growing up in Dublin in the late 60s and 70s, and how now, in the late 80s it had changed almost beyond recognition. She talked briefly of her spells working in London and Brussels, where she had attempted to earn enough money to establish her own genealogy shop in Dublin, but never quite made it. And when she finally did manage to scrape together enough cash, she discovered that the time had passed, and the market had been filled, with several shops catering to, what was principally, a tourist trade. However, she did discover that these shops needed people like herself, genealogical researchers, and she earned a reasonable living as a freelance genealogist. Most of her business came from recommendation and, at the moment, she was in the lucky position of being booked for at least the next six months. But what she really wanted to do was to write; she was nearly there, she'd had a few books published, but all she needed was one good one, just one.

Michael listened to her ramble on, realising that too much wine during the day and not enough food was beginning to take its effect, on them both, as the room began to lose focus around the edges.

'Let's go for a walk,' he suggested.

The fresh sea air hit them like a physical blow, and they both stood in the doorway of the restaurant breathing deeply, almost tasting the salt and seaweed.

'Bottle that and you'd make a fortune.'

Maeve nodded. She walked across the road to lean against the iron rail and look down into the water that was almost lapping at her feet. The fishing fleet was out and so the harbour was almost empty, except for a few rotting hulks tied up close to the shore. Small boats and light cabin cruisers were riding at anchor across the harbour, and she could trace the semi-circle of lights that outlined the harbour, stretching away from her left. Michael moved in beside her, and pointed to the necklace of lights which culminated in a concentration of lights in the distance. 'What's that?'

Maeve frowned, attempting to concentrate, but she was tired, and she had drunk too much of the sweet white wine and the proximity of Michael Cullen was unsettling her. She concentrated harder, her brow furrowing almost comically, and eventually the answer popped into her head. 'Balbriggan.'

Michael nodded and walked away, heading down along the pier. Maeve hurried to catch up with him. 'It's lovely and peaceful here,' he remarked.

'At the moment, yes, but when the fishing fleet comes in, it'll be a different matter.'

Michael looked surprised. 'I didn't think you were that familiar with Skerries.'

'I'm not. But we used to holiday every year in Galway, and it was a great treat to be allowed to stay up and watch the fishing fleet come in. The place was usually silent, just like this, and then suddenly, it would be all noise and bustle, shouting and banging, engines chugging, gulls screaming. It was as if someone had pulled a switch marked "pandemonium".'

Michael glanced at his watch, the luminous hands glowing green, reflecting off his spectacles. 'We'd best head back. Its late.'

They drove back to Blacklands along the coast road. Michael had turned on the radio and Maeve was humming along with a familiar-tantalisingly so-piece of classical music. Once they had driven out of Skerries, the road lights became scarcer and he was driving on full headlights, giving his full attention to the road. Brilliant red and amber eyes regarded him periodically from the road side and after the first start of surprise, he realised they were probably foxes or badgers. The balmy night was alive with fluttering insects, most of whom seemed intent on destroying themselves against his lights. He had become so mesmerised by the sight that he almost missed the turn at the crossroads for the house. Michael hit the brakes hard as they sailed through the crossroads and, quickly checking his mirror, slipped the car into reverse and moved back up the road a bit. He pushed it into first and indicated right at the same time, and then turned hard around the corner, his tyres protesting with a squeak. Blacklands was a couple of hundred yards down the road on the left-hand side now. Knowing he would very probably miss it, he slowed down to little more than a crawl. He spotted the pillars and was carefully turning in the gates, when she appeared.

Raven-haired, pale-white, and naked, she dashed towards the car, coldly, harshly illuminated by the headlights, her arms outstretched, fingers curled, her eyes and mouth wide, teeth long and glistering, saliva threading her lips.

Michael attempted to scream, but all that came out was a brief, strangled gasp. His foot sank to the floor, and the car, which had been in first gear, surged away, fishtailing, spraying gravel and grit behind it. For one brief moment he thought they were going to hit the creature, and then it lifted up, sailing effortlessly over the car. There was a solid thump and then the roof of the car buckled as if under the force of some terrific blow. Michael stood on the brakes and then swivelled in his seat to see what had happened.

The naked woman stood behind the car, the red brake lights casting bruised and bloody shadows across her body. Her perfectly beautiful face was fixed on Michael Cullen, and even across the distance he could sense the ageless malevolence within it. Her right hand lifted, palm upwards, fingers curled.

And Michael floored the pedal again, spraying the creature with gravel as he shot through into the driveway. He stood on the brakes again and the car dipped as its wheels ate into the softer earth beneath the gravel. He sat for a moment, looking in the rear-view mirror before finally turning around to look out through the back window. There was no one there.

'Did I dream that?' he wondered aloud.

'That was no dream,' Maeve said tightly. And then suddenly, she vomited up her meal.

The creature watched the man and women. The human kind. It had been thwarted, but it was patient. It had waited millennia, another few days were as nothing.

And the anticipation of the feast was lending spice to its hunger.

16

'Shit!' Michael ran his hand over the roof of the Volvo. A series of small indentations in the metal culminated in a dipped depression in the exact centre of the roof, and the paintwork was cracked and flaking, shiny metal showing through. It looked as if someone had taken a lump hammer to it.

'Michael, come in, please.' Maeve stood in the doorway, wrapped in Michael's coat, looking pale and miserable. It was all very well to talk of the banshee and fairy folk, and quite another to see the creature. Even Karla's death had been explainable in a vague sort of way, the message on Michael's computer could also be explained away, though not so easily.

But not this.

Michael stood beside the car, a heavy long-bodied torch in his hands, probing the darkness. Every light in the front of the house was on, all the curtains open, flooding the front gardens, lawns and driveways with light.

'Michael?'

The sound of her voice, the note of terror in it, brought him back to his senses, and Michael snapped off the torch, and moved backwards towards the house, unwilling to turn his back on the garden. He wrapped his arm around Maeve and then stood for a final moment, looking out across the night-damp gardens. The creature was out there, he knew it, watching and waiting. He knew he should have felt fear, but all he was feeling now was a deep-seated, burning rage that threatened to boil up and explode.

He followed Maeve into the hall and closed the door behind him. He was hunting for the keys when he felt her stare and turned to find that she was watching him intently. 'We did see it . . . it was there?'

Michael nodded. He knew what Maeve was thinking. Even as he was bringing the car to a stone-scattering halt in the driveway, he was already beginning to doubt that he had seen the creature, and by the time he had helped Maeve out of the car and got her into the house, turned on the lights and pulled back the curtains, he was convinced that it had been nothing more than exhaustion and too much wine.

Until he had seen the indentations in the roof of the car, where something had walked across it.

'We saw it. It was there.' He turned the key in the lock, and then slid home the bolts on the heavy wooden door.

'Do you think that will stop it?' Maeve asked.

'What do you think?' he asked bitterly; simple locks and chains weren't going to keep the creature out.

'I'll go make us some tea.'

'Make it coffee,' Michael said, 'I'm not sure I want to sleep tonight.' He went from room to room, closing the blinds, pulling the curtains across, but leaving the lights on. With the ground floor secure, he started to climb the stairs, and then the reaction set in. His heart began to pound and he experienced a sudden bout of breathlessness. He pressed his hands, the fingers trembling, against his chest and leaned on the banister, attempting to catch his breath.

This shouldn't be happening, not now, not today, in the latter half of the twentieth century, not to some petty New York lecturer. But it was happening, and the only way he was going to fight it was to accept it as real and deal with it accordingly.

The upper floor felt cold. Michael stopped, remembering the chill that had taken Karla's life. Was the creature already in the house? Paradoxically, the pounding of his heart slowed, and his breathing settled, all fear gone now, leaving only the anger in its wake. Using that anger as a spur, he hurried from room to room, wrenching open the doors and then waiting. He wasn't sure what he was waiting for. The bedrooms were empty, the rooms hot and musty, smelling of dust and old clothes, but he found that the bathroom window was wide open, and there was a hint of a sea wind, rich with salt and seaweed, mingled with damp earth, coming in off the fields that bordered the house. He was tempted to lean out the window to look over the gardens, but he resisted the attraction.

And now that he had identified the source of the chill, the anger subsided to be replaced by the fear. He closed the window quickly and snapped the catch across, and then turned to the sink where he washed his hands quickly, the water surprisingly cold. He caught his reflection in the mirror over the sink and stopped, his hands clasped before him in what looked like an attitude of prayer. A wry smile twisted his lips. Aside from his pallor, the black circles beneath his eyes and the size of his pupils, he didn't look too bad for someone who was scared shitless.

Maeve met him on the stairs with a cup of coffee. She had washed the make-up off her face and brushed the loose strands of hair back out of her eyes. But even though she looked calm and composed, Michael saw his own fear mirrored in her bright green eyes.

Handing him the coffee, she forced a laugh. 'I didn't fancy waiting down there on my own, you know?'

He nodded. 'Let's go into the study.'

Unlike the rest of the house, the study was hot and stuffy, stale smelling, but neither of them suggested opening a window. Michael turned on all the lights, including his desk lamp, while Maeve drew the curtains. Finally, with nothing more to do, they turned and looked at one another.

'I wish I'd gone home,' Maeve said with a smile.

'I wish you'd gone home too.' He sat down in the chair before his computer. 'It's after me. So, I think you're safe, but I'm not sure. Well, you know more about these things, than I: does the banshee ever collect souls other than the ones it's supposed to?'

Maeve slumped into the only chair in the room, a much-battered easy chair. 'The creature is supposed to signal the death of a member of a particular family, or alternatively, she is reputed to cause that death by singing its death song, which you and I hear as a wail or a scream.'

'What about Karla then?' Michael said immediately. 'Why was she taken?'

'She was related to you remember?'

'But will the creature recognise marriage as being "related",'

Michael puzzled, and then a terrifying thought struck him. 'But what about the children in that case?'

Maeve nodded. 'There is always the possibility, but I think you've put enough distance between them and it for them to be reasonably safe. No, I think you're the prime target, but that's not to say that anyone close to you or around you won't get hurt in the process. Remember what happened to Paddy and myself the night it struck?'

He nodded, the sudden image of Maeve's near naked body thrashing on the bed flashing into his mind. He felt colour come to his cheeks and to cover his embarrassment, he turned away and flipped the switch on the computer, bringing it to life.

'Are you sure you want to do that?' Maeve asked.

Michael looked from the machine to Maeve. 'You think it might attract the creature?'

She shook her head. 'I don't know, but remember what happened the last time, that information you discovered in the machine memory, but which you weren't able to save on disc?'

Michael frowned. 'I remember, but I don't think the machine attracted the creature. I think, perhaps, the information was accidentally imprinted onto the memory by the presence of the creature.'

Maeve nodded doubtfully.

'So.' He stopped, as a sudden idea struck him. When he turned back to Maeve, there was a brightness in his eyes that she hadn't seen for a while. 'We know the creature's out there, right? So why shouldn't we just leave the machine on, perhaps it might happen again.'

'Perhaps.'

After that, their conversation lapsed, and soon the only sound in the room was the gentle humming of the computer. Michael attempted to read, but the words swam meaninglessly before his eyes. Eventually he sat down before the keyboard and stared at its screen which, except for an orange border along the top giving the file name, his current position, page and character number, was otherwise blank. He could see himself reflected in the screen, with Maeve behind and to his left. Resting both elbows on the table, he rested his head on his fists and stared into the screen, deliberately attempting to concentrate on the young woman, rather than think of the creature. He had his own vague theory that if he thought of the banshee, then he would call her, and he wasn't sure he wanted that yet. Not just now, he wasn't ready for her. The next time the creature came to him, he wanted to make sure it would be its last. And then, suddenly, he thought of his wife's cold body, cold, so cold, with fragments of brittle ice encrusted in her hair and on her face, the bed wet with melting ice. What was the connection between the banshee and the bitter cold and ice. When he'd had his encounter with the creature, he'd felt cold, and when she'd attacked Paddy, he too had very nearly succumbed to the bitter cold. There was obviously a connection, although he wasn't sure what. If she was cold and ice, could she be countered with heat and flame?'

Excited by the possibility, he was turning to Maeve, when the dark screen scrambled to life, shocking him speechless.

At the same moment, Maeve said in a strangled voice. 'It's here.'

Michael stood up suddenly, sending his chair crashing across the room as the debris on the screen began to shift and move, forming groups of letters, that hinted vaguely, briefly, at words.

And then he heard the sounds coming from the house: footsteps, themselves virtually silent, but moving across creaking floorboards.

'Michael . . .' Maeve began, but he nodded. He too had felt the sudden drop in temperature.

The young woman wrapped her arms around him, and he held her close, surprised at the violence of her shivering. She was cold, her skin clammy to the touch, her teeth beginning to chatter. 'She's here,' Maeve said, her voice cracking with hysteria.

Michael nodded, unsure what to say.

'I'm frightened Michael. I'm so frightened.'

'She's . . . she's got a physical body, we've heard her footsteps . . . so she can't just float through doors, she'll have to open them or break them down, and . . .' He suddenly pushed

Maeve away from him, and threw his weight against the heavy filing cabinet, attempting to slide it over in front of the door. Maeve joined him and together they manoeuvred it across the door. 'The windows,' Michael gasped, 'anything that can leap over a moving car is going to have no trouble with first floor windows.'

'Phone,' Maeve said suddenly, 'phone. I'll phone Charley. Maybe he can help,' she added quickly.

Michael pointed to the small, flat phone, virtually buried under sheaves of paper. It had now grown so cold that their breath was beginning to plume before them, and he was beginning to tremble. 'Hurry . . .'

The first explosion stopped them both.

The long, rending, almost metallic, snap took them both some seconds to identify, and it was only when it was repeated, and this time followed by an almost musicial tinkling, that they realised that they were listening to the sound of breaking glass.

'What's happening?' Maeve breathed.

Michael shook his head. He was listening intently, and when a series of rippling crashes reverberated through the house, he guessed that the main windows were shattering.

It took Maeve three tries before she managed to dial the right number. By the time she got a connection, her breath was congealing icily on the mouthpiece.

'This better not be a wrong number,' the voice at the other end of the line murmured sleepily.

'Charley!' Maeve screamed, relief and terror made her voice shrill.

'Maeve! What's wrong?' Charley Woland was wide awake now, the terror in her voice shocking him out of his sleep.

'She's here Charley, she's here!'

'Whose here . . . where? Where are you?'

Michael took the phone from Maeve. It took a deliberate effort of will to force himself to breathe easily, and speak calmly into the receiver. 'Reverend Woland, this is Michael Cullen. Maeve and I are at Blacklands at the moment. We had a terrifying encounter with the creature earlier this evening, and we now believe she's in the house.' He stopped, breathless.

'Shit!'

'Exactly,' Michael said, his voice beginning to tremble. 'The temperature has fallen dramatically, it must be down to freezing now, and we can hear her moving about in the main house, but we're in my study, barricaded in, but there's lots of windows, and there's some sort of rubbish appearing on my machine, like a message, and I don't know what to do, and we need your help, can you help us, help us please.'

'Be calm!' The voice cut through Michael's growing hysteria like a command. 'Now remain calm, keep warm, and do nothing.'

'But . . .'

'I have already encountered the creature. I will attempt a small ritual from here, which should do some good. Now do you have a black-handled knife near you?'

Michael started to shake his head and then said aloud, 'No.'

'Anything made of iron?'

Michael looked around desperately, but everything around him seemed to be made of aluminium or plastic or something similar. And then he spotted the horseshoe on the mantelpiece. 'Yes, a horseshoe . . . a horseshoe would be made of iron, wouldn't it?' he asked hopefully.

'Yes, it would,' the Reverend Charles Woland said encouragingly. 'Now the sidhe-folk fear iron. So if you are confronted by the creature, then try to strike at her with that. And follow a piece of classic advice . . . don't look into her eyes.'

Michael managed a smile. 'Yeah.'

The priest went on to say something else, but the line suddenly dissolved into a mess of static and Michael hung up. He went back to where Maeve was reading through the material which had appeared on the screen. 'The same as the last time?' Michael asked.

'Some sort of narrative,' she nodded, 'similar to the last time certainly.' She frowned as she attempted to make sense of the archaic sentence structure.

'Make a copy in longhand,' Michael said quickly, 'you can translate it later.' Assuming there is a later, he added silently, folding his arms against his body, hugging himself tightly against the insidious chill. It reminded him of winter in New York. It was that same damp coldness that bit deeply into bones and joints.

Maeve's hands were trembling so much that she could barely hold the pencil, and the cold seemed to have affected her brain, she thought as she stared at the screen, attempting to make sense from words and phrases that she knew. Finally she resolved simply to copy them, word for word, letter for letter. She heard a noise and turned to see Michael pulling the curtains from their rods. He wrapped one of the dusty lengths of cloth around his shoulders and carried the second over to her. Although the material wasn't heavy, she was grateful for the little warmth it provided.

Michael went to stand before the uncurtained window, compelled to look down into the garden. The noises in the house had ceased, but he thought it was almost too much to hope for that the creature had simply left. But perhaps Charley Woland's mysterious ritual had worked and he had managed to banish the thing.

The cloaked woman walked out into the garden below.

She stood in the centre of the lawn and lifted her head, slowly, slowly to look up at him. For a moment, he believed that she was a real woman, a creature of flesh and blood, until he saw her face. And the face was totally and completely inhuman.

Everything was as he remembered it. The naked body beneath the cape was that of a young woman in her late teens, thin, gaunt almost, and ice-white. He could pick out the bones, the ribs below the small, high breasts, the prominent shoulder bones and the face. The face from this distance resembled nothing so much as a skull, a bleached skull, but complete with mouth and lips and teeth and tongue.

And eyes.

The eyes were pits in its face, black and bottomless, and although he had looked away almost immediately, he formed the impression that this creature, this banshee, was no ghost, no figment of his imagination. This creature 'lived' if that was the word; it had a physical presence in the world. There was movement and, although the night was airless, the creature's hair, which flowed down its back in a long thick sheet indistinguishable from its cloak, rose slowly and silently upwards, strands twisting and curling, weaving and flowing in some ghostly wind.

And then Michael's eyes misted, and his vision blurred. He blinked, blinked again when the misting remained, and suddenly realised that it wasn't his eyes, the windows were fogging up. He put his hand to the glass and pulled it back – the glass was ice cold to the touch. He stepped away from the windows as the ice thickened on the glass, forming and reforming as the ice encrusted, hardening.

'Maeve . . .' he whispered. He was turning towards her, when the window exploded inwards.

The force of the blow sent him sprawling across the room, and he hit the wall hard enough to topple his books from the shelves down onto him. They probably saved his life. The books absorbed most of the slivers of flying glass, and what struck him were minor. Maeve had an equally lucky escape. She had wrapped the curtain Michael had given her around her head for warmth and that caught most of the glass that went in her direction. The snapping crack of the glass and the sudden implosion of air had toppled her from her chair. She lay on the ground as glass tinkled around her, occasionally nicking her skin with tiny insect-like stings.

And as they both lay shocked and stunned on the ground, they heard the cry of the banshee lacing out into the night. High-pitched and undulating, it enclosed them both, enwrapping them in the terrifying sound, and they both felt its raw triumph.

Michael felt the fear and anger well up inside him and he screamed aloud. Something had happened; the banshee was about to feed.

MJ Cullen watched the digital numeral change on his radio-clock. Eleven-thirty. He tried to work out what that would be in Ireland; they were five hours ahead, which meant it was something like four-thirty in the morning.

And thinking of Ireland brought back the memories, of Mom and Dad and . . .

The scream bubbled up inside him like a wound, exploding inside his head in an agonising ball. He opened his mouth to let it out, but nothing happened. The screaming was trapped inside him, in a solid knot of pain and dread, and unless he released the pressure he was going to burst, to explode. The boy padded down the hall to his aunt and uncle's bedroom, moving silently past the dining room where they were watching a political debate. His uncle's service revolver was in the top drawer of the bedside cabinet, along with his badge and a box of cartridges.

MJ took the .32 Detective Special, turned the chamber until there was a round under the hammer, put the gun in his mouth and pulled the trigger.

The screaming stopped.

17

It lacked a few minutes to seven when the Reverend Charles Woland and Paddy Byrne arrived almost simultaneously the following morning. The two cars stopped in the driveway as both men stood on the brakes, both shocked by what they saw.

Every window in Blacklands House was broken, top to bottom. The glass porch and doorway were shattered, and the morning dew sparkled off millions of tiny particles of glass scattered across the gravelled driveway and out across the lawn. The empty windows gaped like wounds, the damp water stains that darkened the yellowed walls, looking as if the wounds had bled. Paddy Byrne was the first to make a move. He climbed out of his car and walked back to the car that had pulled in behind him, glass crunching underfoot. The car was obviously new, a late 1988 registration Saab Turbo, and he was mildly surprised when the door opened and a tall, bulky gentleman, wearing a clerical collar, stepped out of the car.

The big man grinned as he offered his hand. 'I think it is something to do with the combination of car and collar; people don't expect one to go with the other.'

Nonplussed, Paddy could only nod.

The priest smiled. 'The name's Woland, the Reverend Charles Woland. Call me Charley.'

'Paddy Byrne. I've heard of you.'

The priest nodded quickly. 'Yes, and Maeve has spoken of you too.'

Both men turned to look at the house. 'What in God's holy name happened here?' Paddy whispered.

'Nothing holy, I assure you,' Charley said quietly. He stepped around to the back of his car, opened the boot and then pulled out a long, cloth-wrapped box. Closing the boot, he rested the box on it and threw back the cover, to reveal a highly polished, rectangular, teak-wood box. Lifting the lid, he revealed a long slender sword set into crushed red velvet. As he lifted the beautiful weapon from its cradle, Paddy noticed that it was entirely black, blade and pommel. The clergyman saw the smile on Paddy's lips and grinned slightly, 'Don't worry, all will be revealed later,' he promised.

'I wasn't even going to ask,' Paddy Byrne said, his voice neutral and then he reached in, under his coat, and produced a twelve-inch, all-black, saw-toothed, survival knife.

Charley Woland laughed. 'Black blades. We read the same sources,' he said, suddenly serious. 'I take it you got a call.'

'A little less than an hour ago.'

'Mine was slightly earlier,' the clergyman said, holding the sword in both hands, looking speculatively at the house. 'They were under attack then. I did the best I could, but without visual references for the house it was difficult to construct a sphere of protection around them . . .' he was talking mainly to himself as he looked at the shattered windows. 'No signs of life though,' he muttered, 'and the aura seems placid enough.' He turned his head from side to side as if he were listening. 'There's a slight buzz, but that may be residue from the creature's appearance.'

'Well they were OK an hour ago. Terrified, and a few minor cuts, but alive. They're probably still in the study.' He pointed towards the orchard with the knife. 'We'll go in through the back.'

The windows at the back of the house seemed to have fared somewhat better than those at the front. Nearly all had multiple cracks running through the glass, but only one, the window giving into Michael's study, was completely missing, and the wall beneath it was splashed and streaked with water, which was still dripping from the window-sill.

'Michael? Maeve?'

While Paddy shouted up at the open window, the Reverend Charles Woland squatted down by one of the puddles of water. He touched it with his fingertips, finding it ice-cold, and when he brought his fingers to his lips, he found the water tasted brackish, stale, and smelt faintly of dead leaves and moss.

'Paddy? Paddy . . . thank God you're here . . . and you too Reverend Woland.'

Charley looked up in time to see Michael Cullen's head disappear back inside. He walked over to Paddy Byrne, the sword resting on one shoulder, like a guardsman's rifle. Although the smile remained on his lips, his expression was deadly serious. 'The water is bitterly cold, icy. Undoubtedly the creature has been here, and the chill it seems to generate has wrought this destruction, the glass shattering beneath the intense cold. We have to get our young friend away from this house; he is in deadly danger.'

Paddy nodded. 'I agree with you. However, I don't think it's the house. There are some stories of the banshee haunting one particular locality, but I think these are more correctly ghost stories which have become confused with the banshee legend. No, the creature has locked onto him; perhaps it is something from his family's past.' He looked up at the devastated house. 'Would it help if he left, do you think? Would it help if he went back to America?'

The Reverend Charles Woland shrugged. 'Maybe . . . maybe not. Distance might lessen the creature's hold over him, and maybe living in a city like New York, with its noise and bustle might help also.'

'But you doubt it.'

Charley Woland nodded. 'I doubt it. The creature is part of him; he can never escape it, never destroy it, only exorcise it.'

'You know he has the creature's comb.'

'I know that. The last time I spoke to him, he refused to give it back.'

The clergyman grinned. 'Maybe he'll have changed his mind.'

They both turned as the bolts were pulled back on the back door. 'I doubt it. He's a stubborn streak in him,' Paddy said.

'There's a world of difference between stubborn and stupid.'

The door opened and Michael Cullen stepped out, blinking into the wan morning light. He was pale and visibly shaking, his eyes sunk deep in his head. He held out his hands to both men. 'Thank you for coming . . . thank you . . .' His voice was a reedy whisper.

'Are you all right?' Paddy asked immediately, taking Michael's hand. It felt cold and clammy, and curiously fragile.

'I'm OK,' he attempted a smile, but it never reached his eyes. 'We've had a rough night,' he said looking from Paddy to Charles Woland.

'So I can see,' the priest said softly, looking past Michael to the kitchen which looked as if a bomb had exploded within it, the glass cupboards shattered, spilling broken crockery onto the floor. 'How's Maeve?' he asked quickly.

'She's all right. Shaken, like myself.'

The priest put his arm around Michael's shoulders, turning him back into the house. 'First things first,' he said loudly, 'and that's coffee.' While he was speaking to Michael, he looked at Paddy Byrne and nodded upstairs. The academic nodded, and stepped around Michael, making his way through the devastated kitchen, looking for Maeve.

As Paddy made his way through the house, he began to realise just what the couple must have gone through. Every single item of glassware and ceramics he came across was broken. The lightbulbs were shattered in their holders, pictures broken on the walls, or collapsed onto the ground. A glass-fronted cabinet in the sitting room, which had once held a display of European glassware had been completely destroyed, the beautiful pale-blue glassware now nothing more than pulverised shards. The clockface of the tall grandchild clock in the hallway was cracked in two. Paddy shivered; whatever had done this had been very powerful indeed. He shivered again, and suddenly realised that he was actually cold. A thin cold air lingered in the hallway and rooms, and now that he thought of it, he could actually see his breath pluming before his face. He stopped with his foot on the stairs and turned back to the hall, to where an ornate ship's barometer hung. It's glass face was shattered, the glass lying in broken splinters on the floor, and the thermometer was also broken. The mercury bulb had exploded and tiny globules of mercury nestled in the carpet, like silver marbles. The temperature gauge registered down to minus twenty degrees Celsius; obviously the temperature had fallen way below that with dramatic, and catastrophic, suddenness.

Paddy shivered again, and not with the cold this time.

He started up the stairs, and abruptly realised that the carpet beneath his feet was sodden, squelching with every step. He stooped down to look at the carpet and, what he had first taken to be slivers of glass sparkling in the deep pile, he now realised were splinters of ice.

The door to Michael's study looked as if it had been attacked. Long, deep gouges ran across the panels, splintering the wood in long cracks, and the handle had been wrenched out of the door, and now lay twisted on the floor in a pool of glittering, icy water. Paddy touched the gouges in the wood, attempting to measure the depth of the cuts, and then he pushed the door open, his fingers tingling with the chill, and stepped into the room.

And Maeve screamed.

Michael Cullen and Charles Woland were up the stairs almost before Paddy had a chance to get to her.

'It's OK, it's OK – ' she forced a smile. 'I just saw the door opening . . . and the shadow in the doorway, and I thought . . . and I thought . . .'

Michael took Maeve's hand and squeezed it tightly. 'Everything's going to be all right now. Charley thinks he may have a way to dispose of the creature.'

'Let's leave,' Maeve said suddenly. 'Let's get away from this house. You can stay at my place or I'm sure Charley or Paddy would let you stay with them.'

'Of course,' the clergyman said absently, stooping to look at the computer screen. He tapped it with one, blunt, finger nail. 'What's this?'

'That appeared at about the same time the creature appeared,' Michael said excitedly.

Paddy drifted over to the table. He had been staring down into the garden below, trying to work out something which was troubling him. 'Another mysterious message?'

Michael shrugged. 'I don't know. But I'm almost afraid to

turn off the machine in case it's not stored in the memory. Maeve has been scrolling through it, making a transcription.'

'Would it not be possible to print what's on the screen?' the Reverend Charles Woland asked.

'Usually, yes,' Maeve answered, 'but in this case we don't want to risk it, just in case we lost it. I don't want to have gone through all that last night for nothing.'

Paddy squeezed her shoulder. 'It must have been terrifying.'

Michael Cullen and Maeve Quill nodded together. 'It was.'

Paddy looked at the Reverend Charles Woland. 'This is your field. What do you think happened?'

The priest rubbed his balding head. 'I don't know. It's similar to poltergeist phenomenon, but its not like any poltergeist I've ever seen. Something incredibly powerful raged through this house last night, and yet, unlike a poltergeist, which is usually randomly destructive, this creature was quite selective. I'm not sure of a pattern yet, but I'll make an examination later.'

Paddy Byrne nodded. 'I think you'll find that every piece of glassware in the house has been broken. Even the ceramic tiles in the bathroom have been cracked and split. Furthermore, I think you'll find that they've been broken by intense cold. The mercury in the barometer is lying all over the floor in the hall, where the glass shattered.'

'Now that is interesting.'

'If you look at the side of the house, you'll find it is streaked with water; the carpet is sodden with ice-cold water, and the house is cold, cold.' He rubbed his hands together. 'Can you not feel the chill?'

'I'm so used to working with the chill of the etheric that I rarely feel the mundane cold of this world.'

Maeve reached out and squeezed his hand. 'Charley, you're so pompous. Don't mind him, he doesn't feel the cold because he's so thick-skinned.' She turned back to the machine. 'Now, give me five minutes and I'll have this completed.' The three men nodded and began moving towards the door, when she added quickly, 'Don't leave me on my own.' The panic in her voice was barely disguised by her light tone.

They waited in silence while Maeve continued to work,

transcribing the words on the screen onto paper, her usually small and neat handwriting now ragged and sloping. In the silence, broken only by the humming of the machine, the cold that lingered in the house became more obvious, evidence of the intense chill of the night before. No one felt like commenting that it was still the middle of Summer.

Finally Maeve sat back with a sigh. She dropped her pen onto the notebook and flexed her stiff fingers. 'Finished,' she sighed.

The three men crowded around her. 'Now, see what happens when you try and save what's on the screen,' Michael suggested.

Maeve touched the keys, and a single highlighted word appeared on the screen: SAVING. The screen cleared and the main menu reappeared.

'Now, open the file again,' Michael said, watching the screen intently, seeing only his friends' reflections overlying the orange-lettered menu.

Maeve touched the keys again, and pressed the ENTER key.

The screen cleared as the file opened. And it was blank.

'Nothing,' Paddy Byrne breathed.

Michael nodded quickly. 'Exactly the same as the last time.'

Charley Woland muttered something unintelligible.

Maeve closed the file again, and then reached over to turn off the machine. It shut itself down with a descending hum. She stood up, pressing both hands into the small of her back and then stretched, 'I thought someone was making tea?' she asked.

They had their breakfast sitting on the bonnets of the cars, watching the sun climb higher into the heavens. The sky was already a pale, egg-shell blue, the colour washed from it, and the day promised to be another scorcher. It was actually warmer outside than in the house, where the walls seemed to have absorbed the chill, and were now radiating it back.

Michael and Maeve sat in silence, drinking the strong, sweet tea Charley had prepared, allowing the peace of the place to wash over the events of the previous night, dulling the sharp edges, blunting the terror. Paddy Byrne and the Reverend Charles Woland walked through the dew-damp grass talking quietly together, both men recognising that the couple needed a few moments' peace together.

Maeve yawned, and Michael followed suit, the yawn proving to be infectious.

'I'm exhausted,' she confessed, rubbing her red-rimmed eyes, 'but I'm not sure I want to sleep.'

'I know what you mean.' Michael finished the last of his tea, but kept the cup in his hands, his long fingers locked around it.

'What are you going to do, Michael?' Maeve asked in a whisper.

'My resolve hasn't changed,' he said quickly.

Maeve shook her head, too tired to argue. 'Do you think it's safe to sleep inside?'

He shrugged. I don't know . . . but be careful of the glass.'

'I'm so tired now, I could sleep on a pin.'

'I know the feeling.'

Michael walked her to the door, and then stood in the hallway, listening to her clump tiredly up the stairs, glass crunching under her feet. She was a brave girl, he realised. She had come through that terrifying experience without complaint, and without leaving, and he suddenly thought how lost he would be without her. He didn't want to have to go through another night like last night, but he had an awful premonition that he might have to.

That scream, that creature's scream would remain with him until his dying day. He shivered with the memory of it. When he had heard that wail for the first time he had thought it sounded familiar, almost as if he'd heard it before. But perhaps, if, as Maeve had said, the Cullen family were one of those gifted, or cursed, with a banshee, then he carried the memory of that terrifying sound in his racial memory.

The sound bothered him. It was a pure musical tone, and he had a good ear for music, and yet, try as he might, he couldn't identify the notes. It had been almost vocal . . . he frowned, remembering something about the sound. When he had heard it first, it had been a cry of hunger, of want, of need, but then later . . . later, it had been a cry of triumph, and the agony had turned to exaltation.

At the other end of the hall, the phone rang, startling him. Filled with sudden terrifying foreboding, Michael raced down the hall to answer it. Before he even picked it up, he knew it was bad news.

'Charles, what happened here?' Paddy Byrne stopped and looked back at the house, the gaping windows looking incongruous in the morning sunlight, the gravelled drive sparkling with glass.

'We're up against something very powerful here; something which has access to a lot of power.'

'A ghost?'

Charley shrugged, and then shook his head. 'Not a ghost. A ghost rarely has a tangible existence. This creature obviously has.'

'Poltergeist?'

'Possibly. But one rarely sees the poltergeist. And our young friends have seen this woman, this spirit.'

'You saw it too, I understand,' Paddy said cautiously.

'I saw an image I interpreted as a woman, or rather the three stages of womanhood; maiden, matron and hag.' He paused and then added. 'I've done some research into the phenomenon of the banshee, and she sometimes appears as either maiden or hag, a warning or a threat.'

'And what do we have here?'

'They've seen the maiden.'

'The threat?'

The cry of anguish that echoed out over the quiet morning garden stopped them both in their tracks. They both thought it was the creature, until the sound changed, the voice cracking, and they recognised Michael's grief-distorted voice.

And even as they were running towards the house, they knew there had been a death.

18

The Time of power approached.

A time when the worlds touched, when the membrane of time itself dissolved. A time of strength.

It had fed twice now. Eaten well, but not of the main course. But soon. It felt the presence approach. Return.

It would feed again.

Soon.

Michael Cullen returned to Ireland in late September. He came unannounced, and there was no one at the airport to meet him. At immigration control, the officer on duty had to look twice at the photograph of the man on the passport, comparing it with the man standing before him. The likeness was there, but the photo showed a young man of, he checked the date of birth, yes, in his mid-thirties, while the man standing in front of his desk looked closer to fifty.

Michael Cullen hired a car at the Hertz desk, almost directly facing the arrivals lounge in Dublin airport, and drove straight to Blacklands House in Loughshinny, driving on instinct and memory, surprising himself that he still remembered the route.

He stopped his small Fiesta outside the wrought iron gates, and sat for a few moments in the car, simply looking at the gates and the roof of the house over the top of the trees.

And he felt nothing!

His wife had died in this house. And his son had died because of it, he was convinced of that, and to hell with all psychiatrists' reports which spoke of guilt, delayed grieving, emotive reaction and flawed personality. The banshee had killed his wife and driven his son to death, killing him as assuredly as if she had put the gun to his head and pulled the trigger herself.

But hadn't he been the one to bring them to Ireland in the first place?

The thought was insidious, and had been creeping into his

consciousness over the past few weeks. At first he had dismissed it, but lately it was becoming more and more difficult to ignore. Perhaps it wasn't the banshee who was responsible for his son's death . . . perhaps . . .

Michael turned off the engine and stepped out of the car, standing with his hand resting on the roof, simply absorbing the atmosphere of this quiet, country road in rural Ireland.

It was one of those special, late autumn days, when it felt as if Summer were making a valiant effort to return. The sky was a pale eggshell blue, the clouds high and fleecy, being torn by a wind that remained unfelt on the ground. The sunshine was brilliant, the sun a large, yellow ball low in the sky, sharp and blinding and the air was spiced and invigorating, with salt and warmth. It was a truly beautiful day, reminding him of Fall in New England, if it hadn't been for the vague unspoken menace of the house.

The gates had been closed, but not locked, and opened easily to his touch, flakes of red rust speckling his hands like spots of blood. Leaving the car by the side of the road, he walked slowly up the driveway.

The long gravelled drive was clotted with dead leaves and wood, and vegetation run riot. In the heat of the day it smelled warm and close, with the slightly sweet smell of something rotten underlying it all. At the top of the drive, at the second set of gateposts, he turned to the right, into the garden, and had his first proper look at the house.

The windows had been repaired and the glass replaced. That in itself took the wounded look from the building, but it couldn't disguise the air of menace that hung over it now, like some invisible miasma. There was a general air of neglect about the place, perhaps typified by the leaves which covered everything, and grass had sprouted in clumps between the stones. Unwilling to face the house at the moment, Michael Cullen turned to the right and stepped through the small arched doorway into the orchard. The small enclosed garden was almost stiflingly hot, the air hanging heavy, sickly with the smell of rotting windfall fruit, now hidden in the tall grass. It was also completely silent, and for the first time he realised that he hadn't heard a bird sing since he had entered the grounds.

Stepping out of the orchard, Michael made his way around by the kitchen towards the pool. He knew where it was by sense more than anything else. It registered as a cold patch on his consciousness, and he knew that if he were blindfold, he would be able to point unerringly to the pool. Against the autumnal reds and golds of the trees, he could make out the black water quite clearly. Drawn by an almost macabre curiosity, he made his way through the shedding trees and bushes to stand before the still black water. It was only then that he noticed that, although the ground was littered with leaves from the trees and bushes, the surface of the pool itself was clear, nothing marring its slightly oily surface.

Michael squatted down in the soft muck beside the pool and stared into the black water. The sun was on the other side of the house, leaving this area in shadow. It was cold and completely silent. His fingers found a stone and he dropped it into the water. It disappeared without a sound.

'I've come back,' he whispered.

'I've come back.'

There was a moment of shocked surprise at the other end of the line, and then Maeve asked. 'Michael, Michael Cullen?'

'Hello Maeve.'

'Where are you . . . how are you?'

'I got in today. I'm fine.'

'You should have phoned or written. I would have picked you up at the airport.'

'It was a sort of spur of the moment thing.'

'You're keeping well?' Maeve asked, and then immediately realised how lame it sounded.

'I'm well.' There was a pause and then he added. 'As well as I can be. I suppose.'

'Where are you now, Michael?' Maeve asked, suddenly feeling a sense of foreboding, which solidified into a solid knot of fear when she heard his answer.

'I'm at Blacklands.'

'Why have you come back?' she whispered.

'I've some business to finish,' he said quickly, and then hurried on. 'I'd like to have dinner with you tonight, if that's all right.'

'Yes . . . yes, I'd like that.'

'Somewhere quiet, where we can talk. A hotel . . . someplace like that. I'll pick you up at your flat at eight.' He paused and added. 'And bring the transcripts you made of the creature's last visit.'

Maeve stared at Michael Cullen for at least thirty seconds without recognising him. The tall, gaunt-faced man standing at the door bore little resemblance to the Michael Cullen she remembered. He had aged; his hair, now shaved close to his skull, was almost white, and his eyes had sunk deep into his head, giving him a cavernous appearance. He was dressed in a three-piece black suit, white shirt and black tie, which only emphasised his funereal appearance.

'Hello,' he attempted a smile, but it never reached his eyes. 'Don't look so shocked,' he continued, when she remained silent.

'I'm just surprised,' she said eventually. 'You . . . you're early.'

'I misjudged the traffic.' He tilted his head slightly. 'Can I come in?'

'Of course.' Maeve stepped to one side and allowed Michael to walk into the tiny two-roomed flat. Abruptly realising that she was still wearing her bathrobe, she stepped in, out of the hallway, and closed the door behind her, following him into the room. She suddenly felt nervous with him in the room, but for no reason she could put her finger on. She had always felt comfortable in his presence, never threatened. But something about him had changed and it wasn't just his appearance, that change was shocking enough. He now exuded an aura of . . . of what?

Michael turned suddenly, catching her staring at him, and Maeve suddenly realised what was different about him. It was his eyes. She remembered his eyes as being grey, soft warm grey, like cloth, but now they were hard, hard and flat like polished stones. They were the eyes of a dead man.

'Have you got the notes?' he asked abruptly, his voice harsh, sounding slightly cracked.

Maeve looked around the room in confusion. Michael's presence was unsettling her. She had rooted out the notes earlier and placed them in an envelope for that evening. She finally spotted the package on the small table beside the window. 'You'll find them there, in a large brown envelope.'

Michael nodded and turned away without waiting for her to finish. He crossed to the table, his long fingers trembling slightly as he lifted the envelope, opening it, pulling out the single-spaced type-written page which had been clipped to her original hand-written notes. He hooked out the typist's chair with his foot and sat down on it, leaning his elbows against the table, and began to read.

'I'll go and finish getting dressed,' Maeve said from the other side of the room. There was no reply.

> 'The first sacrifices were of blood. And that alone was sufficient. Blood and faith.
>
> 'Faith lends substance.
>
> 'The belief made me strong, calling me forth from the darkness of the void, calling me back into being.
>
> 'The early believers were primitives, little more than beasts. The land the Princess Caesir Banba had claimed from the sea and invested with such beauty had succumbed to animals. They came from the lands to the north and south. Some were pale of hair and light of eye, others dark featured, dark skinned. Their customs, clothing and mannerisms were different. But though they called down the Gods and Goddesses by different names, they were conjuring the same beings. Some were creatures of power, others little more than elementals, petty spirits.
>
> 'I was one of those.
>
> 'But I was cunning and my power waxed. The primitives worshipped me, sacrificed to me, made me

grow with their sacrifice and faith. I became strong, growing from a petty creature, haunting the bloody battlefields, to the status of a Goddess, a creature of blood and fire, of death and destruction.

'Great was my power.

'I became the Morrigan, Macha and Badb, War, Death and Madness, the Three that are One, the Tripartite Goddess.

'And then the robed ones came.

'Small men, small in stature, dark skinned and small in intellect. They brought with them the word of a new God, a God of peace, but who had died by violence, a God of love, but who had died hated and reviled. They spoke of a God who had died and rose again, as if this were some extraordinary feat, but the old Gods performed such feats. They preached love and the ending of war, though these men were not above enforcing their beliefs with the sword; they spoke of kindness and gentleness, but many of the robed ones were not kind and were often ungentle. And the people, fools that they were, listened to them.

'Many were lost to the old ways.

'And with the loss of Faith, many of the old Gods went into the Shadow, some, never to return. I was sorely beset, and my power, my strength was stripped from me piece by piece. The food of battle, the blood, the lust, the anger, the fear, the excitement, were denied me, starving me. There were still enough bloody, violent deaths to provide me with such sustenance necessary for my continued existence. But the days when my name struck terror into the hearts of men were gone, stolen by the robed ones. Gradually, they took away the last vestiges of my power, reducing me to a cypher and to denigrate me even further, they took to naming me: 'woman,' they called me, though it had been a long time since I had been called woman; 'fairy folk' they said, although I had never been one of the Shining Ones; 'myth' they said, 'legend', and I could not deny that, for I had always been legend.

'What little power I had left I used. I sang the Deathsong outside their windows, calling them to the Shadowland. I taught the robed ones that there was a power other than their White Christ. And when they had gone on, and I remained, I took an especial pleasure in feasting upon the descendants of the robed ones, teaching them to fear my cry. Soon, the name they had gifted me with assumed a new power, the power to terrorise.

'They had called me fairy woman, bean-sidhe, a title of mockery. I made it a name of terror . . .

'I'm ready.'

Michael looked up, startled, the pages slipping from his hands.

Maeve was standing in the doorway, looking curiously ill at ease in a formal, midnight-blue evening dress. 'I thought since you had dressed up . . .' she began, and then stopped in confusion as he started to shake his head. 'What's wrong?'

'Nothing.' He attempted a smile. 'Only now I'll have to take you somewhere grand to match that dress.'

'It's the best I have,' she confessed.

'And you look gorgeous,' he said, a degree of warmth creeping back into his voice, a trace of the old Michael Cullen returning.

'Thank you,' she said cautiously, unsure how to take the compliment. She was aware that the dress was perhaps a little too revealing, and emphasised her large bust, and she felt perhaps too self-conscious in it to be really comfortable.

'Where shall we go?' he asked, stooping to gather up the pages he had dropped. He stood up slowly, stiffly, and looked at her. 'A good restaurant mind.'

She nodded. 'I know just the one. Have you got a car?'

'I hired one at the airport. It's parked just down the road.'

'Let me lock up.'

'You've a lovely apartment,' Michael said looking around as he moved towards the door.

'Flat,' Maeve corrected him. 'Its a flat. An apartment is something much grander altogether.' She stopped and looked around the room. 'But it's not bad,' she admitted. 'I've two rooms: a sort of kitchen-cum-dining-room-cum-sitting-room, and a tiny bedroom with a small loo off it. It's fine. It suits me,' she said, nodding decisively as if to convince herself.

Michael opened the door and stepped out into the hallway and then stood back, waiting for her to lock the door. 'Have you been here long?'

'A few years, four, five, something like that. Every year I promise myself I'll find someplace else, or that I'll buy myself a house, but I guess I'm just too lazy, and of course houses are so expensive.' She realised she was rattling on, her nervousness making her talkative. Throwing a coat over her bare shoulders, she pulled the door closed behind her, and then hunted for her keys with which to lock it. 'I hope I haven't left them inside,' she muttered, 'no, here they are.' She turned around and stifled a scream. Michael Cullen was standing behind her, his face barely inches from hers.

'What's wrong, Maeve?' he asked gently.

'Nothing . . . nothing.'

'You're as nervous as a kitten.'

She shook her head. 'No, no, just . . . just surprised at your return.'

'You knew I would come back,' he said softly, his breath on her face was cool, smelling of mint.

Maeve stared at him in the semi-darkness of the hall, and then shook her head. 'No, Michael, I didn't think you'd come back. I didn't think you'd come back at all.'

'I said I would.'

'I didn't believe you. You had nothing to come back to, had you?'

His face hardened into a mask. 'I told you. I've some unfinished business.'

'The book?' she began.

'Fuck the book!' he snapped. 'I've come back to destroy the creature.'

'Michael!'

'I'm going to destroy the banshee!'

She started to shake her head, and then his hands came up, gripping her elbows almost painfully.

'And I need you to help me.'

'No . . . I've told you, no. This is madness.'

'Perhaps. But it's madness for a woman to freeze to death in her own bed. And it's madness for a thirteen-year-old boy to put a gun into his mouth and pull the trigger.' His voice was calm, measured; if he had shouted and ranted, she would have found it easier to accept, but the very fact that he was so calm, so controlled, she found terrifying.

'I can't help you . . .'

'We'll talk about it after dinner,' he said, suddenly changing the subject, 'let's not have any unpleasantness now.'

Maeve nodded, unwilling to argue with him. Obviously, his son's terrible death, coming so closely on the heels of his wife's, had made him irrational, unstable. She was determined to do her best to keep the conversation light over dinner and avoid the subject of the banshee completely.

They had dinner in a tiny French café, in one of the side-streets off St Stephen's Green. The food was delicious and Michael seemed to unwind a little during the meal. He talked about university life both as a student and later as lecturer, and encouraged her to talk about herself and her plans. Maeve drank sparingly, although Michael polished off two bottles of a crisp, white wine without showing the least sign of drunkenness. However, he quickly agreed when she suggested a walk around the exterior of the Green, the park gates being closed for the night.

After the warm, food-and-drink scented atmosphere of the restaurant, the night air was refreshing. It must have rained whilst they were eating; the streets were sparkling, and the shrubbery smelled damp and earthy, overlying the acrid exhaust fumes which tainted the autumnal evening.

'You know,' Michael said suddenly, when they had almost

completed one circuit of the Green, 'you know, we wouldn't be able to do this in New York.'

She looked at him silently.

'I mean, two well-dressed people, out for a stroll, are obvious targets for the low lifes.'

'That doesn't mean you're perfectly safe here,' Maeve said with a smile.

Michael stuck his hand in his pocket and pulled out a small, snub-nosed revolver. Without saying a word he put it away again.

'Jesus!' Maeve breathed. 'How did you get that into the country. That's illegal. I mean you can't . . . you're not allowed to . . .'

'It's only illegal when they catch you.'

'But how did you get it into the country in the first place?' Maeve persisted.

'I posted it to myself,' Michael smiled triumphantly. 'I sent three parcels of books, one after the other. The final parcel contained a hollowed out book with this little toy.'

'What do you want it for?'

He shrugged. 'Protection, security.'

'It won't stop the creature,' Maeve said gloomily, 'quite the contrary. If you hurt the creature it will only redouble its efforts to get you.'

'So what will hurt it?' he demanded.

She shook her head defiantly. 'No, no, you're not going to dupe me into discussing the banshee,' she snapped.

'I never mentioned the creature,' he smiled coldly. He patted his pocket. 'But if the gun is handy the next time it appears, then I'll use it.'

'A black-handled knife or sword is the traditional method of killing one of the fairy folk, steel is the great enemy of the Sidhe.'

'Is there any other way?'

'I'm not even sure of the first way,' she said numbly.

'I'll see the Reverend Charles Woland tomorrow; perhaps he would know the correct way of trapping and destroying the creature.'

Maeve stopped. 'I don't think you'll ever stop it or destroy it. Charley says if you destroy it, you will destroy part of yourself.'

Smiling, Michael started to shake his head, when the scream lanced out from the depths of the park!

19

It was dark in the park. The lights from the surrounding city streets provided a brief illumination around the perimeter, and a vague ceiling of light over the park, which obscured the stars, but left the interior in darkness. Stepping into the moist darkness was like stepping into another world.

The sound had come from ahead and to his left and Michael Cullen moved resolutely through the undergrowth towards it. The gun was in his hand, although he wasn't aware that he had pulled it from his pocket.

There was another scream, muffled this time, but it fixed the distance and destination in his mind's eye. He was also able to identify the sound as being definitely human and female. The banshee's eerie cry could never be mistaken for anything else. Vaguely disappointed, he stopped and was about to turn away when he realised that he was going to walk away from an obviously terrified woman. The banshee may have taken his wife and son, but it hadn't robbed him of his humanity. Appalled by his own callousness, he pressed on.

He came across them on the banks of the lake. At first, he thought they were simply a drunken couple, fumbling at one another. Then he realised that the man, although obviously drunk, was far too determined in his assault on the woman, and she was equally determined to resist him. He stood in the shadows, watching them, his rational self presenting arguments to counter his emotions: this was none of his business, there was no reason for him to get involved; he didn't know what was happening here, they seemed to know one another, she knew his name.

He walked out of the bushes, moving silently across the path and onto the grass, his rubber-soled shoes making no sound, his black evening dress rendering him virtually invisible against the night.

The woman attempted another scream and this time the

man struck her across the mouth, the sound loud and sharp in the silence.

And then Michael Cullen was behind him, the muzzle of the small pistol pressed into the soft flesh below his ear.

'Get up,' he hissed softly.

There was a moment of shocked immobility and dumbfounded silence, and then the man surged backwards off the girl, rearing up to his full height, which was a little over six foot.

Michael stepped back and pulled back the hammer on the pistol. The double click stopped the man in his tracks.

'Say mister . . .' he began.

'I don't want to know.' The gun was rock steady in his hands.

'Look . . .'

'Turn around,' Michael whispered.

'Now listen . . .'

'Walk into the lake, or I'll blow your fucking head off. Walk in there and keep walking, until you're chest-high in the shit.' The man didn't move. 'Do it, or By Christ I'll shoot you.'

Slowly, reluctantly, the man began to inch his way down the gently sloping bank and into the water. Michael Cullen suddenly stepped up behind him, and shoved him hard, sending him head first into the mud. Without another word, he turned and walked away into the night, leaving the man floundering in the cold water and the woman lying bemused on the bank.

Maeve was still standing in the same spot when Michael jumped over the rail, moments later. Relief, mingled with anger, made her voice sharp. 'Just what the hell was that all about?' she demanded. 'Who was screaming?'

'You wouldn't believe me if I told you.'

'Tell me!'

'And you mean to tell me, he simply walked out into the lake?' Maeve demanded incredulously.

Michael smiled. 'What else could he do? The way I read it, it was an amorous encounter that got a little out of hand. Perhaps she decided he was a little too drunk, or too rough, and perhaps he thought she wasn't willing enough. Anyway, no matter how their encounter was going, having some maniac appear out of the night and put a gun to his head was sure to ruin his evening. And if someone sticks a gun in your face, you'll be inclined to do what they say, and that includes walking out into the middle of a lake.'

'And the girl said nothing?'

'Not a thing.'

'I wonder if it'll be in the papers tomorrow.'

'Don't count on it.'

Maeve smiled. 'Ah, but you're thinking of a headline which reads, "Mysterious Gunman Saves Girl From Vicious Assault," while I'm thinking of something like, "Maniac With Gun Threatens Courting Couple."'

Michael spotted a parking space and deftly pulled into it. He had mastered the right-hand drive cars and the fact that they drove on the wrong side of the road, relatively quickly, and it was only roundabouts, junctions and parking which caused him any real problems. Especially parking.

They walked slowly towards Maeve's flat, which was about ten yards from the parking spot. Even at this late hour, Rathmines was bustling, and the smell of cooking from the dozens of takeaways lingered on the air, making their mouths water even though they had recently eaten. Maeve was debating whether to invite Michael in for coffee, wondering if he would misconstrue it. Although he had relaxed as the evening had worn on, that strange episode around the Green had convinced her that he was unstable. She couldn't help wondering if the man had refused to walk into the water, would Michael have shot him? She was half inclined to believe he would.

'Did you leave a light on when we left?' Michael asked suddenly, startling her.

'No!' She looked up at the window of her flat in surprise. And stopped. There was a white light shining through the juncture of the curtains.

'You're sure?' he demanded.

'I'm sure; I can't afford the price of the electricity. Shit, it's probably a burglar; this is flatland remember?'

'Stay here,' Michael commanded, walking away.

'Not this time,' Maeve snapped. 'This may be your night for playing hero, but I'm not standing around waiting for you. And remember,' she added quickly, seeing his hand disappear into his pocket, 'no guns, please. This is Ireland; the police get very nervous where guns are concerned.'

'I didn't think your police were armed,' Michael said softly, as Maeve carefully fitted the key into the front door and turned it in the lock. The door opened without a sound.

'They're not, maybe that's why they get so nervous.'

They padded silently upstairs, their feet making no sound on the worn carpet. The gun was in Michael's hand now, looking like nothing more than a toy in the wan, reflected light from the street.

Maeve's room was on the first floor. The other two doors were dark, but an intense, white light outlined Maeve's door.

She stopped, suddenly frightened, and reached out for Michael's arm when he went to approach it. 'I don't have a light that bright,' she whispered.

'Maybe it's one of those high-power torches,' Michael murmured, not really believing it himself. 'Give me your keys.'

Maeve dutifully passed over her keys and Michael approached the door cautiously, gun in one hand, key in the other. When he touched the handle, he immediately knew who was inside.

It was ice-cold.

'Maeve . . .'

He managed the one word before the door split right down the middle, like a card torn lengthways. One half of the door smashed back on its hinges, while the second half sailed over Michael's head, missing him by inches, to embed itself into the banisters, shattering them, slivers spraying across Maeve in the process. An icy gale whipped out from the room and across the landing, scattering objects from within, everywhere. The everyday objects of her life battered at them both, while the wind tore at their clothing. Michael took the brunt of it; ice-tipped and freezing, it stung at his eyes, spattering across his cheeks, and coated his glasses with a thin film of ice.

The light from within the room intensified, turning into a solid block of pure white light, intense enough to hurt.

And then the shape appeared.

It blotted out the light in a tall, regular black shape, and then suddenly the figure took on a form and definition all of its own. Arms, legs and a head separated from the rest of the blackness. The arms raised up, and the cold intensified. The lightbulb exploded with a dull pop, and the plaster on the walls and ceiling split and cracked with intense cold. With every breath a searing agony, Michael Cullen tightened his frozen finger on the icy metal of the gun, and fired.

Against the howling of the wind, the detonation of the gun was virtually inaudible, and the shape in the doorway staggered. Michael fired again and again, and continued firing until the weapon clicked empty. With each shot the shape disappeared further and further into the room. When the final shot struck it, it vanished, and with it, the bitter cold and the freezing wind.

Michael turned to look at Maeve, his face a death-mask, ice in his hair, coating his eyebrows, his glasses coated with rime. His eyes blazed with triumph as he held the gun aloft. 'I told you it would work.'

Maeve slumped to the stairs and began to sob.

The Reverend Charles Woland had just settled down in front of the empty fireplace for the night, with a glass of very fine brandy and a passable cigar, when he felt the chill on the back of his neck. He remained seated in the large leather armchair, the glass still poised in his right hand, the cigar in his left, waiting for something else to happen. He never even considered that someone might have broken into the house; as well as the usual locks and alarms, he had had several other slightly nastier and certainly illegal devices installed. And if it wasn't a person . . .

He put down the cigar and brandy and then, sitting back into the chair, he began to breathe deeply, performing the ritual that had become second nature to him over the years. Gradually disassociating himself from the physical world, he entered an almost dream-like state, in which the physical world appeared only as a vaguely perceived shell. He turned to look at the empty fireplace, the vestiges of old fire and heat trembled against the brickwork, the ghostly flames shimmering blue-green. He lifted his hand before his eyes. He could see the skeletal structure beneath the skin, and the skin itself was outlined in a ghostly red-blue aura. Lifting his head he stared at the wall directly in front of him; it was sheathed in light which, even as he looked, grew dim and transparent . . . and then he could see beyond the wall, through the wall . . . and he was looking out over Killiney Bay. The waters of the bay were a kaleidoscope of colour. As the myriad forms of life which swarmed beneath the surface gave off their own distinctive auras.

Satisfied that the transition was complete, the Reverend Charles Woland stood up and turned around.

There was a woman standing behind him. She was standing partially in shadow, although the ghost-world Charles Woland now inhabited had neither light nor shadow in it, her arms by her side, her fingers splayed and pointing downwards. She was naked except for a white gauzy shift, which barely concealed her young body. Woland guessed she was not long into her teens.

'Who are you? Why have you disturbed me?' The questions went unspoken, but Woland knew that she would be able to understand him.

The woman moved forward, her diaphanous gown billowing in some unfelt breeze and, although her body came into the light, her face and head remained in shadow. As she neared him, he noticed that there were five ragged holes in the cloth, and even as he watched, five puncture wounds appeared on her body, three in her breasts, one in her stomach and one high on her thigh. Thick, black ichor appeared in the holes. The woman's arms came up, palms upwards, pleading.

'If you are unquiet, or have died by violence, then tell me

now or where your corpse lies and I will do what I can for you,' Woland said calmly, and then he frowned with the realisation that something was amiss. He had seen what were commonly called ghosts and spirits before, and while he had initially thought that's what this was, some unquiet spirit roaming the astral looking for a contact in the physical world, now he wasn't quite so sure.

The creature moved closer.

'Have you left this plane of existance recently?' Charles Woland persisted, 'are you in need of a guide?' Sometimes the newly dead needed help to counter the trauma of having passed over.

The woman's long-fingered hands turned, the nails long and black, and then delicately, almost gently, one touched against his face.

And there was pain.

Knife-sharp, ice-cold pain.

The woman moved atop him, her embrace like that of a lover, her arms wrapping themselves around his body, her hands at the back of his head. One leg came up and twined around his leg, pulling him even closer, rubbing its groin against him, and then it moved against his face, its lips, ice-cold and bitter, against his . . .

Succubus!

Charles Woland grasped at the thought, concentrating on it, using it as a lure to call forth his own arcane knowledge. Succubus, a female spirit that took sustenance from human men while they slept, a psychic vampire. But he wasn't sleeping, he wasn't some defenceless soul.

The pain intensified, in his chest, his stomach, high in his thigh. But there shouldn't be any pain in his astral form, nor should there be pleasure. He could feel his body responding in a purely physical way to the creature's lewd embrace, and that too was impossible. That shouldn't be happening. He wrenched his head away, looking at the wall, and it was solid, the room dark and heavy, the brilliance of the auras gone. And Charles Woland realised he was back in the physical world. Somehow, someway, the creature had pulled him back to the real world . . . and that meant . . . that meant . . .

The pain was incredible, and the roaring in his head was making coherent thought difficult. He felt moisture on his chest, his stomach, his leg.

And then the creature was moving away, pushing him backwards. He staggered, stumbled and fell to the floor. He could see her clearly now, could see the long thin face, the high pronounced cheekbones . . . and the eyes, deep, dark, pitiless, inhuman eyes. There was something else about her, something different. He brought his hand up to his chest, touched pain and moisture and then lifted it to his face. His fingers were thick with blood.

And then he realised what had changed about the creature: the wounds, the five punctures in her bone-white skin were gone, the cloth of her shift was still rent, but the holes in her flesh had vanished.

And as the creature threw back her head and screamed triumphantly, Charles Woland knew that his own body was punctured in the same places, knew that he was dying.

The creature screamed and screamed again, the frenzied baying of a beast that has just pulled down its prey.

It struck Michael like a physical blow. His first reaction was to hit the breaks, the second to swerve into the side of the road. Luckily there was little traffic at this late hour, and the two cars that had been travelling reasonably close behind him, went past with horns blaring.

'What happened. What's wrong?' Maeve had been dozing in the passenger seat, exhausted by the evening. The violent lurching of the car had woken her.

Michael was gripping the wheel so tightly his knuckles shone whitely in the light of the passing cars. His face was a rigid mask, his spectacles mirroring the light of the oncoming cars.

'What's wrong?' Maeve demanded again.

'Didn't you hear it?' he whispered.

'I was dozing.'

'I heard it. The creature. The banshee. It's just fed.'

20

Michael Cullen replaced the phone on the cradle, and turned to look at Maeve, who was sitting dejectedly on the bottom stair.

'Nothing,' he said softly.

Maeve looked up, puzzled. 'What do you mean, nothing?'

'I've 'phoned home and Chrissy is fine. So is every other member of the family as far as I could find out.' His eyes were wide and haunted.

Maeve stood slowly, joints cracking and protesting. 'Perhaps you imagined it,' she suggested gently.

Michael shook his head savagely. 'I did not imagine it. I heard the creature. And she has fed.'

Since hearing the cry of exaltation on the airport road, Michael had driven like a maniac, completing the journey to Blacklands in under ten minutes, although it was usually a twenty-minute drive. He didn't know what he had been expecting at the house, the banshee rampaging through the house, the windows shattered, the air sharp with ice? But Blacklands was quiet and felt empty. He couldn't define it, but he instinctively knew the banshee wasn't there. He had then spent the best part of an hour on the 'phone, desperately trying to contact the States, convinced that Chrissy had been attacked by the creature. Finally, after a long crackle and static filled conversation, he had discovered that she was physically well, although very quiet and withdawn, still numbed by her brother's death.

'Well if you're convinced that the creature fed, and if it's not a member of your family, who is it then?' Maeve demanded.

'I thought these creatures only followed one particular family or clan?' he asked.

'Usually, yes. But this is obviously not the common or traditional banshee. Mind you, I don't know of anyone else who has antagonised one in the same way you have.'

'You mean its doing this out of spite?' he demanded. 'I thought these were unthinking spirits.'

'I never said that,' Maeve said tiredly. 'Usually, they sing and someone dies, sometimes the hearer of the song, sometimes a relative. And it's as simple as that.'

'Isn't that what's happening here. I hear it sing, and a member of my family dies.'

'I suppose so,' she whispered. 'But you have its comb, it will not rest, it will not leave you until it has recovered that.'

'But if it's victimising me for that,' Michael said very slowly, 'might it not then be petty enough to attack my friends also, striking at me, hurting me by hurting my friends,' Michael continued, not listening to her.

'You have very few friends in Ireland,' Maeve observed.

Michael was already dialling Paddy Byrne's number.

'Paddy. Thank God? Paddy, it's Michael, Michael Cullen . . . no, I'm not back long. Listen to me, has anything happened tonight? Anything unusual?' His shoulders slumped. 'Nothing? OK I'll be in touch tomorrow. Go back to sleep.' He hung up.

'I can see him getting some sleep,' Maeve said wryly.

'I can't think of anyone else,' Michael said, tiredness suddenly washing over him, enclosing him in a thick woollen blanket, making even the simplest thoughts difficult to follow through.

'Charley Woland,' Maeve said slowly, looking up at Michael. 'Give Charley a ring.'

'But I don't really know him,' Michael protested.

'He came here when the creature rioted through the house,' Maeve reminded him.

'All right, what's his number?' he asked numbly.

'It's unlisted.' She scrabbled through her notebook until she found the clergyman's phone number and then carefully read it out.

The phone rang twice and then an answering machine cut in, Charles Woland's deep voice echoing slightly on the line. 'This number is unattended . . .' There was a click as someone picked up the phone at the other end, followed by silence.

'Hello . . . hello . . .?' Michael looked at Maeve in alarm.

'Help me!'

It is eighteen miles from Loughshinny to Dublin City and Killiney lies another eight miles beyond that. Michael Cullen and Maeve Quill completed the journey in just under thirty minutes, neither of them speaking much, except when Maeve gave terse directions.

The roads into the city were practically deserted, and Dublin's streets were empty under orange streetlamps, which gave the place a curiously abandoned feel, even the brightly lit shops looking forlorn and deserted.

The gates of Charles Woland's cliftop mansion were closed, a tiny red light glowing on the electronic lock, shedding an eerie light on a small numeric keypad. The lights sunk into the lawn, at the edge of the driveway, were also on and the decorative bulbs scattered throughout the trees were burning, but when Michael looked at Maeve, she simply shook her head. 'They're on a timer.' She touched the lock with her fingertips, pressing the keys. 'I hope he hasn't changed the combination.'

'You know the priest very well,' Michael observed quietly, without inflection.

'He was a good friend to me when I needed a friend,' Maeve said, and then nodded as the gate clicked open. 'A very good friend.'

They walked up the driveway in silence, their footsteps crunching on the gravel. The house, which looked so warm and inviting during the day, took on an altogether more sinister appearance at night, with the recessed garden lights casting long shadows upwards into the night. There were no visible lights showing in the house.

'What do we do?' Michael asked, his voice dropping to a whisper.

Maeve rummaged in her shoulder bag and pulled out a bunch of keys. Silently, she lifted one up, holding it to the light.

Michael lifted the small, snub-nosed revolver from his pocket and thumbed back the hammer.

Maeve fitted the key in the lock and turned. The door opened a couple of inches and then stopped. Maeve slipped her hand in, her fingers busy at the wall just inside the door. 'Another alarm,' she muttered, and then the door opened all the way.

Michael touched her arm, stopping her, and then he stepped into the hall before her, the revolver held in both hands, close to his body. Maeve stepped in behind him and gently closed the door.

'Lights?' she murmured, her mouth so close to his ear that he could feel the moisture on her breath.

He shook his head, and then turned to whisper, 'Any idea where he'd usually be? And remember, its someplace close to a phone,' he added.

Maeve pointed, her bare arm pale and vaguely luminous.

Michael padded silently down the long hallway, his shoes virtually noiseless on the polished wooden floors; Maeve had taken off her shoes to follow him. He stopped at the door Maeve had indicated. It was closed, and when he put his ear to the wood, there was no sound from within. Taking a deep breath, he turned the handle and gently pushed the door open.

The smell hit him, wet, cloying, metallic. He gagged, identifying and rejecting it immediately. Blood.

'Stay here,' he whispered, pushing Maeve back and then, holding his hand across his nose, stepped into the room, and clicked on the light.

The room looked like a charnel house.

There was blood everywhere. The carpet was sodden underfoot, the wall streaked high with it, the windows blotched, even the ceiling was speckled with long streaks of dark arterial blood.

Maeve looked into the room, and then collapsed onto her knees and began to vomit.

Michael found him behind the couch, twisted and curled like a stillborn foetus. Lying in a vast pool of tacky blood, the big man looked shrunken, smaller, as if his bulk had drained out of him with the blood. Michael knelt on the sodden carpet and gently turned him over.

'Oh Jesus!'

There were five holes in the man's body, five punctures through the fabric of his clothing, five gaping exit wounds. Michael Cullen didn't need to be reminded that he had shot at the creature five times, hours before.

'I'm sorry . . . I'm so sorry,' he whispered.

And Woland's eyes flickered open. For a single moment they swam unfocused before they locked onto the American's face, with an intensity that was close to insanity. The lips moved, bloody froth bubbling against his teeth, and then his right hand came up, wrapping itself around Michael's throat, dragging him down with terrifying strength, until the younger man's face was almost resting against his bloody lips.

'Spirit . . . can . . . cannot be harmed. Physical can,' he panted. 'The word made flesh. Made flesh. Make . . . it . . . flesh.'

Michael started to shake his head, but the big man's grip tightened, threatening to choke. 'It feeds . . . on memories. Feed it . . . make it real . . . and then kill it.'

'Charley?'

'Kill it!' Woland came upright in a move that sent Michael floundering across the bloody floor. 'Kill it. Kill it. Before it kills you and everyone associated with you, family, friends. The more it kills the stronger it becomes, it feeds on blood and memories.' The blood on his lips has turned darker, and his every breath exuded a sweet stench. 'Feed it's presence with memories, make it's presence part of this world. Make it whole. Kill it. Ki . . .'

Michael managed to catch him before he slumped to the floor.

Maeve reappeared in the doorway, but didn't step into the room. 'I've phoned for an ambulance.'

Michael didn't move; didn't seem to understand.

'Michael?'

When he looked up, his face was virtually unrecognisable. 'There's no point,' he said, bending his head.

* * *

It was a little after dawn when Michael Cullen and Maeve Quill returned to Blacklands. They had spent the last three hours with the police whilst their story was checked and double-checked. They had received a phone call from the Reverend Charles Woland, asking them to come out quickly. When they had arrived at the house, they had found him lying in a pool of blood on the floor, and they had then phoned for an ambulance, who had contacted the police when they saw the nature of the dead man's injuries. It was close enough to the truth to make no difference, and they both realised that to bring anything else into the story would only complicate matters and possibly implicate them in Woland's murder.

It was a murder investigation, or at least it had been until it was discovered that there were no bullets in the bullet-like wounds in Charles Woland. The five punctures were simply that, holes in his body. There were no metal fragments, no burning or scorching around the flesh, no evidence that five slivers of lead had ripped through his body.

With nothing to hold them on, the police had finally allowed the exhausted couple to go free, on the understanding that they hold themselves ready for questioning.

They had driven home in silence, the traffic still relatively light, most of the cars heading into town to begin another normal day. Michael found himself wishing it was just another normal day, with none of the strangeness, but he didn't think he could remember his last normal day. What was normal and natural in his life had shattered with the first notes of the banshee's cry all those months ago. Still, he couldn't shake the idea that this was simply a dream, a nightmare from which he would awake eventually, with Karla in the bed beside him, and the two children arguing together down the hall.

Michael slowed as the pale, cream coloured walls of Blacklands appeared over the tops of the hedges. He turned right, between the tall gateposts and made his way slowly up the shadowy tree-lined drive, and then stood on the breaks as a figure appeared in the pathway!

'Jesus!'

Maeve came awake with a scream, and she continued to

scream as the figure approached the car. It was still shaded by the trees and difficult to determine any features. Then, Michael flicked on the lights and the figure threw up an arm to shield its face.

'It's OK . . . It's OK . . .' Michael touched Maeve's arm, and she flinched from his touch. 'It's Paddy . . . it's only Paddy Byrne.'

Dr Patrick Byrne came around to the driver's side and leaned down to look in. The smile froze on his face. 'God in heaven, what's happened?'

'It's a long story,' Michael said tiredly.

'Go up to the house. I'll close the gates and ensure we're not disturbed.'

Paddy Byrne came jogging up the drive moment later, as Michael was helping Maeve out of the car. He came around and scooped Maeve up, into his arms with surprising ease. She closed her eyes and rested her head against his chest, her arms going around his neck, taking comfort from his presence.

Michael slumped against the car. 'I'm afraid I can only carry one,' Paddy said, eliciting a vague smile.

'You go on, I've opened the door. I'll be right behind you.' He watched Paddy kick open the door and carry the young woman into the house. And then he turned and looked at the trees and bushes that girded the lawn. Now, with their Fall colours upon them, they should have looked their best, serene and restful. Instead, with the bare branches poking through, and their leaves turning to mulch on the sodden grass, they looked withered and diseased. Death and disease; Michael Cullen nodded silently, that was fitting.

There had been pain.

But the pain had been welcome, for the pain was sensation, and it had not felt sensation for so long now.

But the pain had been paid for.

And then there had been pleasure.

It was aware of pleasure, when it sang the Song, when it cried the Call, there was pleasure in the feeding that followed, but a muted pleasure, an abstract, almost uncertain pleasure. This sensation had been purer and the more powerful for all that.

And that pleasure, far from sating it, only made it crave more.

It would feed again.

And soon.

Maeve was asleep on the couch, Paddy Byrne's coat thrown over her, when Michael entered the room. Paddy was standing with his arms folded, looking down at the woman, his face pinched and tight, his eyes tired. He hadn't had much sleep since Michael Cullen's phone call earlier. Michael crossed to the bar, hands blindly reaching for bottles that were no longer there. He looked into the empty space, tiny flecks of glass still sparkling in the crevices, and remembered that he hadn't restocked after the creature's last visit. 'I was going to offer you a drink,' he mumbled.

'What happened, Michael?' Paddy demanded.

Michael Cullen shook his head. 'I don't know,' he said after a long silence. 'I don't think I can make sense out of it anymore. The creature was in Maeve's flat,' he said carefully, choosing his words, finding them thick and leaden on his lips. 'It came at us, and I shot it.'

'You shot it!'

Michael took the gun from his pocket and silently turned it over in his hands before putting it away again. 'I shot it, and it fell back into the room and disappeared. And that was that. But Maeve's flat was destroyed, so she accepted my offer to stay here while she found herself a new flat. And on the way here, I heard the creature sing.' His voice caught and he took a moment before continuing. 'I thought . . . I thought . . .' He took a deep breath and continued. 'I phoned the States, but Chrissy was fine, and so were all the other reasonably close relatives I could think of. And then I thought the creature might strike at me through my friends, and that's when I phoned you. But you were OK so the only other person I, or rather Maeve, could think of, was Charles Woland. But the creature got to him first. He was lying in a pool of blood, with five holes, five puncture wounds, in his body. I thought they were gunshot wounds at first, but they weren't bullet wounds.' He stepped up to the older man and stared deep into his dark eyes. 'Paddy, his wounds matched the bullet wounds I put into the creature.'

'So, it transferred its wounds to Charley?'

Michael shrugged. 'I don't know. I suppose so. It must have.'

'Did Charley have a chance to say anything before . . . before he passed on?'

'He told me to feed its presence with memories, make its presence part of this world.' He frowned, remembering. 'And when it was whole, he told me to kill it.' He shook his head. 'It doesn't make any sense.'

But Paddy Byrne shook his head. 'I think it does. He told you to feed its presence with memories?' he asked.

Michael nodded.

'Obviously, your presence here in Ireland activated the creature, whoever, whatever it is, and it draws sustenance from your memories. This creature feeds on memories; like some sort of vampire, it is feeding off your history, both personal and family, and thus gaining in strength and substance. I think Charley was advising you to concentrate on your past, research your ancestors, relive their lives, and with those memories, the banshee will gain strength, and substance. And once it enters this physical world, it can be slain by physical means.'

Michael looked at him numbly, unable to generate any excitement for his friend's hypothesis. 'And what happens while I'm drawing this creature into this world with my memories. It'll grow stronger, and more dangerous.'

'That is the risk you'll have to take, Michael. You have no choice.'

21

There was a shaft of wood sticking out of his body.

Turning his head slightly, he could see the long length of wood protruding from the centre of his chest. Slowly, with difficulty, he raised his eyes, following the wood, and saw the ragged feathers threaded into the sides close to the end. Arrow. It was an arrow.

And with that realisation came the pain. It lanced through his body, exploding in his chest in a solid ball of pure agony. There were other cuts on his body, a slash on his thigh, a gash deep into his side, a lesser slash across his left arm. He could feel them all now, feel their individual pain, their separate agonies, could differentiate between the levels of pain, the degrees of agony.

And, as the pain took him, he heard the cry.

It echoed flatly across the plain, across the river that ran red with blood, across the piled corpses in their tattered colours and cloths. It was the sound of a soul in torment, the wail of a mother who had lost a babe.

He looked up, past the shaft in his chest, and he saw the figure come up over the small, rounded hills. It was a woman, a woman in white, with long black hair streaming behind her in a breeze which he certainly didn't feel on his face. Her long-nailed hands clawed at her face and as he watched, she threw back her head and screamed.

And he screamed too.

The scream was still echoing flatly in the darkened bedroom as Michael Cullen jolted upright. He was bathed in sweat, and his heart was hammering in exactly the same spot as the arrow had been in. The door suddenly burst open and this time Michael shouted aloud.

It was Maeve.

'Jesus, but you scared the shit out of me,' Michael said through chattering teeth.

Maeve came over and sat down on the edge of his bed. 'It

was nothing like the fright I got when I heard the scream. I thought . . . I thought it was . . .'

Michael nodded. 'I know. I was having a dream . . . a nightmare,' he amended. 'What time is it?' he asked suddenly, lifting his arm, squinting at his wristwatch, attempting to focus.

Maeve shook her head. 'Late afternoon, I think.' She stood up and crossed to the window, pulling back the curtains to allow the late afternoon sunshine to stream into the room.

Against the sunshine, the long teeshirt Maeve was wearing was almost transparent, exposing the outline and curves of her full body. With a deliberate effort of will, he looked away. 'Where's Paddy?'

Maeve shook her head. 'I don't know. I'm not even too sure what's happened over the past . . .' her voice trailed away. 'It wasn't a dream, was it?' she asked very softly.

Michael shook his head.

'Oh Christ!'

'You were exhausted when you got back from the station, so Paddy put you to bed,' Michael explained quietly, attempting to pull her away from the memories of the past twelve hours. 'We talked together for awhile, and I got to bed around two in the afternoon I suppose. I looked in on you, but you were sound asleep.'

She took his wrist in her hand and turned it to look at his watch. 'It's five, I'd better get dressed.'

'Why?' Michael asked suddenly. Catching Maeve's startled look he added quickly, 'I mean, where are you going to go?'

Maeve started to answer and then shook her head.

'I mean you can't go back to the flat, can you? Where else can you go?'

'The flat might be . . .' she began.

'Stay here. There's plenty of room, plenty of space. And I'd like the company,' he admitted softly.

Maeve hesitated just long enough for Michael to realise that something else was bothering her.

'It's a genuine offer,' he said carefully. 'No strings, no hidden catches. No ulterior motives.'

Maeve smiled. 'All right then. On those terms.'

Michael smiled in return. 'On those terms.'

'If I didn't know you two better, I'd be thinking terrible things.' Paddy Byrne stepped into the room, carrying a tray with three steaming mugs. 'Everyone's getting tea,' he said, putting the tray down on the end of Michael's bed, passing one of the cups to Maeve, the second to Michael. 'Did you both sleep well?' he asked, looking from one to the other.

Both shook their heads.

'Bad dreams,' Maeve said.

'Nightmares.'

Paddy sipped his tea. 'It might be useful to share them,' he said, looking first at Maeve and then to Michael. He raised his eyebrows in a silent question.

Michael grimaced. 'I dreamt I was on some sort of plain, flat, with rolling hills, and a river . . . there was definitely a river. And I had an arrow through my chest.' He paused and drank some more tea. 'There were other cuts on my body . . .' Even as he was speaking, his hand was touching his chest, arms and legs 'And it hurt, it hurt like hell. There had been a battle, I'm sure of it, a big battle. And then I heard a cry across the hills. And it was terrifying. The pain intensified, and it was as if the two were in union, linked, and when I looked up and saw the creature, I felt as if . . . as if . . .' he shrugged. 'I don't know what I felt like, but it felt terrifying.'

'Describe the creature,' Paddy said softly, looking at Michael, 'was it the creature you've already encountered?'

But it was Maeve who replied. 'No, this was a mature woman, with a broad high-boned face, long black hair streaked with silver. Large full breasts . . .' she touched her own breasts instinctively, 'and a slightly rounded stomach.'

Michael's eyes were wide. 'That's the woman!'

Paddy turned to Maeve, his face expressionless.

'I dreamt I was standing on a hill,' the pale-faced woman said softly, her arms now wrapped around her body. 'And I was . . . older,' she frowned. 'I remember thinking, knowing! that I was older. There were bodies all around me, men and horses, flags, guns, and all I could feel was a terrible loss, as if my own children had died in that battle. I remember turning, and there was a river to my right in a broad gentle valley, a river that was tinged with red.' Maeve stopped suddenly, her eyes widening, and when she continued, her voice was so soft that the two men had to strain to hear it. 'I moved across that battlefield, looking for someone, a relative, a husband, a son . . . something like that.

'And I was crying.

'I saw him then, lying propped up against a low grassy bank. I was a good distance away, but I could see him clearly, I could make out his . . . wounds. There was an arrow in his chest, and below it a deep cut in his side, which continued up and across his left arm and down onto his right thigh, as if he had been cut in a long slash by a sword or something similar.'

'They were my wounds,' Michael said loudly, startling them both. 'I mean in my dream, I had those wounds. But I didn't connect the wound on my arm, stomach and leg as being one long cut.'

Paddy turned back to Maeve. 'Anything else?'

She shook her head. 'Nothing.'

'What have we just experienced Paddy?' Michael asked, his voice beginning to shake now with reaction.

Paddy ran his hands through his white hair, drawing it back off his face. 'You've studied the mythologies of the various primitive peoples. I would have thought you'd know what it was.'

'Communal dreaming. The shared dream?' Disbelief made Michael's voice sharp, demanding.

'What's so surprising?' Paddy asked, standing up and crossing to the window, to stare down into the garden below. He turned and perched on the edge of the window-sill, watching them both carefully. 'The shared dream is a common enough phenomenon amongst the various primitive peoples of the world. And man, despite all the evidence to the contrary, hasn't advanced much beyond that primitive mind. We like to think we're civilised, but civilisation is a very thin veneer. I would suggest that all it needs is a disturbance, similar to this, to shock it back to its primitive state. This is straight out of the cave-dwelling days, the formless howling in the darkness, the half-seen shapes in the mist. Your minds have reacted accordingly.'

For a single moment, he looked very much the academic, lecturing to his students. 'You know it has been suggested that our ancestors possessed some additional senses, which were not only necessary, but almost essential for survival. With modern society, those senses have, except in a very few cases, vanished almost completely, existing now as nothing more than intuition. The Aboriginal peoples of Australia, for example, possess an extraordinary degree of what we would call telepathy, and they speak with absolute confidence of the Dreamtime . . .

The frost formed so quickly on the window that neither Michael nor Maeve could understand what they were seeing. The late evening sky turned milky as the whorls and spider webs of shimmering tracery danced across the glass.

'PADDY!'

Michael was out of the bed and had Paddy Byrne half way across the room before the first crack appeared in the glass. He shoved Maeve ahead of him, out onto the landing and slammed the door shut.

With a thunderous crack, the windows exploded inwards. Slivers of glass embedded into the walls and the soft wood of the door, shredding the curtains, razoring through the bedclothes and pillows.

And even above the sounds of the breaking glass, the mocking, high-pitched laughter was clearly audible.

Pale-faced and shivering, Michael turned to Maeve and Paddy. Neither of them were conscious of his nakedness. 'If we don't destroy this creature soon, it will destroy us. It won't stop until we're dead: all of us, me, my family and my friends.'

Maeve, her arms folded under her breasts, licked her dry lips and said, 'then we have to bring it into this world, and to do that you have to concentrate on your past, your family's past, and that's only going to draw it closer to you, make it even more dangerous.'

'It's timing,' Paddy smiled wanly. 'You have to strike when it has become part of this physical world, but before it gets too powerful to destroy you.'

'It's powerful enough for that already,' Michael said looking at the door.

There had been times in its existence when it had been thwarted; not often, admittedly, but those times still rankled.

The Hound of Ulster had disregarded her warning, and her revenge had been terrible. He had provided her with sustenance for a long time; his memories, his strengths and powers had been great indeed.

The Emperor of the Irish, Brian, had ignored her cry and he had paid her price. He had been a man of power and she could still remember the taste of him, the strength that had flooded into her with his demise.

The clan O'Neill, always rich in warriors, had kept her in existence for generations. Warriors, scholars and scribes, they had all fallen for her hunger.

The pirate-woman, the O'Malley had defied her for far too long, even after she had taken her husband and her children. She had been old and feeble when she had broken, but even then her memories had been enough to sustain the creature for an age.

Latterly, the Harper had successfully kept her at bay for a time. The blind man had retreated into drink to numb the sounds of her, and used his harp to defy her call, but even he had eventually fallen.

When the Time of Hunger, the Famine, was upon the land, she had fed well and often. The memories of the peasants were thin, like a watery gruel, but they had sufficed.

She had fed too in the Time of Revolution; the feeding had been good then, and she had walked the burning halls of the building known as the General Post Office, exalting in the destruction.

She had experienced her own lean times and her times of plenty. The times of plenty had been in a different age though, a time of belief, when the very faith of the people was enough to give her strength. That time was gone now, and the few she took in these more modern times were often of so little account, that there was small satisfaction and even less sustenance in them.

Until now.

This one was different. There was strength here, and terror too, but terror was a sauce to be savoured and his memories were rich and varied. It had fed of his companion and taken something of him in that feeding, and then it had fed of his child, and taken more. There had been the other feeding, the man, but that had been a bonus, for a man of strength like that to succumb so easily was a rare enough occurrence. There had been no sustenance in that feeding though; there were memories, but they were concealed, locked in some recesses which even the trauma of death could not unlock.

It would take the two companions now; the man and the woman. Then its knowledge of the feast would be complete. Then it would feed properly and it would be a feast to be savoured.

The Time of Power approached. It would feed then.

She could walk away.

And go where?

It was a question she couldn't answer. Maeve Quill stopped dressing and looked at herself in the long mirror in what had formerly been the Cullens' bedroom. The bed, the bed in which Karla Klein Cullen had died, was gone of course, and a single bed put in its place, but otherwise it remained the same. The wardrobe and the chest of drawers were still filled with the dead woman's clothing, and Michael had instructed her to take what she needed. She had protested until Michael had pointed out that she possessed nothing except what she stood up in.

It had felt a little ghoulish looking through a dead woman's collection of clothing, but her initial reluctance had changed to astonishment at the quantity and quality of Karla's huge collection of clothes, most of them designer labels, and nearly all of them new.

She sorted through the wardrobe, finally picking out a pair of black leather trousers – she had always wanted a pair of leather trousers – and a dove-grey silk blouse to complement it. There was a pair of short black leather boots in the bottom of the wardrobe as well; they were half a size too big, but they would do.

Pulling off the long tee-shirt, she stood naked before the mirror, running her hands down her body, smoothing her skin. On impulse, she undid the clips that held her hair back in a bun, and shook it out, allowing it to flow down her back; it reached almost to the base of her spine.

Her hair was her finest feature, she knew. Few people nowadays had the patience to cope with all the work that long hair entailed. Constant washing, treating and continuous combing had combined to lend her hair a luxurious glow, like polished wood, and in certain light, when the sun took it properly, it glowed with an almost purplish sheen. However, it was her breasts that most men noticed first, she conceded, bringing her hands up, cupping them. She had always thought them too large, and God alone only knew what would happen to them if and when she ever became pregnant.

She blinked, a rippling film moving across her eyes. She looked at the mirror again, frowning now. Her breasts were large, but firm, her skin pale, the nipples equally pale. But in the mirror . . . the mirror showed her breasts as looking even heavier, purple veins prominent, the nipples dark and puckered. She looked at her face, and a scream caught in her throat.

The face in the mirror was hers and not hers.

Her face was oval, with strong pronounced cheekbones, a straight nose and bright green eyes. The face in the mirror, superimposed over hers, was broader, the cheekbones equally high and pronounced, but older, definitely older. And the eyes were black, coal-black, stone-black, night-black. The hair, as thick as her own, was streaked with grey and silver.

The rippling again, like oil on water, and now the face had aged. The clear skin was gone, buried beneath a mass of deeply grooved wrinkles, leaving the cheekbones even more pronounced now. The eyes were no longer so black, a translucent grey, watery membrane now covered the black pupils. In the mirror, her skin was wrinkled and flaccid, her breasts hanging shrivelled against her chest. Her hair was grey, the colour of old stone, and clung to her scalp in scabrous patches.

Maeve's mouth opened and the mirror-image mimicked her.

'Beware the Maid, for she is Death.'

And Maeve screamed!

When Michael and Paddy found her, she was crouching, naked, in a corner of the room, the bedclothes pulled down over her.

She was in shock, shivering uncontrollably, ice-cold to the touch and incoherent, threads of saliva on her chin.

'She needs a doctor,' Paddy said immediately.

'No,' Michael said quickly, 'we can't . . . I mean, there's been enough police and medical activity around this house. Don't you think they're going to start asking questions if we call them in for this. What are we going to say?' he demanded, his eyes wide and compelling. 'What have we got here anyway . . . a naked woman, two men, a lonely house, one death under mysterious circumstances . . . the newspapers would have a field day.'

'All right, all right, I see your point. OK. What she needs now is to be kept warm and liquids, sugary liquids. I'll go and make some tea.' He stood up and looked down at the shivering woman. 'What in God's name happened to her?'

'I heard nothing,' Michael said slowly.

'All I heard was the scream.'

'No, I'm not talking about that. I heard her scream too, but I didn't hear anything else.'

'No banshee wail?'

'Nothing.'

'What happened then?' Paddy asked again. He knelt down beside Maeve, and took her face in both of his large gentle hands. Looking into her wide, terrified eyes, he put the question gently, his voice barely above a whisper. 'What happened, Maeve? Tell us. What happened?'

The woman stared at him blankly.

Michael leaned over. 'Was it the creature? Was it the banshee?'

Paddy shook her head. 'I doubt if she's even hearing us. She looks like death.'

Maeve's expression suddenly solidified, her eyes blinking back into momentary focus. Suddenly, she opened her mouth and screamed, '*Beware the Maid, for she is Death!*'

22

Mick Cullen winced as the bullet spattered into the heavy sandbag, almost directly below his chin. He felt his breath catch somewhere deep in his throat at the realisation of just how close to death he had come. A heavy hand fell onto his shoulder, startling him, 'Are you all right, son?'

The boy looked up, and then suddenly scrambled to his feet, recognising the figure of Patrick Pearse, the leader of the rebellion. 'Yes, yes, sir. Thank you, sir.'

Pearse nodded quickly, ducking his head slightly with a nervous movement. 'Good. Good lad. Stay away from the windows. Keep close to the walls.'

'Yes, sir. Thank you, sir.'

Pearse squeezed his shoulder again and moved on, pausing to have a few words with the next man in line. Mick Cullen lay down again, the Lee-Enfield rifle propped up beneath his chin, one eye on the broad expanse of Sackville Street, the other on the retreating figure of Patrick Pearse.

When Mick Cullen had left home earlier that morning, Easter Monday, 1916, he had thought he was going out on just another exercise with the Volunteers. The Irish revolutionaries had been talking of an uprising for months, years now, and there had been marches, parades and numerous secret, and not so secret, organisations, which the authorities and the ordinary Dublin people had looked upon with some amusement. But there was going to be an uprising, there had to be an uprising if conditions were to change. For the system to change there had to be a new beginning; a blood sacrifice, Pearse had called it. Well, Mick Cullen was prepared to make that sacrifice, for Ireland.

Only his younger brother, six year old Tom, had been awake when he had crept out shortly after dawn. In the other bed, his two younger brothers, Robert and Seamus, were still asleep, while in the next room, his baby sister, Nuala, slept with his parents. The family of seven lived in two rooms, and the room the boys used as a bedroom doubled as a kitchen-cum-dining room during the day. But they were lucky enough; in some of the other rooms in the tenement, in the mean streets behind Dublin's main thoroughfare, larger families were living in smaller rooms.

The republican movement had found many converts in this breeding ground. Dublin's tenements, where death and disease ran riot, where lack of sanitation and a proper water supply ensured one of the highest infant mortality rates in Europe, where the largest brothel district in Europe flourished. The people here were not looking for luxuries, only the basic necessities.

Mick Cullen had gone out on that Easter Monday to take part in what he had been told was only an exercise, but when he discovered that the exercise was suddenly for real, it didn't bother him, he didn't ask permission to leave, to return to his home. Instead, he had been part of the group which had taken the General Post Office in the heart of Dublin, the prime target, the most public target in the public's mind, the very heart of the British administration in Ireland.

There had been little activity that day. They had taken over the General Post Office on the stroke of noon, and then later, in the early afternoon, a troop of mounted lancers had attempted to charge the building. Mick could only stare down the barrel of his heavy rifle and watch in amazement as they galloped their horses nearer the building, their lances levelled.

And then the shots had rung out and the men had fallen, and for the first time Mick Cullen realised that this was no game, this was real. This was now a matter of life . . . and death.

His family would be sitting down to tea about now, bread and butter, tea with milk, and cocoa for the younger children, and he felt his own stomach rumble hungrily. Although the rebels had organised a kitchen within the Post Office buildings, Mick hadn't been relieved from his post and hadn't been able to report there for anything to eat.

He was only sixteen years old, but he wasn't the youngest there. A few of the Fianna boys, a movement modelled on the ancient Irish order of knighthood, and borrowing a little from the Boy Scouts, were in the Post Office, although most of the other units were scattered around the city in the other rebel holdings, Liberty Hall, St Stephen's Green, the Mills and the Bakery, Mick wasn't sure which. He wasn't sure how many men had marched out to join the rising, nor how many of the positions had been taken and held. He knew the Four Courts hadn't been taken, and neither had Trinity College, so he suspected that the rebels' hold on the city was not as complete as they would have wished it.

The first day passed relatively quietly, but the night was a different matter altogether. For their own protection, the police had been withdrawn, and for the first time ever, there was no police presence on the streets of Dublin. And so the slums and tenements behind the main streets emptied, and the crowds moved into the heart of Dublin.

The rioting and looting went on long into the night.

Eventually, the rebels had sent their own men out to attempt to restore order, and there were several running battles between rebels and looters.

Mick remained at his post in the General Post Office and saw his dream of a free, independent Ireland turn sour before his eyes; he suddenly realised that the people he was fighting for didn't care. They just weren't interested!

The following day the army arrived, and the fighting began in earnest. That day he watched people, friends, comrades, die.

Mick Cullen first heard the sound late on the Tuesday afternoon. At first he thought it was nothing more than the wind howling through the broken glass, but when he concentrated on the sound, he realised that it seemed to be coming from behind him, and that it was far too regular, and the pitch too variable to be the wind. He had the strangest feeling that it was the sound of someone singing!

There was sniping that night. In the darkness, shots would ring out and a bullet would ricochet off walls, sparks exploding across the brickwork, or glass would shatter overhead, and the men below would hold their breath, waiting to see if it would be followed by a thump, as a body hit the ground.

In the darkness, still at his post by the window, staring out at the deserted Sackville Street, Mick Cullen heard the sound again. And this time it was close enough for him to identify.

It was the sound of a woman singing.

There were women in the General Post Office, members of the women's movement, the Cumann na mBan, other supporters and nurses, but Mick Cullen instinctively knew the sound didn't come from one of them. Its quality was too pure, too ethereal, to have been made by a human throat.

On Wednesday, the fighting intensified, and Mick, suddenly terrified and trembling, fired his first shots at the enemy. The singing was with him now, a constant companion, a keening, crooning, that was not completely unpleasant.

And it never occurred to him that he was the only one hearing the sound.

Shortly before dawn on the Thursday morning, he

saw the woman. She was moving down the long staircase to his left, stooping to look at the bodies slumped, either in sleep or death, on the stairs. She touched them briefly, her hand white and almost translucent, and then moved on. Mick squinted, trying to make out some details. He got the impression of youth, of sharp, hard features, of long, black hair, but it was difficult to form any lasting impression of the woman in white.

And then she was looking towards him, and he saw her lips curl in a peculiar expression. She began to move towards him, and Mick noticed for the first time that she was not actually walking on the ground, but rather gliding about a foot or so off the marbled tiles. She reached for him when she was still about six feet away, both arms outstretched, fingers splayed. Her mouth opened, her teeth white and glistening against blood-red lips, and she mouthed his name, 'Michael . . . Michael . . .'

Mick Cullen chambered a round into the heavy rifle and was actually pointing it towards the creature, his finger curled around the trigger when she spoke again, 'Michael Cullen, come to me . . .' And then the voice changed, becoming harsh, demanding, vengeful. 'You are mine!'

The boy started to shake his head and his pressure on the trigger increased, when a heavy calibre bullet took the top off his head. He was dead before he hit the floor, and his last abiding thought in this world, his last conscious image, was of the creature's head thrown back in victorious laughter.

'My uncle Mick fought and died in the General Post Office with Pearse in 1916. He was only sixteen years old himself, and I can clearly remember my own father telling me how he watched him leave on that sunny Monday morning, in his green uniform with his Sam Browne belt and rifle.'

Maeve nodded, not looking at Michael, her eyes on the

screen, her fingers deftly tapping the keys. 'And he was the eldest?'

'He was born in 1900, and my father was born ten years later . . .'

'Was there any other family?'

'I had two uncles, Robert and Seamus, and an aunt, Nuala. The boys were older than my father, the girl younger. I'm not sure of their actual ages, but my aunt Nuala, my father's sister, is still alive and I'm sure she'd know.'

Maeve looked up, moving her large round glasses with her fingertip. 'If this genealogy is to be complete, I will need proper dates of birth if possible.'

Michael glanced at his watch, gauging the time in New England, where his aunt lived.

'Did she marry, does she have children?'

Michael shook his head. 'She never married.'

Nuala Cullen loved the Fall.

It was the best time of the year, a time of peace and contentment, when even time itself seemed slower, and the two extremes of Summer and Winter were buffered by the softness of Fall.

Nuala Cullen did her best work during the Fall. She was a writer of children's books. It was said Michael, her nephew, had discovered his love of books and writing from her, and during the Fall, she wove the plots of the half dozen books she would write in the long Winter and Summer months. She did very little writing during the Fall, inasmuch as any writer could not write, preferring to wander the woods that came right up to the back door of the small, discreet, mock-alpine bungalow that nestled in a niche above a dark, placid lake. The woods were full of ideas then, and she had based her very successful series of Irish folklore stories in those woods, using them as the basis for her creation, Seamus Ban the Leprechaun.

Seamus Ban had made her wealthy. It had been more than twenty years ago now, but she still clearly remembered the day she had conceived the character. She had been walking through these woods, thinking back to the vaguely remembered days of her childhood in Dublin, realising that this must have been what Ireland was like before it became modernised. The leprechauns, the cluricauns, the luricauns and the Fir Darrig would have wandered through dark woods, very similar to these. Erin had been governed by the small folk then. If she closed her eyes, she could almost see the man, small and stout, with a round, red face.

It was as simple as that.

And so, she had created the wise old man, calling him after her nearest neighbour, Jim White, but using the Irish version of his name, Seamus Ban. Now Seamus existed in sixteen different languages, had appeared on four calendars, and in a series of animated cartoons, a serialised newspaper strip, teeshirts . . .

The old woman strode along, a smile on her thin lips, remembering. Seamus had started as a small, single book idea and now it was an industry. Digging her hands deep into her pockets, and ducking her head against a chill, northerly wind, she walked the high ridge over the lake, thinking that what she really needed now was another idea like that. Not because she needed the money – but just because she so enjoyed the craft of writing, and the pleasure it gave to her and so many others. One of the greatest joys, she had discovered, about writing children's books, was the huge volume of fan mail that flooded in.

The moment she heard the sound, thin and high, the ghost of a noise through the trees, she knew she had her new idea. She would write a story about a banshee, a lost soul.

When she heard the eerie sound again, she stopped, realising that it wasn't the sound of the wind through the trees. Pulling down her hood, she turned her head from side to side, listening, wondering what had made the noise. Perhaps an animal had got caught on some wire or in some thicket. Of course, it might be nothing more than a fluke, a cry from the valley far below, carried upwards on an errant gust of wind.

The next time the cry was nearer.

The fear washed over her in an icy blanket.

She had spent her whole life writing about Irish folklore, and she had created a vast amount of fiction based around characters and creatures from it, and so perhaps it wasn't altogether unnatural that she should suddenly think of the banshee.

Nuala turned back on the path, her mouth suddenly dry, a hollow iciness in the pit of her stomach. It was nothing more than a lost dog or the wind whistling up from the valley below or the breeze in the branches of the trees. She repeated the excuses to herself, desperately trying to convince herself, but failing. Dusk was falling, and the trees in their autumn golds and bronzes were taking on a grainy texture, becoming indistinct and vaguely ominous. Her eyesight was not the best and now, in the twilight, she lost her ability to make out both distance and detail.

And then she saw the figure in white, standing amongst the trees.

And she heard its cry.

She turned and ran, her boots digging into the soft mulch of the soil. She could feel her heart pounding painfully in her breast, and she was breathing so quickly, she was afraid she would hyperventilate. She was afraid, terribly afraid. She desperately attempted to recall what she knew of the creatures known as the banshee, the bean-sidhe, the fairy woman.

To hear their cry was to die . . . or did one die because one had heard the cry . . . or did their cry forewarn death . . .?

Trees loomed up out of the gloom like sentinels, branches snatching at her with cruel fingers, plucking at her clothing, her skin, entangling her hair. The paths she knew so well, the simple, safe, gentle paths that led from her home to the lakeside, the wooded walks, the river, the stream, now became treacherous. It was as if they had taken on a life of their own, and like malicious servants, now twisted and curled back upon themselves. She fell once, a root she had never before been aware of, catching her foot, dropping her to the ground with enough force to snap one of the small bones in the base of her foot, cracking a rib as she fell, scraping flesh from her face and hands.

The cry continued, now contemptuous and mocking in turn,

like a child taking innocent pleasure from torturing some small animal. There was both pity and amusement in that cry.

The cry was one of hunger.

And it was closer.

Nuala Cullen staggered to her feet, a thin, whining moan escaping from her lips as she put pressure on her damaged foot. Crying with the pain, bent almost double with the agony in her side, she limped on up the track. Now that she had been forced to go slower, she thought she recognised some of the twists and turns on the way, and some of the stumps and twisted trees seemed almost familiar.

She heard the phone ringing.

The sound was so innocuous that it shocked her motionless. The ring was high-pitched and piercing on the still evening air, and it was coming from directly in front of her, and the only phone on the mountain was in her house. With renewed hope, Nuala Cullen struggled on.

She crested the top of the rise and the house rose up before her, dull and white, grey and dusky, like a badly exposed photograph. Almost blind with tears she staggered up the packed earthen path and pushed open the unlocked door.

The sound of the phone was louder now, and unconsciously, she turned towards it, groping blindly on the small table, beneath the window that looked out over the lake. She picked up the instrument and for a single moment, static howled and echoed down the line, and even through her agony, she recognised the noise of a long distance call.

'Nuala.'

The voice shocked her motionless. It came from directly behind her, a whisper, the merest breath of sound, the voice mouthing her name so softly, and with such a strange accent that, for a moment, she thought she had imagined it.

'Nuala?'

And this time her name was echoed down the line.

'Nuala.'

The old woman turned towards the sound, the phone forgotten in her hand. She was still aware of the pain in her foot and side, aware of the burning in her lungs and the stinging on her face and hands, but it was as if the pain were unimportant, as if they were no longer part of her.

There was a woman standing in the doorway; a tall, thin woman, dressed in a gossamer white robe. She reached out with a bare arm, and Nuala felt compelled to go towards her.

'Nuala?'

The voice cracked through the phone, and even with the distance and distortion on the line, the fear and anxiety could be heard in it. The voice was familiar, but Nuala Cullen knew it wasn't worth while even thinking about trying to identify it. She took a step towards the creature, and she noticed, almost unconsciously, that the woman cast a partial shadow on the ground . . . as if her shadow had been dusted onto the floor in grey chalk and then some of that chalk blown away.

'NUALA? AUNT NUALA!'

She nodded, recognising the voice over the crackling of the instrument. It was Michael . . . her nephew, Michael. But what matter, eh?

'NUALA? AUNT NUALA!'

Static howled down the line, and then Michael heard the phone clunk against something solid. He turned to look at Maeve, terror in his eyes. She crossed to him and wrapped her arms around him, holding him tight, resting her head on his shoulder. He was trembling so badly she thought he was going to collapse, and then they heard the sound of the instrument being picked up at the other end.

'Aunt Nuala?' Michael said, his voice cracking with relief.

The sound that echoed down the line was a paean of triumph, barely human, and yet too pure for an animal sound.

It was the cry of a hunting creature that had fed.

23

Michael Cullen kneeled on the wooden floor and wept, his head on Maeve's lap.

He had never felt so impotent, so defenceless in all his life. When Karla had died, he had been devastated, but the shock of her sudden passing had numbed him. His son's death had saddened him, and Charles Woland's had only puzzled him. But his aunt's death terrified him, enraged him, left him shivering and exhausted – and lost. Hopelessly lost.

He was losing his family, one by one; and there was nothing he could do about it.

Paddy Byrne came and stood in the kitchen door, looking at the tableau in the hall, and then he turned away. He didn't need to be told.

Paddy walked out into the quiet, autumnal garden, his hands deep in his pcokets, knowing there was nothing he could do, nothing he could say that would do Michael any good now. Maeve would help, and he was glad she was there. This was the time when a woman's touch was essential. He grimaced, the sudden memory of the time the banshee had touched him, revolting him. Almost unconsciously, he found he was heading towards the small, dark pool. He ducked beneath the bare branches and, with the brambles scratching and catching at his clothes and sleeves, pushed his way through until he was standing beside the pool, which was now swollen with the heavy autumn rains. Its surface was impenetrable, but curiously, completely devoid of leaves or any of the other growths that should, by rights, have been scattered either across its surface, or along its banks.

Paddy stared into the pool for a long time, deliberately not thinking of the creature, concentrating on the pool and its surroundings, taking in every detail, memorising it, conscious of something lurking at the back of his mind, refusing to come to the surface. Finally, he turned away, and stopped. A ghost of a smile touched his lips, and he turned his head to look back at the still, black waters. Then with a quick nod of satisfaction, he hurried back into the house.

Paddy found Michael and Maeve in the sitting room. Michael was staring out through the large windows at the lawn, his face set, his eyes red-rimmed and slightly swollen. What little colour there had been in his gaunt cheeks was gone, and he looked almost wraith-like himself. Maeve was standing just behind him, barely touching, there if he needed her, but not intruding on his grief. She looked up when Paddy appeared.

'I think I know how we may destroy the creature,' he said quietly, calmly.

After a moment's hesitation, Michael turned to look at him. 'Tell me,' he said softly, his voice without inflection.

Paddy stepped into the room and crossed to the chair before the unlit fire. 'Come here both of you and listen to me, and you can tell me then whether I'm crazy or not.'

'It can't get any crazier,' Michael said. He rubbed his hands across his face, digging the heels of his palms into his eyes, blinking hard, and then crossed to the chair, moving like an old man. Maeve took up a position behind him, her hand resting lightly on his shoulder.

Paddy leaned forward, resting his elbows on his knees, his hands, palm to palm in an attitude of prayer, resting against his lips. 'Maeve can tell me if I'm wrong, but from the little I know of Irish folklore, the banshee is a woman of the Sidhe, a fairy woman, and the fairy folk have always been associated with the Tuatha De Danann, the magical people who came across the seas from the west to Ireland.' He looked up at Maeve for confirmation, and she nodded.

'Now, when the time came for them to leave the country, when man with his iron tools and weapons arrived, they went into their secret places, the hidden valleys, the sunken islands, the barrows, the hollow mountains . . . and beneath the lakes.'

'Myths . . .' Michael murmured.

'Michael, you've seen a myth! The banshee is legend, and yet you've seen it, walking, touching . . . killing! You've heard its voice. And if that much is true then why not the rest of the legend? What's to say that the banshee isn't a member of the fabled Tuatha De Danann? Walking, talking, feeding, but in a way that neither you nor I would comprehend?'

'The De Danann are the most mysterious of the invaders of ancient Ireland,' Maeve said gently. 'The *Lebor Gabala Erann* details all the invaders of ancient Ireland, tells us where they came from, gives us lists and genealogies, but even it knows little of the Tuatha De Danann, and they were the only invaders credited with magical powers. They were said to come from the lands to the west of Ireland, and some of the fringe folklorists believe that they came from the island of Atlantis.'

Michael said nothing.

Maeve looked from Michael to Paddy. 'What are you suggesting?' she asked.

'I'm suggesting that the banshee is one of the De Danann folk, who has managed to survive on down through the ages by feeding off . . . I don't know what. Blood, energy, emotions? I don't know. But I believe she may, like the legends tell us, be living beneath the pool.'

Michael laughed, a harsh barking sound.

'Have you ever looked at the pool, Michael? I mean have you ever examined its surface closely, and looked into its depths . . . and before you answer, remember, it was at the side of the pool that you first encountered the creature!'

Michael opened his mouth to reply and then closed it again. There was nothing he could say and what was the point in applying any sort of logic to this situation. Finally he nodded. 'I remember the pool.'

Paddy leaned forward. 'Well if the creature is somehow living within or beneath it, then surely all we have to do is to destroy the pool, to destroy the creature!'

Michael Cullen said nothing.

Maeve looked down at Michael, squeezing his shoulder for emphasis. 'I think it's worth a try. We've nothing to lose.'

'No, I suppose we haven't,' Michael said bitterly. 'We've lost enough already.' He looked at the older man. 'How do you propose to destroy the pool?'

Paddy shrugged. 'Drain it?' he suggested.

Michael Cullen breathed deeply, steadying his nerves. Now that he had something he could concentrate on, he didn't have to listen to that terrible screaming, the crackling hollowness of the phone line. 'Is . . . is the pool fresh or saltwater?' he asked.

Paddy considered, then shook his head. 'Fresh I should imagine, but I see what you're getting at. If it's salt then it might prove impossible to drain.'

Michael nodded.

'All right then, let's suppose it's impossible to drain it, then can we not destroy it in some other way?'

'In legend, an enemy's fields were sometimes sown with salt,' Maeve suggested.

Paddy made a face, and then looked at Michael. 'It's worth a try.'

But Michael shook his head. He turned to look up at Maeve. 'What has the power to defeat the fairy folk, the Sidhe?'

Maeve crossed the room to stand before the window, looking out across the garden, but seeing only her own reflection in the glass before her face.

'I think we have to differentiate between the Sidhe and the fairy folk,' she said seriously. 'The Sidhe is a term used to denote the fairy folk, a sort of generic name, but the fairy folk is a much looser term. And surely we've been discussing the banshee as one of the Tuatha De Danann?'

Paddy's reflection nodded. 'Tell us the difference.'

'I think the De Danann gradually became associated with the Sidhe by the common people, and the Sidhe in turn became the fairy folk. But I think there is an important difference here. The fairy folk can be defeated by holy water, a relic . . . indeed any of the traditional implements used to defeat latter-day manifestations of evil spirits or the Devil. The De Danann however, were defeated by ordinary men wielding iron. They had no protection, no defence against the metal. And in traditional lore,' she added, 'the banshee is something overthrown by a black-handled knife with an iron blade. It is also effective against other members of the Sidhe.'

'A black-handled knife or iron blade,' Paddy mused. 'I knew about the black-handled knife.'

'So, what do we do, drop a black-handled knife into the water and hope it hits the creature?' Michael interrupted bitterly. 'No, no,' he surged to his feet, 'why don't we drive a car into it. That's metal, that would rust in the water, and it might even crush her as it falls.'

'Sit down Michael,' Paddy said tiredly, 'we're only trying to help you.'

'What's wrong with my car idea?' Michael snapped, rounding on him.

Paddy smiled grimly. 'There's not enough iron in cars these days.'

Michael glared at him for a moment, and then, his aggression spent, his shoulders slumped and he sank back into the chair.

Maeve stepped away from the window. 'Could we sow the water with salt?' she said softly. 'If it's a freshwater pool, then by polluting it with salt, might it not render it uninhabitable for the creature?'

Michael started to shake his head and then stopped.

Paddy Byrne had opened his mouth to protest, and he too stopped.

Finally, they both looked at one another, and then at Maeve.

The memories were life to it. The memories brought strength, and the strength in turn brought other, older, memories, and they too were sustenance of a sort.

And with the memories came presence, a physical sense, a corporeal body, with feeling, with sensation, with emotion.

With enough memories, it would become whole again.

It had taken the old woman; her memories had been a morsel, her experiences curiously limited for one so aged. In the time past, age was revered, for age meant experience, and experience was nourishment. But not now, not in time present. It needed to feed again, and soon.

'I got it from the fish-packing factory in Skerries,' Michael said, hefting the coarse bag from the boot of the car. 'God alone only knows what they think I wanted it for. I told them the grounds were overrun with some really difficult weeds and back home in the States we made our own weed-killer from solutions of salt and seaweed.'

Maeve smiled. 'And did they believe you?'

Michael grinned for the first time in days. 'What do you think? They're no fools. If I'm lucky, they might just think I'm a harmless American eccentric, but then again, they might send the police up to investigate.'

Maeve came down the steps and kissed him on the cheek. 'And what do you think they'll charge you with, possession of a couple of bags of pure salt.'

'A salt dealer,' Michael grinned.

'How much did you get?'

'One hundred and twelve pounds, that's,' he did the quick calculation, 'eight stone.' He looked at Maeve. 'Will it be enough do you think?'

She shrugged expressively. 'How do I know? I've never poisoned a pool before.'

From the Four Cities they had come, in their ships of metal, in that time past. The cities each had their own tribes, their own customs, cultures and histories, but were united in their worship of the Goddess Dannu. They had united in the New Land to form a single tribe and they had prevailed over the savages for generations . . . until the barbarians came, with their blades and implements of iron. The De Danann folk had no defence against the metal, and so they left the New Land.

Some had sought shelter beneath the ground, others in the hidden valleys and caves, some had gone to the islands, and some went beneath the waters.

She had chosen the waters; cool, cleansing water, it's gentle touch like a lover's caress, its constant susurration a soothing paean of love. In the Times of Desolation and Pain it had served her well, a refuge from the world, a place of repose, alone with her memories.

Until now.

It had felt like fire, like ice, a cold burning that etched deep into the core of her being.

She had felt flames before; she had taken the memories, fed off the essence of those who had died by fire, by burning, but this was different, so different. She was acquainted with death in its many, myriad forms. She had brought death, forewarned death, accompanied death in the times past and times present. In her embodiment as the Maid, she was death incarnate.

And so she was all too familiar with its silken touch. This was death; this ice-fire touch, these invisible flakes of crystal.

Expanding her consciousness, taking in her surroundings, she immediately became aware of the man and the woman who were mate and not-mate. They were standing over the pool, cloth sacks in their hands, emptying white powder into the water.

It billowed downwards in a swirling cloud, like twisting shifting fog-banks.

And it burned.

The banshee threw back her head and screamed.

The water froze.

It had been cloudy with the salt, the matt, black surface suddenly grey with the concentrated crystals, the water radiating a subtle damp chill, that both Michael and Maeve could feel seeping up through the soles of their feet.

Michael wasn't sure if there was any value in what they were doing, he was simply doing it because there seemed to be nothing else to do, nothing else he could do. He was trapped now; even if he fled back to the States, then the creature would still pursue him. He had called up a demon, and it would not be laid to rest.

The scream pulsed up through the ground in a shock wave that sent them both staggering back into the bushes. Michael had been in Turkey once during an earthquake, and for a brief moment, he thought he was experiencing another tremor and then he remembered that Ireland wasn't on any major fault line. He crashed into a bush, scattering salt everywhere, and he was suddenly conscious that he couldn't hear. He looked for Maeve. She was lying on the ground a few feet away from him, both hands pressed to her ears. Her mouth was open and she might have been screaming but he could hear nothing. He was crawling over to her when he saw the water freeze over. At first glance he thought it was nothing more than the salt swirling in the ebon depths, but as he looked, a scum formed on the surface of the black pool, a crust, which hardened and thickened.

The salt, he thought, and then, like a speeded-up film, the surface of the water iced over with a thick, hard crust that immediately cracked, splinters of glass-like shards flying upwards, as if under great pressure, then the cracks and splits iced over again.

The ice creaked and cracked, and Michael suddenly realised that the dreadful pressure against his ears was gone and he could hear again. When he turned to help Maeve to her feet, he was jubilant. 'We can do it,' he said excitedly, his voice sounding numb and distant in his ears, not realising he was shouting. 'The salt hurt her, that's why she froze the water, to protect herself. She can be defeated, we can destroy her.'

He held Maeve tightly, and then with a start realised that there was blood running down the side of her neck. He brushed back her hair and found her ears were bleeding a pale, watery fluid. The neck and shoulders of her blouse were sodden.

'You're hurt,' he said numbly.

Maeve shook her head, and brushed her fingertips across his top lip. They came away red and sticky with blood from his nose. 'The scream . . .' she began.

'What scream?'

'You didn't hear it?'

He shook his head.

'It was a scream,' she said simply, 'a terribly, terrifying scream. I thought it was an explosion. It was the loudest noise I've ever heard.'

Michael shook his head. 'I never heard it, all I could feel was a pressure against my ears, in the back of my head.'

'That must have been it.'

'We were hurting her,' Michael said looking at the pool, 'hurting her so badly she had to react, to drive us back from the pool, and then freeze the water into a solid block of ice to prevent us throwing any more salt into it.'

Maeve nodded. She suddenly felt tired, very, very tired.

'And that means we can kill her. We can kill the banshee!'

24

Paddy Byrne stood before the tall glass windows in his rooms in Trinity College, looking up the length of Dawson Street towards St Stephen's Green. Sluggish rivulets of rain snaked their way down the window, and the sky outside was leaden with unshed rain. It was going to be a dirty night, he reflected.

It was at times like this that he regretted giving up cigarettes. He could feel the tension sitting in the pit of his stomach, in a solid knot, and the pressure behind his eyes had intensified since lunch. Without looking at his timetable he knew he had two lectures left this afternoon, and unfortunately, there was no way he could bow out, not at this late stage anyway.

With his hands deep in his pockets, he rested his forehead against the cool glass, and closed his eyes, wondering how, in God's Holy name, had he managed to end up in this situation. He had reached the time of life when he should be slowing down, relaxing. By now, he should have experienced most of what life had had to offer, he shouldn't have to go through this. No one should have to go through this.

Michael Cullen was an old friend, a dear friend, but right now, right this minute, he actually hated him. Michael had brought the banshee into his life, he had been the one responsible for resurrecting the ancient legend or whatever it was. And for whatever reason the banshee was responsible, directly or indirectly, for several deaths.

And Paddy Byrne was afraid. Terribly afraid.

He had dreamt of his ex-wife last night. He had been divorced from Marion for twenty-two, going on twenty-three, years now and she rarely entered his thoughts. She still sent him Christmas cards, which he always acknowledged with a card and a small gift, but otherwise there was no communication between them. And that was the way he wanted it. Every Christmas he promised it would be the last time, and every year he sent off the gift towards the middle of November so that it would arrive in plenty of time for the festive season. This year he swore he would send her nothing, but he already knew what he was going to send her.

But he had never dreamt of her. Not even in the early stages of their divorce, when there was still a little of the love that had initially brought them together left, had she entered his dreams.

Until last night.

He couldn't even remember the dream, only that she had been in it, and the very formlessness of it frightened him. Was it a warning, or a threat? The banshee had struck at Michael and his family, and had certainly made an attempt on both Maeve and himself; would she or it or whatever it was, now attack them and their families? He didn't want to find out.

Shaking his head, he turned away from the window, glancing up at the clock on the wall; he had just under an hour before his next lecture. Plenty of time for a walk up to the Green; perhaps the fresh air would clear his head, ease some of the tension that had wound him tight as a watch spring. He was shrugging on his coat when the phone rang. It was Michael Cullen.

'Paddy, listen it worked. Your idea worked. We can kill the creature. We've hurt her!'

'Michael . . . Michael,' Paddy stopped him, squeezing the bridge of his nose between forefinger and thumb. 'Not now, eh? Not now Michael. Ring me later.'

Michael looked at Maeve in astonishment, holding the buzzing phone in his hand. 'He hung up on me.'

'You told him about the scream?'

'I didn't get a chance to. He hung up on me.'

Maeve took the phone from Michael's hand and replaced it on the cradle. 'We've got to warn him Michael.'

'How?' he demanded.

She shook her head quickly. 'I don't know . . . I don't know. But I've got a terrible feeling.'

Michael nodded hopelessly. 'I think its already too late.'

* * *

Paddy stopped outside the bookshop in Dawson Street and stared in at their new display of recently published paperback and hardback fiction. He smiled grimly at the four or five horror titles; whatever terrors their authors had imagined could in no way approach the reality.

He was turning away when he became aware of the commotion approaching down Dawson Street, coming from the direction of St Stephen's Green. Looking up the street, he noticed the articulated lorry coming down Dawson Street, it was unusual to see one of the really big trucks in the city centre, and he also noticed that it seemed to be moving unusually fast. Even as the idea flashed into his mind, he saw the light at the corner of Duke Street and Dawson Street had changed to red. The truck slammed on its airbrakes, and the wheels locked and the truck kept coming.

Paddy Byrne's last conscious thoughts were that the sound of the locking brakes and the sliding wheels were of the same pitch and intensity as the banshee scream – and then the truck mounted the footpath and ploughed into the bookshop.

Eighteen people died in the freakish accident and thirty-two were injured, some of them critically. Paddy Byrne's body was only identified from the contents of his wallet.

Michael Cullen and Maeve Quill watched the nine o'clock news in silence, too numbed by the events of the past few days even to shed any tears.

As soon as they had heard the news of the accident, they had both known, instinctively, automatically, that Paddy had been involved. They had attempted to contact him both at the college and at home throughout the day, but with no success and his absence only confirmed their worst suspicions.

The terrible accident in the heart of Dublin was headline news both at home and abroad, and they had listened to the news bulletins throughout the evening and on into the night, hoping against hope that they were mistaken. The television news had shown Dawson Street looking as if it had been bombed. The lorry, now canted to one side, was embedded into the front of the building, while its back had slewed across the road and footpath, effectively cutting the street in two. The lights from the various rescue crews lent the area a curiously artificial aura, more so since power to the district had been cut off and the street lamps demolished by the truck.

'. . . latest reports can confirm that the death toll in the Dawson Street tragedy is fixed at eighteen. The last victim to be identified was Dr Patrick Byrne, a Trinity College lecturer. It would seem that Dr Byrne had stepped out for a stroll between lectures when he was struck down. This is Tom Killeen for RTE . . .'

Michael leaned forward and snapped the television off, and then sat back into the chair and closed his eyes. And opened them again, an image of his friend's mangled body flashing into his mind. He turned his head slightly to look at Maeve, but she was still staring blankly at the grey screen.

'Just you and me left,' he said hoarsely.

When she turned to him, her eyes were huge and wild. 'For how long?' she suddenly screamed. 'How long will it be before she takes us? There's no escape now, she's too powerful.' There was spittle on her lips, white froth gathering in the corners of her mouth. 'She's too powerful. We're dead Michael. Face it. We're dead. Far better for us to slit our wrists and die with dignity than let this bitch take us her way!'

'Maeve!'

She turned and ran from the room, slamming the door hard enough to crack one of the panes of glass in the windows. Moments later he heard the door to her room slam upstairs, followed by the creak of bedsprings, as she threw herself onto it.

Michael wrapped his arms around himself and shuddered. He knew what she was saying was true.

Maeve sat shivering in her bed, her knees drawn up to her chin, her arms wrapped around them. She was staring blankly at the grey wall in front of her, her eyes wide and unblinking, her pupils dilated.

'Our Father, who art in Heaven, hallowed be Thy name . . .'

The words wouldn't come, and yet as a child, she had known

them all by rote. Maeve Quill had been educated in a convent school in the heart of County Kerry. The Sisters there had had high hopes for her, apparently, and were already beginning to consider her as a potential novice when she had finished her second-level schooling. But she had ignored their hints and later their more direct suggestions that she should join the convent community. When she had left school, she had found she had little enough to thank the nuns for, except a deep and abiding interest in religion. And not just the Catholic Faith in which she was raised, they had sparked an interest in her for all religions, and from there, the drift into folklore studies seemed almost a natural one.

She was dismayed though that she couldn't remember the words of even the simplest prayer. There was one though, one she couldn't forget: Saint Jude, Patron Saint of Hopeless Cases. She had gone through all of her exams praying to Saint Jude. She put her successes, some of them with distinctions and honours, solely down to the fact that the saint was never known to fail.

'Saint Jude, Glorious Apostle, faithful servant and friend of Jesus, the name of the traitor has caused thee to be forgotten by many, but . . . but . . .' But what?

The thought slid into her mind, cold, insidious, like the whisper of sand across grass, as chilling as the touch of ice: why pray to the New Gods? The banshee represented the older, darker, elemental forces, and surely to control her, to intercede with her, one would have to call down the older Celtic Goddesses?

Maeve began to rock to and fro, the merest wisp of an idea drifting through her mind. She attempted to catch it, but it kept shifting, drifting, like a fog-wrapped ship.

'Beware the Maid, for she is Death.'

Maeve actually gasped with shock when she heard the sentence, as clear and as cold as if someone had whispered it in her ear. But at the same time it solidified the idea in her head like congealed ice. The only maiden that symbolised death was the Morrigan, one aspect of the tripartite goddess of the old Celtic Faith.

The banshee was the Morrigan!

The idea left her feeling slightly breathless and she became aware that her heart was thumping wildly. Taking a deep breath, she thought the idea through; she wanted to have all her facts, if that was the right word, prepared before she presented it to Michael. Knowing the identity of the creature brought them no closer to a solution, or did it?

In the old Celtic religion, the tripartite goddess was the Maid, the Matron and the Crone; the Morrigan, Macha and the Badb, the Goddess of War, the Slain and Madness respectively. And of these, the most powerful, the most feared and fearful was the Morrigan.

'Beware the Maid . . .'

But who had warned them? What had warned them? Who was doing the killing? Michael and Paddy had both seen the maid, beware the Maid, for she is Death, so the Maid was the killer. But what then of her other selves, Macha and the Badb, the Matron and the Crone? What part did they play? Were they somehow opposed to the Morrigan killing? Were they attempting to warn . . . to . . . to . . .

Maeve's eyes fluttered and she drifted into a light uneasy slumber.

Maeve Quill was seven years old. The noises had awoken her, drifting in through the thin bedroom walls. The young girl pulled the blankets up over her head to drown out the sounds of her parents arguing, but even sticking her fingers in her ears, she could still hear the raised voices. There was a sudden sharp sound, a slap, and then another, softer sound of a punch. The long silence that followed was eventually broken by the sound of her mother sobbing.

Maeve Quill was thirteen. She had come home from school unexpectedly early to find her mother and father arguing again, indeed, she didn't think she could ever remember a time when they weren't arguing. The screaming and shouting was audible in the street and as she turned her key in the lock, she heard her father shout 'she's your daughter . . .' There had been the sound of a blow and then a series of crashes. And, as

Maeve raced into the hall, she was in time to see her mother end up in a tumbled heap at the bottom of the stairs. Her father's face was a rigid mask of hate, and until the day he died, two years later, she never forgot, never forgave him that look. Her mother had remained in a coma for three months after that fall. If people suspected how she had come to fall, they never spoke about it, and when Maeve herself was questioned by the police and hospital authorities later, she shielded her father. And hated herself for it.

Two years later her father was killed in a tragic accident, although Maeve was convinced that his death was suicide; those who knew him and who were suspicious of his wife's fall and death said it was justice of a sort, God's own justice. He had fallen down an elevator in a shopping centre, a simple slip, which someone else might have walked away from, but his hair had become entangled in the moving steps when he reached the bottom, and his neck had snapped.

The insurance and settlement Maeve had received had enabled her to go through college.

And that was why she had felt so guilty.

Down through the years, whenever she was tired or depressed, the thought would come back to haunt her. Her parents' death, both of them, had enabled her to enjoy a life-style that would ordinarily have been denied to her. If her mother hadn't died, she would probably have ended up in the convent, and if her father hadn't died, she wouldn't have had the money to come to university in Dublin.

And what had her father meant all those years ago when he had said that she was her mother's daughter? Was he somehow blaming her for something, was there something she said or did, something which gave rise to his foul tempers? And of course, if she had been home just a few moments later, if she hadn't hesitated with her key in the door . . . and if she hadn't felt so glad, so pleased, when she had learned of her father's death . . .

Too many 'if's'.

Too much guilt.

Maeve felt the pain well up inside her in a black wave-like filthy bile, suffocating, choking.

She awoke sobbing, her cheeks and face wet with tears. She was shivering, not with cold now, but something else, a deeper, more intense chill, that came from deep within her soul. She attempted to blink back the images, the countless, hitherto unremembered, images, incidents from her past, the petty jealousies, the tempers, the little lies, the hurts.

Maeve heard the sound coming from her throat, and it frightened her. It was a long, low keening, a cry of absolute anguish. Staggering from the bed, she dashed into the bathroom and flipped on the light. Squinting against the harshness, she stared at her face in the mirror, blinking shortsightedly. She looked wretched. It was as if the foul memories, the guilt within her soul, had eaten away at her features, stretching the flesh across her cheeks, sinking her eyes into her head, giving her flesh a faintly yellowish tinge. Maeve leaned across the sink on rigid arms, her head bent, feeling wretched. She turned on the hot tap to splash some water onto her face, and then gasped as it came out steaming.

The idea came to her so easily, so naturally, that she was surprised she hadn't thought of it before. She was tense and naturally so after the events of the day, and so what would be more natural than a bath.

A nice warm bath. Hot, steaming, relaxing.

Although Blacklands House had been completely refitted inside, the present owners had been careful to maintain the style and fittings of the original, and one of the bathrooms now boasted a deep, high-backed, copper bath. Maeve turned the levers, and the pipes chugged once before steaming water thundered into the metal bath. She stood for a few moments, breathing in the warm steam, before retreating to the bedroom to strip off her pyjamas and pull on a heavy, towelling dressing gown. She stepped back into the bathroom, blinking hard against the steam that almost completely obscured everything. She tightened a towel around her thick hair, and tested the water with her toe. It was scalding. Turning off the hot tap, she ran the cold, and then she stood watching the bath fill with water.

Although the bathroom was hot and moist, she still felt cold, chilled through to the bone. There was an ache across her shoulders and in the pit of her stomach, and she wrapped her arms around herself, hugging herself. She felt sick inside, heart-sick, soul-sick. She felt guilty. She knew, deep in her heart and soul, that she had been responsible for her parents' deaths, and she also knew, with an absolutely terrifying finality, that she would never be rid of this feeling. She was sobbing again, but with self-pity this time. How could she go through life feeling like this? She looked at the swirling water again and the idea crept into her unconscious.

She tested the water again and found it was satisfactory. Shrugging off the robe, she pulled open the door to the mirrored bathroom cabinet.

The water was as warm as a lover's caress, skin soft, silk smooth. Maeve sank deeper into it, deliberately holding her legs and arms down as they attempted to rise to the surface. Now that the decision was made, she felt calm, restful, some of the bitterness inside her gone now.

She had heard that this was the most peaceful way to go, a mere drifting away, a painless sleep.

Beneath the surface of the water, the safety razor glinted dully. With surprisingly sure fingers, she slid off the head and then in one swift deep movement, dragged it lengthways up her arm, slicing into the arteries and veins. She drew three even lines from her wrist almost up to her elbow on the left arm and then, switching hands, managed to make one deep cut on her right arm before the blade fell from tingling fingers. Closing her eyes she lay back in the scarlet-touched, cloudy water.

There was no pain. There was nothing. The bitterness, the fear inside her, began to recede, drifting out of her body with her life's blood. Maeve became aware of something else too. For the first time in a long time the sound inside her head was gone, the shrill high-pitched buzzing sound that she had thought was a hearing problem. Now, in her last few moments of life, she recognised it as a scream. For the past few months she had been hearing a scream inside her head, a scream of absolute, final despair.

Maeve Quill opened her eyes, and was somehow unsurprised to find a second figure in the bathroom. The blood and the memories had drawn her. She squinted, attempting to make out the creature's features, but found she couldn't. She closed her eyes; it was of no matter. It was unimportant. She flinched, however, when something ice-cold touched her face. Opening her eyes, she found there was a hand before her face, a long-fingered, long-nailed, ice-white hand. But as she stared at the hand, she noticed it was speckled and blistered as if the flesh had been burned. For some reason she thought of salt. But that too was unimportant.

The bath water was now a thick, purplish red, the water sluggish with her fluids. But it was warm. Blood warm, Maeve smiled and closed her eyes for the final time . . .

25

Maeve Quill opened her eyes.

There had always been a future. When he had been teaching, he had known exactly what he had to do for the coming term, and there were the field trips to be organised, researched and arranged. When he had been working on a book, there had been deadlines to meet; proofs would have to be returned by a certain date, and there would be a publication date further down the line. His life had been mapped out, times and dates, futures.

There had always been futures, until now.

Michael Cullen sat before the humming computer, staring at the blank screen, and realised that there was no future ahead of him now, and before there would be, before there could be any future for himself, he would have to slay the banshee. Everyone was dead, except Maeve and himself, and the only way they were going to stay alive would be by killing the creature, destroying it completely. They had hurt it today, he was convinced of that; what they needed to do now, more than anything else, was to press home the attack. Tomorrow morning, he would attack the pool with a vengeance, and destroy it by any means possible.

However, before he did that there was something else he wanted to do.

His fingers tapped the keys slowly, almost reluctantly, typing out the document carefully, his lips moving with the words that appeared on the screen.

'This is the last Will and Testament of me, Michael Cullen . . .'

He wasn't sure what the correct formula of the words was, but he was sure this would do. It was simple enough in any case; his last remaining relative was his daughter, Chrissy, and if anything happened to him, then everything, and God knows but it wasn't much, went to her. The text of the Will took exactly one paragraph. When he was finished he signed and dated it, '10.31 . . .' and then he stopped, realising he had used the American form of the date. Today was the thirty-first of October.

Michael stopped, the smile that came to his lips freezing into a rigid mask. The thirty-first of October. All Hallows Eve, Halloween, the time when traditionally, the gates between this world and the next opened, a time when the country people believed the fairy host rode forth in all its splendour. At any other time he might have scoffed, but now.

He printed up two hard copies of his Will, signed both and addressed two envelopes, one to his attorney, the second copy to Chrissy. He stuck stamps on both envelopes and stuck them into his jacket pocket; he would post them tomorrow morning. Then he began hunting through the folklore notes Maeve had previously prepared, looking for information about the feast of All Hallows. There was nothing. He went searching through his own collection of folklore, both what he had brought with him, and the books which Maeve had bought earlier in the year. He was reaching for volume one of a two volume set intriguingly called the *Festival of Lughnasadh*, Lugnasagh being one of the great Celtic feasts celebrated on the first of August, when he came across the comb.

It was resting on top of the book on the top shelf and, although he had no conscious memory of placing it there, he knew immediately, instinctively, what it was when his fingers touched the cold, smooth surface. He felt his breath catch in his throat, and it took him several long moments before he lifted it off the top of the book, holding it between finger and thumb, and blew away the dust. Cupping it in the palm of his hand, he prodded it with his index finger, almost as if it were a species of insect. But it was a comb, nothing more, a simple bone comb, dating back to, to when, a thousand years, two thousand years, more? He didn't know; wasn't even sure he cared, all he knew was that this was his one tangible link to the creature. Was this what had kept the banshee on his trail? Paddy, Maeve and even Charles had thought so, but he wasn't quite so certain himself. Or perhaps he didn't want to believe that if he had returned the comb in the beginning, all this would not have happened. No, he was convinced that the creature had latched onto him simply because of his name and ancestry. He was convinced of it.

Michael Cullen slipped the comb into his shirt pocket and returned to his computer terminal. He realised, of course, that he was doing nothing useful. He was merely marking time, keeping himself busy until . . . until what? until the banshee appeared?

And what then?

Michael sat back into the swivel chair and pulled the comb from his pocket again, looking closely at the workmanship. It was surprisingly crude, and yet immediately recognisable, the basic design of the comb hadn't changed much since man first parted his hair with a twig. It was semi-circular, with about twenty teeth protruding from the inside of the circle. Turning it slightly, he could see the merest outline of a design which had been etched into the bone, but obviously time and usage had worn it smooth. There was also a slight discoloration within the design, which suggested that it might have been coloured at some stage. Lifting it to the light he turned it around in his fingers, and a hand plucked it out of the air!

Michael leapt out of the chair in fright.

'Jesus, Maeve, you scared the shit outa me.'

Maeve Quill ignored him, concentrating on the comb in her hands. She was wearing a thick white bathrobe, a towel wrapped around her head, water droplets still glittering on the backs of her hands and across her forehead.

Shaking his head, Michael turned back to the screen. A flicker of movement caught his eye and he suddenly realised it was scrolling furiously, screen after screen, full of random characters. He tried to break into the programme, but nothing happened, and then he tried to clear the screen, again with no results. The hairs on the back of his neck begin to crawl. 'Maeve,' he whispered, 'She's close. The screen's gone crazy.'

Maeve Quill leaned across his shoulder to look at the screen, her cheek almost touching his, her left arm draped across his left shoulder. She smelt of soap and . . . something else, something vaguely bitter, not quite a perfume, not even a scent, but which tantalised by its very familiarity. She rested her right hand on the table, beside the keyboard, and Michael noticed that she was still holding the comb.

'I'm going to try and reboot the machine,' he muttered, using the three key combination that effectively restarted the computer without having to turn it off. The screen blanked for a moment, and Michael saw himself and Maeve reflected eerily in the soft blackness of the empty screen, and then it started to run its memory test. It finally blipped once, signifying that it was ready.

'Let's go into the banshee file,' Michael suggested, touching the keys gently. 'It should be empty.'

It wasn't.

When there is hunger we must feed. And our food is blood and memories.

We feed upon the Family, those of the Sons of Men who once accepted our kind into their midst, who fed us in return for our lore and learning, our strength and skills.

In time past there were many. Now there are few and we are forced to feed upon their descendants.

'Maeve?' Michael asked, looking up at the woman, but she was staring intently at the screen, her lips slightly parted. He turned back to the moving text as another line appeared, the letters marching right to left.

And the text was in English.

He felt the change from Old Irish to English was significant, but he wasn't sure how or in what way.

Ageless I am, yet aged.

I have been maiden, mother and hag. Men and women both have I taken, children too have fed me, but their blood is thin and their memories unsatisfying. Kings and commoners have provided me with sustenance, and yet the purest food is those who bear the name of the Families and carry its blood within their veins.

And now one has approached, calling me forth from the depths of my pool. From the clan O'Cuillean, but far-travelled, with little respect for the last of the De Danann folk. He has fought me at every turn, and I have fed off his companions and family, a thin tasteless gruel, but now he is mine. This eve I will feed upon the man.

Michael found he was shivering so violently he was afraid he would fall out of his chair. Maeve's grip around his shoulders tightened and he hugged her close in turn.

'What am I going to do?' he whispered. 'What can I do? I want to kill this creature, I have to kill this creature. But how? In God's name, how?'

Maeve turned his chair slightly, bringing him around to face her. Her lips brushed across his cheek before settling on his lips, her tongue probing.

Shocked, motionless, it took him seconds to respond, and then his arms tightened their grip, pulling her closer, down on top of him in the chair. One hand went to her thick hair, pressing against her head, the other settling into the small of her back. They kissed passionately for some moments, and then abruptly, Maeve pulled away, pushing him back into the chair, with enough force to send the chair back on its castors. He blinked furiously, wondering what had happened. Not quite sure what to do, almost embarrassed to look at her, Michael pulled his chair back to the computer and looked at the screen.

It was littered with random letters and symbols.

'Maeve . . .' he began, and then stopped. Maeve Quill had pulled the towel off her head and had shaken out her thick, black hair, allowing it to flow down her back. It seemed to be darker than he remembered it, but he supposed that was because it was still damp. She was watching him closely behind hooded lids, a curious look in her sharp, green eyes. Her hands reached for the belt around the dressing gown and Michael Cullen was already rising to his feet as she tugged it open. The dressing gown parted down the middle.

'Maeve . . .?'

She was naked beneath the dressing gown, and she stood quite still her hands limp by her side, silently watching him. He tried to concentrate on her face, but his eyes were drawn downwards, along the length of her throat, down her chest, the curves of her breasts hinted at by the open gown. Down her flat stomach, her navel deeply indented, and into her groin, the hair as thick and as dark as her head.

And then both hands came up and reached for him, palm upwards, fingers spread.

Michael blinked and blinked and blinked again, attempting to clear a film that had misted his eyes. He felt a stirring in his groin, and was all too aware of how long it had been since he had slept with a woman. Something plucked at his consciousness, and somewhere deep inside him a warning bell went off.

But then Maeve had stepped up close to him and, pulling back her dressing gown, allowed it to fall to the ground. Her hands went around his head, pulled it close to her and her mouth opened as their lips met, her tongue wet, darting.

He fumbled with the buttons on his shirt, two skipping away as he pulled it off. Maeve's cold hands ran down his body, leaving a faint tingling sensation in their wake, and then her fingers worked at his belt.

As she stripped him, pushed him to the carpeted floor and straddled him, impaling herself upon him in a frenzied rush, he became incapable of conscious thought. He was only aware of the sensations that flooded his being, the fire that coursed along his veins, the pounding in his head and throat, the pulse in his groin. He remembered the first girl he had ever kissed, the same girl he had touched intimately; he remembered the first woman he had ever slept with; he remembered the first time he had met Karla, their first kiss, the one and only time before their marriage that they had slept together.

He remembered her death.

The passion left him as quickly and as powerfully as it had taken him, leaving him shaken and slightly sickened. He looked up at the woman sitting across him, noticing her overlarge breasts, blue-veined, the thickset thighs, and then he looked at her face, and saw for the first time the vacant expression, the slack mouth. Was she drunk or drugged?

'Enough,' he croaked.

The woman didn't move.

'Maeve . . .'

Her head turned, looking down on him, and Michael was abruptly aware of just how heavy she was across the pit of his stomach, thighs and groin. He brought his hands up, wrapping themselves into the soft flesh just below her breasts and attempted to heave her off him. She didn't move, and Michael had the sudden impression that she was actually growing heavier. He could feel the constriction across his chest, and the pressure on his ribcage forced him to breath quicker.

'Maeve,' he snapped, 'for God's sake!'

Maeve tilted her head so that her long, black hair trailed across his face. Her mouth opened and closed several times before she managed to speak. '*Which God, yours or mine*?' she asked, and then she laughed.

The sound froze his blood. It was somewhere between a cry of delight and a scream of pain. It was a wail that sliced through his consciousness right to the core of his being, and he suddenly remembered what had been so familiar about Maeve's gesture. When he had first seen the banshee, she too had reached for him, palm upwards, fingers outstretched.

With a monumental effort, Michael heaved upwards, attempting to dislodge the woman, and then, almost at the same time, she began to move in a slight rhythm.

'MAEVE!'

The eyes snapped open, and they were black, coal-black, night-black.

The scream that began deep in his stomach never reached his throat. The creature's hands closed around his throat, the long nails drawing blood from his flesh, and Michael Cullen realised that Maeve Quill didn't have long nails, didn't have black eyes.

He looked up into the woman's face.

The Maid looked down. '*You are mine!*'

It was Maeve and yet not Maeve. Although she was still recognisable, something else had moulded her features, deepening her eyes, heightening her cheekbones, lengthening her face. Her breasts were smaller now, the nipples darker, her stomach flat and hard, her ribs pronounced. The mouth opened, showing small, white teeth, some of them looking too pointed to be natural, and the tongue that touched the lips was sharp and flickering.

Michael screamed, and the woman threw back her head and howled with demented laughter.

When her head came forward, she had aged; lines had etched themselves into the face, and the body had thickened, the breasts grown larger, the stomach slightly rounded.

Michael Cullen flailed at the creature with fists and nails; his nails tore strips of flesh from her which healed over even as he was looking, and his punches and blows only succeeded in hurting his own hands; they had no effect on her.

The woman's eyes now sparkled with something approaching life. They were no longer pitiless, black stones; somewhere deep, deep within them, something moved, an emotion of some sort, pity, amusement?

She began to move more quickly, almost urgently on top of him, and against his will he could feel his body beginning to respond. He struck at her face, attempting to gouge her eyes, but her hands wrapped themselves around his wrists, pinning them to the floor at an angle that threatened to rip his arms from their sockets. He screamed again, and when the woman laughed, he felt sure he detected a touch of genuine amusement in it.

Her hair had fallen over his face, across his eyes and when she lifted her head, she had aged. If any vestige of Maeve Quill remained within this creature, then it was Maeve in her late eighties, her body shrivelled, her breasts withered, skin stretched taut over prominent bones and yet the same fire still burned in the eyes, and her grip on his arms never slackened. And the woman continued to move atop him.

He could feel himself building towards a climax, was powerless to prevent it and he knew with absolute certainty that when he had achieved climax, the creature would kill him, and what then? What would happen to her? By giving a portion of himself to her, was he making her more powerful, giving her a physical body. And what then?

With a sudden effort that cracked two of his lower ribs, Michael Cullen wrenched his arms free and heaved himself upwards, almost, but not quite, upsetting the creature. His flailing arms struck the table with enough force to break every bone in his left hand, and the table leg. The computer slid to the floor, the screen exploding in a shower of sparks, the motor winding down with a ominous whine.

Sparks danced across the old woman's withered skin, and she immediately changed again, becoming the Maiden, young, vibrant, merciless and deadly. Her teeth were bared in a grimace as she worked herself against him with quickening rhythm.

'*You are mine.*' Her tongue was dark and moist against her lips.

Michael felt the release begin deep in his groin, as his questing fingers found the bone comb, his body began to spasm into orgasm, and then he drove the comb up into her jugular vein!

The twenty bone spikes shredded the vein, bathing him in warm, salty blood. He wrenched the comb free as her hands closed around his throat, and stabbed it home beneath her breast.

The banshee flickered through her tripartite stages in blinding rapidity, maiden, matron, crone, until elements of each became inextricably, grotesquely confused.

And all the time the banshee was howling: an ear-shattering, terrifying, terrified sound, that shattered every glass object in the house, that drove every cat and dog in a three mile radius into a bloody frenzy, that brought children terrified from their sleep, that brought others to their knees in prayer.

The cry of the banshee, once heard, is unmistakable.

You are mine now and forever, part of me for all eternity!

Michael Cullen attempted to speak but the pain in his throat, in his oxygen starved brain was tremendous, and he never managed to tell the banshee that he had won before she snapped his neck, with a single, savage twist.

EPILOGUE

They found the bodies of Michael Cullen and Maeve Quill, wrapped together in death two weeks later, when one of the neighbours noticed a strange smell emanating from Blacklands House. Thinking the septic tank had packed up, he strolled up to the house. When he saw the devastation that had been wrought across the front of the house, he turned around and walked away.

Fifteen minutes later the first of the police arrived.

Suicide pact was the initial verdict of the police who discovered the bodies, and this was confirmed when Michael Cullen's Will was found in his pocket. It was only later, when the extraordinary nature of Maeve Quill's wounds were revealed that questions were asked. Both her wrists had been opened from wrist to elbow, her jugular had been torn out and an ancient bone comb driven through her ribs into her heart. And yet she had still managed to break Michael Cullen's neck.

Subsequent investigation revealed the curious events surrounding the last few months of Michael Cullen's life, and although suspicion now fell on Cullen as the prime suspect, no evidence was ever produced that linked him with the deaths.

Christine Klein Cullen walked away from the simple grave and didn't once look back. She knew if she looked back she would break down and cry, and once she started . . .

They were all gone, mother, father, her brother, even her aunt. She was the only one left.

It wasn't fair; it just wasn't fair. Why had she been left behind; why hadn't she been taken with the rest of her family. What sort of God?

But her aunt had attempted to explain what sort of God took a twelve-year old girl's family, and left her to fend for herself. It hadn't been a very good explanation.

She felt like screaming, like throwing back her head and

screaming her anguish to the empty skies. The need was so bad, that deep inside her she could already hear herself howling, could already hear the cry of pain echoing across the skies.

Closing her eyes, she felt the scream well up inside her . . .

· ACKNOWLEDGEMENTS ·

I would like to thank the present owners of Blackland House, Robert and Celeste Vogel, for the use, and abuse, of their home.

I would also like to acknowledge the assistance of the real-life counterpart of the Reverend Charles Woland, whose knowledge of the tripartite goddess was invaluable.

A special word of thanks to Eddie Taylor and Philip Donnelly who saw the Banshee, and then made her!

The places mentioned in *Banshee*: Skerries, Loughshinny, and Blackland House, all exist.

The characters are, of course, fictional.

Only the existence of the banshee remains in doubt.

A Selected List of Fiction Available from Mandarin Books